OUT OF COURT SETTLEMENT

Lucy Rutherford

Cover designed by Peter Clinton.

ISBN: 978-0-244-42606-4

PublishNation
www.publishnation.co.uk

Also by this author:

A Bunch of Lies

This is dedicated to all victims of crime.
It shouldn't have to be like this.

Prologue

TUESDAY 6ᵀᴴ NOVEMBER 2001
12.45PM

The rapist had got off again. Grinning broadly, Darren Sutton stood in the wintry sun on the cracked concrete steps of Brighton Magistrates Court. He lit up a victory cigarette and gave his solicitor, Ms Cavendish, a high five. True to his type he'd used a woman to defend him. The Bench were wet liberals with cholesterol ridden soft hearts and it was always better to have a victim torn into by one of their own gender during cross examination. That's if it got that far, which it didn't very often.

The Crown Prosecution Service had done him a favour by lowering the charge to assault by beating. It was all good. Better still, the long loving and long-suffering Lisa had done him another by not turning up to give evidence. He knew the police had been gutted because they had plenty of injury photos that were useless without old Lisa. He hadn't been totally sure she'd stay away, so he'd given her a couple of smacks last night in places that wouldn't show, and it'd helped her to decide. She'd even fooled the Witness Care Officer who'd rung to support her and had promised she'd be in court this time. Lisa might get lucky tonight, whether she fancied it or not. It all depended how much celebrating he'd done first.

He nodded at his brief when she said, 'See you again Mr Sutton.' She'd got her Legal Aid and he'd got a result. His tattooed fingers automatically started texting his mates on his mobile to tell them the good news and make arrangements. Beating the system, as well as Lisa, always felt good. There was nothing like it. It was going to be a good night.

In all his excitement he didn't notice the pair of eyes watching him as he blew out a gust of smoke into the air and still smiling, he swaggered across Edward Street.

Chapter One

SUSSEX POLICE HEADQUARTERS

Assistant Chief Constable, Anne Lancaster never told her officers the reason she wanted a meeting with them. Instead she would begin with her favoured opener. 'Do you have any idea why I have asked to see you?' This was a clever tactic which often had already anxious police officers incriminate themselves over minor misdemeanours in a kind of confessional response. She obtained a great deal of information this way and she never filled a silence with anything other than an intense blue-eyed stare.

While waiting to see her, Detective Sergeant Lorcan O'Leary paced the managerial grade thick navy blue carpet and heard the ACC giving a list of instructions to her staff officer. He looked round the wood panelled room and noticed photos of his superior taken with 'the great and the good' at various events, including one of her with an Elvis impersonator. Lorcan smiled to himself. So, she did have a soft side, and didn't spend all her nights lying in a coffin waiting to suck the life blood out of her junior officers. He idly picked up what appeared to be a set of vintage Elvis playing cards on a bookcase. Years of drug searches saw him automatically open the box and start flicking though the cards. Hearing the senior officer start to return, he hastily thrust them back in the pack, but not before two cards sprang out, and which he swiftly kicked under the bookcase as he turned to face her.

'Well, Detective Sergeant O'Leary why do you think I've called this meeting?'

'No idea ma'am.' His Northern Irish accent was still strong. A few things came to mind, but he had no intention of suggesting them.

She looked hard at him. 'Last Friday – road traffic accident. Want to tell me your side of things?'

'There's not much to tell – it's all in my report. I was travelling in plain clothes about fifty yards behind the incident on my way home. I could see it was a bad collision, so I stopped my car and ran to assist. Upon arriving at the scene I phoned the emergency services, which I knew would be delayed due to rush hour traffic. The passenger in the Golf, that I later learned was stolen, had sustained massive impact trauma. Her body was in the crushed car, but her head was on the hard shoulder rather than on her own as it were.'

'Go on.'

'The driver was critically injured and was trapped in the car. He smelt strongly of alcohol. I tried to reassure him while we waited that it would be OK, though I knew it wouldn't be. He died just before the other services got there. His last words were, 'I suppose you bastards are going to nick me.' Given the circumstances I felt it appropriate to set his mind at ease, so I said, 'not this time mate.' Of course, if he'd pulled through, it would have been a different matter. He'd have had the book thrown at him. When colleagues arrived I explained the situation, and then pretty much left them to their job.'

'Will you be surprised to learn that we've had a complaint from the Fire Service about your insensitivity? I have no doubt that you saw some dreadful situations when you worked for the RUC in Northern Ireland but doesn't excuse you for what you said.'

Lorcan threw his arms up, 'Just what am I being accused of here?' His forty-eight years melted away and he felt like a small boy being admonished by the Jesuits again.

'The fireman said you pointed at the girl's torso and her other body part in the road and said, 'heads or tails' as you left. Did you feel that was appropriate?'

Lorcan gamely tried to explain about the necessary level of black humour that sustained the emergency services on operational duty in such a way that the ACC was implicitly criticised for her desk bound job. 'Usually fire officers aren't so precious, ma'am. Right enough they're good for a laugh.' His voice grew louder. 'I needed to keep it together, as do my colleagues in whatever way we can, while on this occasion I find myself having to hold the hand of a drunken thieving scum bag who shat himself while dying.'

The ACC turned her head slowly towards him and her voice was low, but he could sense the underlying anger. 'Unfortunately, your remark was also overheard by a member of the public who was asked to comment by the press, and we came out of it badly. You forget that you are an ambassador for the Force and your so called

4

coping strategy was not appreciated by bystanders. Unsurprisingly, the Fire Service is very keen to distance itself from this. We shall issue an official version that it was a misunderstanding, but I must tell you this is a warning, officer. Keep a handle on your blarney. The rest of it was a good job by the way.'

The ACC didn't look like an Elvis fan, nothing would shake her up, he thought as he drove back to the grubby CID office with its thin stained carpet tiles. A DC handed him a mug of tea and another colleague snapped a gingerbread man in half and said, 'Heads or tails is it, Lorcan?' He didn't answer as he'd already grabbed a greasy doughnut out of the birthday box by the kettle and the viscous synthetic apology for strawberry jam was inevitably making its way down the stubble on his chin.

Chapter Two

THE GIN HOUSE

It wasn't that she necessarily wanted them all dead, though a lot of them deserved it. Guardian reading Circe Byrne was pathologically unable to tolerate unfairness. But years of working in the criminal justice system, or the 'criminal injustice system' as she preferred to call it, had systematically eroded any sense of compassion for the offender. Magistrates were required to dispense justice without fear or favour and that justice needed to be seen to be done. Circe was renowned for her fairness. She always went by the book, but in the political climates which operated over the last twenty years that she'd been on the bench, it was obvious that the book wasn't fair to victims of crime. Her view was that the system was loaded in favour of the criminal no matter what social class they came from. She had absolutely no bias in that regard, as she saw them as all 'getting away with it.' Not everyone would think this was an ideal quality for a local magistrate, but her opinions were sustained by her strong feelings and experiences that successive governments of all political hues, had put the victim so far away from justice that it was now almost necessary to book a long-haul trip to get in touch with them.

However, while it's one thing to say at dinner parties over your fourth glass of red wine, 'I could kill all the bastards!' It's quite another to do it.

It was dark when Circe got home from court to the Victorian house she bought years back before the fashionista of incomers to Brighton and Hove drove up the prices. She still loved the place as much as when she first saw it. The property had a wealth of original features, stained glass and open fireplaces and she'd restored it to its original blousy splendour. She eschewed the minimalist white walled populist trends with their stainless-steel operating theatre style kitchens and clattering wooden floors. She went for colour and clutter and visitors often suggested that its authenticity meant it could be used as a film or TV set without much change or alteration.

A large elm tree, planted by the Victorians, stood on the street outside the house. It survived the characteristically understated 'storm' of 1987 and was part of the watch and wait programme of Dutch elm disease control bravely adopted by the city council. Its branches, illuminated by the street lamp, cast shadows of varying depths and shapes into the house. Old houses have their ghosts and a slowly dying tree was no threat. Although Circe owned the house she still felt like the caretaker of a piece of history, as everything in life is technically on loan, and in time becomes someone else's property.

Her home was a little on the large side now that Alice had left for Cambodia, but Circe had no plans to move. She walked round the house glancing at her daughter's unneeded winter coat as it hung on the hallstand and made her way to her computer. Emailing Alice was a lifeline and she wrote often. It was early evening, and as usual the curtains were open, allowing the shadows from the elm tree's branches to twist and writhe across the walls in her low-lit study. The ice chinked in her red glass goblet. She looked at the bubbles imprisoned in the recycled glass. It was more of a bucket than a glass, but since Oxfam had two for sale at three pounds and they were so dramatic and suited her Gothic study, she couldn't resist them. Circe tried to sound upbeat when she wrote, despite her heavy heart.

From: Circe Byrne MBE JP < circe@blueyonder.co.uk>
To: Alice Byrne <alice@cambodiahumanrights.com>
Date: 6 November 2001 at 18.15
Subject: Angry and still overweight...

Well Alice, it's not every day that you see a rapist walk free from court, is it? Although we all know from the pitiable conviction figures it happens all the time, we don't usually get a ringside view of the bastard punching the air in triumph with his solicitor. Despite appearances to the contrary there's a link with this and my weight which I'll explain.

I've decided I really AM going to lose that stone (or so) of fat and have researched the best diets on the internet (and I do know what you'd say if you were here.) So, this week it's going to be the watermelon diet where you get to eat - that's right - just watermelon! As much as you want apparently, including the skin!

Well, things haven't gone exactly to plan today, which is why I'm sitting here writing to you, with my favourite old drink - a very large Bombay Sapphire, soda, and a big healthy chunk of fresh lime and a sprig of mint. I'm not counting the calories as I consider it's very nearly a health drink.

Now, where was I? After morning court I went up to Kemptown to get some watermelon for lunch. I'd reckoned I'd be fine with a biggish slice, but since it worked out cheaper to get a whole one, that's what I did. Honestly Alice, it was massive - the size of a bloody floating mine! I heaved it into my 'I'm an old bag' shopper that you so kindly gave me and made my way slowly back to the courthouse with aching arms. Tragically I never even got to eat it because the bottom fell out of the bag and the sodding great thing landed on my foot, bruising my toes as it exploded - red mush ruining those pointy black suede shoes of mine. As I was rubbing said foot I found myself mobbed by every seagull in Brighton, all of whom seemed very keen to have a change from fish, or old dustbin contents.

It was while I stood there in front of the court building, with the massacre which was my lunch at my feet, that I spotted Darren Sutton celebrating with his slime ball brief. He's a total flat-liner as far as responding to punishments go and is euphemistically labelled an IPPO. Yet another government acronym meaning Identified Prolific Priority Offender. When anyone has a record like he does, of over 150 offences, it's stating the bleeding obvious that he's a known prolific offender, but apparently all the agencies are supposed to leap into action to 'support' his rehabilitation and prevent him re-offending. Judging by his paean of triumph on the court steps I deduced he must have got off his latest charge.

I checked the court list later and it seems that instead of rape, the CPS had gone for the usual lesser charge of assault on his partner, despite the strong evidence. How do I know he's a rapist? Quite simply from Lisa herself. When she was in my court earlier this year on yet another case, she said that

8

his idea of foreplay was to use her as a punch bag. So, the brief gets thirty pieces of state silver, and Sutton gets off. Lisa won't be likely to call the police again now, will she? Defence lawyers are morally bankrupt and I wonder how they can look at themselves in a mirror? What collective noun would best describe them? (Yes, I'm still collecting those and inventing more for that little book I'm going to write – like me, it will be a slim volume!) An unscrupulousness of lawyers? A greed? An instruction of lawyers?

Before afternoon court I chewed the cud with my colleague Hugo. Well I didn't exactly chew anything as my lunch was in the gutter, but we both know there are too many people who get away with crime these days. The victim is no longer at the heart of the criminal justice system despite what politicians claim. The guilty go free and the innocent victims serve a life sentence of fear, their apprehension and pain garnished with an overwhelming sense of injustice. Guess you know that from working on the Khmer Rouge reconciliation trial eh? I do admire you all at Cambodia Human Rights, though I think we have enough human rights abuses over here and you don't need to travel overseas for the glamour of theirs. Poor old Lisa has human rights too, doesn't she?

Sorry about this rant. I see that the weather over in Phnom Penh is hot and humid – a bit like my mood!

I've got a shift at the Samaritans tomorrow. Hope it's not too busy. I'm not sure the watermelon diet will sustain me.

Consider yourself hugged, love you. Mum xxx

Circe moved away from the laptop and snapped the lid shut. The painful tug of a strand of her hair caught inside made her fling it open again and toss the offending lock back in line with the rest of her luxuriant wavy hair. She still wore it long despite her forty-five years, though of late she was required to take steps to ensure that the increasing number of white hairs were blended into the bright copper mane. Only she and her hairdresser knew the truth. She wasn't prepared to be invisible just yet. Its vibrant colour and extreme length had always invited comment. She grew proud of its distinctiveness and dismissed the childhood bullies with their

9

unexceptional hair in shades of muddy browns. She carried light and fire with her always.

Her father, Hector, had been a bohemian type and it was he who named her for the colour. He and his girlfriend Sheenagh, 'the camp follower', as Circe always referred to her, stared at their new born baby with her cloud of golden red hair. He said, 'we'll call her Circe after Helios, the Sun God's daughter and enchantress.' He made a few random strumming noises on his guitar as if to emphasise the decision. Sheenagh agreed because she always acceded to Hector's requests. And it was just as Circe's eyes had turned from blue to their permanent amber that Hector left for the States to catch the 'zeitgeist of the fifties' as he called it. That was the last they heard of him. When Circe was still a small child, Sheenagh went to London to catch the second wave, which was how Circe came to pass into her unwilling grandmother's care and to spend her childhood in a convent.

Circe made her way into the kitchen across the black and white tiled floor and poured herself another Bombay Sapphire, soda, mint leaves and lime cocktail. The 'BSC' as she always called it, eased the bullshit of the day. Returning to her study she placed the glass carefully away from her paperwork as she sat down at her substantial dark wooden desk. It was second hand, though well chosen, like the majority of her possessions. Most of her wardrobe came from charity shops, as long as it was black and good quality. Circe never wore colour except in the form of an occasional accessory.

She moved the piles of papers on her desk shifting the unread Guardian and disturbed two of her three cats lying amongst them. Her work was stacked in a kind of system she always said. The largest tower of files was the Victim Support Scheme for whom she'd worked for years. Despite this she was surprised and rather taken aback when she was awarded an MBE two years ago in recognition of her efforts. 'I'm not the kind of person that gets noticed,' she said to the charity's auditor. He looked over his half-moon glasses at the woman with her burnished curls piled on her head like a bright halo of red gold and her stylish black suit and black suede stilettos and smiled.

'Indeed? Perhaps the powers that be got you mixed up with someone else. An easy mistake to make!'

Her visit to the Palace with Alice as her invited guest, was now a distant memory. She had nearly declined the so called honour as they were such staunch republicans. Seeing it for what it was, she accepted the MBE to highlight the work of Victim Support. Alice, who brought light into her life had now left Circe's existence in comparative darkness since her travels.

As she started going through her papers she absently ate cubes of watermelon grimacing every time the magenta flesh yielded up its bitter seeds into her mouth. 'This can't go on' she said loudly. 'It really can't.'

Chapter Three

THE POLICE AUTHORITY

Lorcan's day wasn't going well again. He and a colleague were due to give a presentation entitled *Improving Rape Convictions* at Sussex Police Authority's meeting in County Hall, Lewes. The SPA was comprised of local politicians, magistrates and independent members. Their duties included overseeing the strategic direction of the Force and setting the budget. Most serving police officers didn't have a lot of time for the Authority and saw it as a government imposed irrelevance. The Chief Officers attended the meetings along with the Force directors and Lorcan hoped that the effort he and the team had gone to would satisfy the meeting that they were doing all they could. Lorcan loathed having to do PowerPoint presentations. 'It's death by PowerPoint,' he'd say. 'I'm a police officer, why the fuck am I wasting my time on this shite?'

The council chamber in County Hall had purple seats and a purple carpet. It was an unimpressive room in an unimpressive building. The serried ranks of SPA members and staff faced each other while at the top of the room the Chair of the Authority sat with the Chief Constable and the SPA's chief executive Ralph Wendover. The latter was a man who put himself first and not only relished the status of his publicly funded job but saw to it that he was getting as much as he could by way of perks, ranging from the wide screen television in his office to having manoeuvred his way into the Chief Officer's medical and remuneration scheme. He loved nothing more than a 'fact finding' trip in the Force helicopter with the Chair of the Authority followed by an extended lunch at an expensive hotel on the high street. No one dared challenge his extravagance, except Circe.

Lorcan and DC Steve Tibbs stood facing all of the Members and Chief Officers. The Chief Constable gestured for him to begin with an irritable wave of the hand. The figures didn't make good reading.

A sample of some of the police serials was discussed. In one, the caller said, 'I think I've been raped. There's a strange bloke in my bed and I don't remember anything as I was mullahed last night...'

It was to be regretted that many women, young and old, who reported these offences, were under the influence of drink or drugs. Certainly, in no way could they have been deemed to have given their consent, but proving it was going to be difficult and the CPS struggled with victim witnesses like these.

As the Chairman of the Authority adjusted his red bow tie and smoothed his yellow waistcoat he couldn't help remarking on it. 'Well, I may be getting on a bit but we were always told that a young lady should be conscious during relations. It says a great deal that young men don't care for any participation from their partner. Sad state of affairs. Shall we break for lunch? Thank you for your talk Detective Sergeant O'Leary.'

Lunch was waiting for Authority Members and Chief Officers in Westfield House, a small Georgian mansion adjacent to the 1960's council building. The participants would stand around balancing china plates and glasses while shaking hands and chatting to invited guests such as the Lord Lieutenants and High Sheriffs of East and West Sussex. The food was always a pretentious buffet which was tricky to eat and to remove from their teeth afterwards.

Lorcan started packing up prior to making his way back to the CID office knowing he would only have time to grab a petrol station sandwich. The police's beloved canteen had long been sacrificed for economic reasons. No warming food for the night shifts now. Pot Noodles and Cuppa Soups were all that held cold wet bodies and souls together, that and syrupy smelling Oats So Simple.

As he shovelled papers into his briefcase he became aware of one of the magistrate members of the Authority walking over in his direction. He had noticed her during his talk and technically knew her identity, as all SPA members had their photos and names up in every department of the Force, though he'd never spoken to her. She was in her mid-forties which made her younger than the others, but he thought she had striking looks with that amazing copper hair that went below her waist. She seemed to be intelligent and to understand what was going on and didn't have a political axe to grind. This made her quite exceptional, as did the fact that she wasn't racing to

Westfield House to plant her trotters in the collective trough which had resulted in the stampede from the room a moment earlier.

He straightened up and smiled in a professional way. 'I hope the talk was OK? Sorry about the PowerPoint – it's almost Force policy...' He stopped, realising that she sanctioned Force policy.

She returned his smile and he noticed her eyes were the same colour as her hair. 'Mmm... but it's a part of our lives, like the conviction rates. Depressing figures. I wanted to ask you if I could have a copy of your slides?'

He promptly withdrew them from his case and handed them to her with the crib sheet. 'Here, you're welcome, I've got the originals on my computer.'

'Thank you, Detective Sergeant.'

'Lorcan, please.' But she had turned on her heel and was making her way noiselessly across the purple carpet to the door. He looked at the seat she had recently vacated. The sun was casting long lines across it from the slatted vertical blinds and it illuminated her name, CIRCE BYRNE MBE JP. How do you pronounce Circe he wondered? Byrne made her Irish too, he reckoned – bound to be with all that red hair of course. He didn't say anything to Steve Tibbs who was mowing his way through the leftover biscuits by the jugs of cold coffee.

'What?' he said, spraying crumbs, as he saw Lorcan watching him. 'We don't get hand-crafted biscuits like this.'

'We don't get jack shit.' The shafts of sun had gone and Lorcan had a serial rapist's case file on his desk and a community meeting on the Stoneleigh estate to attend.

Chapter Four

STONELEIGH ESTATE

Brighton is famous for lots of things. Not its council estates though. Stoneleigh, just to the west of the city, is one of the worst. Even on a sunny day Stoneleigh estate has a bitter wind whipping round it, the cold air needles through the blocks of flats and down the rat runs of streets. Anywhere else that was three hundred feet above Brighton would have lovely views, but this place exuded such negativity that it was almost a dark fog on the horizon.

No amount of redesigning Stoneleigh or the millions of pounds that was pumped in for regeneration made any difference. Stoneleigh could teach the country's now infamous councils a thing or two about abusing children. The estate no longer even had a secondary school following three failed incarnations before it finally shut; all the head teachers having been broken in the process. The feral children and their indifferent parents had won a hollow victory, for which society paid the price. Multi-agency meetings would try to address all the problems including teenage pregnancy, which exceeded the national average. It was an unpleasant truth that a child born in Stoneleigh was known to have a life expectancy which was eight years shorter than other Brighton residents.

The estate's streets were characterised by young girls chatting on mobiles, pushing prams and pausing now and again to light up a cigarette while the child whined. Hooded young men drifted in packs and loitered. Using the crime reduction forum, the police and council did manage to succeed in substantially reducing the number of pubs in the area. They considered this a minor achievement against antisocial behaviour, though the corner shops still regularly sold alcohol to under-age drinkers.

One public house that did remain had as little character as a metal coated Nissen hut. The Black Dog, known as *'The Dog'* was a drinker's pub and Jason pushed open its door on the damp November evening. He wasn't the kind of man to notice the virus sharing sticky residue on its filthy handle. The heavily patterned carpet was as greasy as a spaniel's ear and pockmarked with cigarette burns and the smoke hung heavy in the air.

Looking round at the pathetic examples of humanity slumped in various stages of inebriation, he spotted Mohammed Khan sitting in the corner with a half-finished pint in front of him. Jason's small stoat-like eyes met Mohammed's hooded ones. He went over to him with his confident strut and pulled up a grubby stool. Mohammed gestured to his son, Ali to get him a drink.

'I'm guessing it's a lager, Jase? You see I've been here long enough to understand you white men,' he kept his voice upbeat.

'I'm not fucking drinking with you, and it's a funny thing for a devout Muslim to be doing ain't it? Drinking alcohol. You usually keep that behind closed doors don't you, like a lot of other stuff that doesn't fit with the old Koran?' He ran his fingers through his short gelled spiky hair. His racist little eyes fixed on Khan.

'I'm involving myself with the British community in their time honoured tradition of drinking ale, Jase. It's local integration you understand?' He smiled ominously baring purple shrunken gums and six large gaps where his teeth should have been.

Jason took a breath and clenched his weak jaw. His plan was to keep things calm.

'It's been a week now, where's Amina?' he demanded.

'I was going to ask you the same question, Jase.'

'Stop fucking using my name, I ain't got dementia and don't need to be reminded of it every other word. You weren't going to ask me anything and you know why. What have you done to her? Some bloody so-called honour killing?'

'Jase, there is no need to take that tone with me.' The voice was silky. 'She's my daughter and so precious. I just don't want her to spend her life with the likes of you....'

'She's eighteen and chose me and can make up her own mind, alright?' Despite himself his voice grew louder.

'You want to ruin her, and the family won't let that happen.'

Jason lowered his voice. 'What have you done with her? I'll fucking call the police on you!'

'Will you now boy? Ali, hear what he's saying to a man of my age who is respected in the community and who looks after his family.' Khan spread his arms wide to illustrate his point. His son glared hatefully.

Jason felt the power shift. 'You've got a big mouth and a big fist and you live off the state. Remember that.'

Khan tried to regain balance. 'But also please remember we have friends in our home country who help us out when we need it.' He put his face close to Jason who reeled back at the smell of his breath.

Jason adjusted the gold chains on his arm and moved the sovereign ring to a more central position on his middle finger. 'Look old man, just tell me where Amina is.'

'I was, as I said, expecting you to answer that question yourself. Attack is the best form of defence and you look like a rattlesnake, Jase.' Having not read Jason's body language Khan leant closer again and whispered, 'Now boy we gave you a considerable amount of money, and we are, as you say, a poor family. We wanted you to leave Amina alone. You took it and our business deal is closed.'

Jason uncoiled and leapt, 'No, she is my business old man. Hear this! Amina and I had an arrangement, so I took the money to set her up in a flat where she could entertain her punters as and when she wanted—'

'My daughter is a prostitute! Ali, you hear this about your sister?'

Jason cut in. 'Exotic dancer, old man, who enjoys the company of her gentlemen friends.'

Father and son Khan gave the appearance of genuine shock. 'You were not her only boyfriend?'

'Boyfriend? Nah, I pimped her out along with all my other girls. But she was a good worker like all you lot are and I want to know what has happened to my investment.' He couldn't help but smile as he dropped the depth charge.

Chapter Five

FRIDAY NIGHT IN STONELEIGH

Even though eleven years had passed, pensioner Elsie Standish was still afraid and shook at every noise that occurred outside her little bungalow. At the time it happened, she and her husband Syd had only lived on the Stoneleigh estate for eighteen months and didn't consider themselves typical Stoners by any manner of means. The council had only moved them there because of Syd's problems. These were never officially proved but the rumours still hung on, and she'd always hated it. What a rotten place to spend your last years, but what choice did they have?

The bloody tree was far too close to the house. If it blew over or was knocked down, which was a real possibility on that junction, it would flatten the 'bungaloid', as she called it. It blocked the sun out and every year shed its horrid leaves that then blew into her porch, menacing them with its presence. It was hard work, she said. It was all hard work.

Syd later said that he never heard any noise going on around midnight that night. He was only ever roused by his over-active bladder these days. But Elsie knew it was the local feral youth shouting and carrying on as usual. Despite her age she had good eyesight. Hearing a bottle break on the wall outside her home she crept to the window and peered nervously through the net curtains, keeping her lights off. The street lamp just outside made it seem like day anyway. The branches of the tree had yet to break into leaf as they writhed, and their shadows moved like a web over the young people. There were about eight of them yelling and taunting. *Slutty girls and drunken boys*, she thought. One wore a white baseball cap and he ran up the road opposite her, then a short time later he came back with another boy in tow. Then a second bottle broke. Should she ring the police? It would take them too long to get here, and the kids would be gone by the time they arrived, and besides she might get picked on by her neighbours. Best to stay out of it. Things were bad enough as it was. But Elsie still rested her trembling old hand on the phone. Then she saw a boy get up from the ground, and he shouted as someone seemed to punch him. As clear as day she saw a massive carving knife sticking out of the back of his football shirt. He fell flat on his face. He didn't move again.

Still Elsie didn't dare come out of her property, but clearly heard one of the group shouting for someone to call an ambulance. So that would be alright now, he'd get help, though he was bound to need stitches. The loud voices were different now, and there was some girl crying loudly saying, 'Oh my god, oh my god' over and over again. Well, what did the silly little cow think would happen with all that noise and fighting? It was bound to end in tears.

Elsie heard later that he was beyond help. He died outside her house, in the dog's mess, did Luke Marchant. Sixteen years old and with five years of youth offending behind him. But he didn't deserve a death sentence according to his mates. He was a diamond bloke with a cheeky smile and would do anything for anyone, so the tributes said.

Now that horrible tree had a shrine to him at its base. All tacky plastic shit and football banners. Right there every day. She had no choice but to look at it. No question of taking it down. More than her life was worth. The branches still waved and mocked her.

On Friday nights the kids still hung round there, drinking and smoking weed and taking pills. Luke's former girlfriend even had sex up against the tree with one of his mates, so he'd feel part of the old group and to get his blessing on the brief drunken union. It wasn't fair, Elsie had been through too much already. She hardly dared leave the bungalow any more, and only went to the mini-mart on the corner for milk, bread and a few ready meals first thing in the morning before the others woke up. Luke Marchant had once shouted at her, 'watch your back, you'll be next.' And even after some time had passed since his own back had been stabbed, she could still taste the fear his words provoked. No resting in peace.

Chapter Six

BRIGHTON MAGISTRATES COURT

The watermelon diet gave way to the grapefruit one. Circe reasoned that this made a lot of sense in that a grapefruit before every meal reduced the appetite and supposedly helped to break up the fat deposits in one's body. It was going to be better than the watermelon diet which had left her so hungry that she invariably ended up supplementing it with a cheese sandwich or two. The scales showed a net gain of four pounds that week.

When she went into court she was listed to be in Fine Enforcement. She was down to chair the session with two recently appointed magistrates as 'wingers', neither of whom had sat in fines before. Circe explained to her colleagues that fines were at the lower end of the sentencing structure and the Bench were issued with guidelines and tables so that they could equate the defendant's income with the seriousness and type of crime. In this way it was understood that the punishment was supposed to fit the crime and the fine was due to the court on the day that it was imposed.

The female winger was an older lady who dressed the part of a magistrate. She wore pearls, a safe navy blue twin-set with her stiffly permed iron grey hair and her swollen ankles forced into tight black patent shoes. Circe thought how no one would try and see the reflection of her knickers in those, as the nuns had warned her back in the day. The man was younger than many of their colleagues, his *Independent* newspaper protruded from a briefcase and he exuded earnestness and understanding for the defendants. While his colleague's occupation was a housewife, he worked in Social Services.

Circe took a sip of the grapefruit juice she had brought in and rather than have a biscuit as her fellow magistrates were with their coffee, she unwrapped a few segments of grapefruit.

'Many defendants claim that they can't pay on the day as they're on benefit or in other financial difficulty', she explained. 'They're then given time to pay by the Bench and a weekly sum is set and, as you know, we aren't allowed to charge interest on unpaid amounts. So in their minds it becomes very low priority. I know I'm going to sound cynical, but since I've been doing this for so many years, I feel it's appropriate to stereotype a little and let you see what many of the politicians of all colours ignore. The public expect that those fines as well as any compensation due will be paid, otherwise it makes a mockery of the whole system. However, a huge number of people avoid paying for years and we're told to keep giving them more opportunities. We, as magistrates, have a truly dreadful rate of fine collection. You couldn't run a business like that. We don't have the resources to check what the defendants tell us about their means. No bank would lend you money without knowing a lot more about you than we, as an organization do, and in fining someone we are effectively expecting to be paid without evidence of finances. The judiciary have always been promised that there would be an alternative for fine defaulters such as unpaid work, or community service, as it used to be called. But that has never happened. The government are forever changing the names of disposals so that you can't keep reliable statistics of what isn't working. So we're left with the unenviable task of enforcing fines for people who clearly don't want to pay. Can't pay and won't pay, if you like. Some of them clearly have funds but chose not to pay.'

Social Worker opened his mouth to cut in, his caring brow furrowed. Circe's amber eyes narrowed. 'So, just look for some of the following: out of season tan, designer clothes, logos or sports gear - even though the only exercise they get is running from the law - expensive hairdos, false nails, jewellery, tattoos, handbags. It's all there. Just keep your eyes open.'

Twin-set piped up. 'How do we know they aren't gifts?'

'A good question and often this is what they say when challenged, *my mum bought it for me/my friend did my hair*, and so on. You have to use your judgement to see if you believe them. Remember every person who comes into fines court is a volunteer. They chose to be here by committing the crime. They were convicted and now need to pay their debt to society. If they don't, as many chose not to, then there's nothing to remind them to stop offending in the future. Any punishment has to have bite, and it needs to impact on their lives. Many criminals become serial offenders collecting masses of fines, which add up to thousands owed to the public purse. We are then told that it is 'in the interests of justice' - don't get me started on whose justice this is – that the fine should be paid off in twelve months. So if they're on benefit the rate is set at £5 per week and so how much does that work out per year?' Circe looked at the social worker.

'£260.'

'Right, so what do you think should happen to a serial offender who has accrued fines for say motoring offences, assault, travelling on the railway without paying and so on? Let's say that in the last six years he's racked up fines of £2,500. What do you think the Bench's solution is? And bear in mind that each fine was set according to his means and these include up to one-third discount if he pleads guilty. Let's say we've tried deducting the fine directly from his benefit before he gets it, but this has failed because the DWP tell us he owes council tax and has taken out a social loan, both of which they recover from his benefit first. The court fine is last and that's why no one takes them seriously and why we've ended up with a situation where the crime rate is soaring and no one does anything about it.'

'So what happens to someone like this?' Twin-set smoothed her hair off her powdery face.

'The government tells us that we have to remit, or write it off, if you will. So you effectively don't punish him for his offending and give him a gift of the outstanding £2,240. The idea is then that hope against hope that he pays the paltry £260 that he is deemed able to budget for. But why should he comply? What sanctions do we have? Eventually after years of chasing we can impose a suspended sentence and if they still don't pay we can finally make an attempt to send them to prison. In the old days this used to work because as soon as they didn't pay their fines, as ordered by the Bench, they'd be down the cell steps and allowed one phone-call. The money was almost always produced and the courts were self-financing. Now we have rafts of administrators who are employed solely to do the paperwork relating to warrants, enforcement and writing off.'

Twin-set and Social Worker looked increasingly bleak.

'The best ones are the young fit men.' Circe continued, 'Say between the ages of eighteen and twenty-six, who as I call it, live off their mother's love. We find they don't always claim benefit as they can't be bothered or they're working 'on the black' or making a living from crime. Their mothers give them board, lodging, clothes, money for fags, drugs and booze, and there is no way that we can get the fines owed off them directly.'

'What happens in those cases?' Twin-set asked.

'Well it was hard to set a fine in the first place since besides their stupid myopic mothers they have no visible means of support. So I generally encourage them to go out and get a job.'

'How do you do that, we aren't a Job Centre?'

'No, but I try and make the experience in a fines court as unpleasant and intrusive as possible. I put on my imaginary surgical gloves and probe deeply to find out where their money is and why they haven't paid. The idea is ultimately to get them to pay rather than having to endure a barracking. This court is reserved in the main for those who have the means but won't pay. I just need to shift their priorities for them.

Social Worker looked crossly at Circe. 'This doesn't sound very nice.'

'Who said it was? I'm here on behalf of a society that is sick of people getting away with crime. In addition, there are often a lot of poor victims who need compensation paid to them. Facing their responsibilities, by whatever means, is the first sign of a criminal's rehabilitation.'

As Circe ate a segment of grapefruit, the juice from its skin made its way into Social Worker's eye.

'Sorry about that,' Circe handed him a tissue to dab the streaming tears.

'I've nearly lost a contact lens,' he moaned.

Twin-set adjusted her pearls anxiously and brushed off some of her dusty skin which had settled on her shoulders. Meanwhile Social Worker looked balefully out of his one good eye.

Chapter Seven

FINE TIMES

The courtroom set up for the first defendant had been carefully choreographed by Circe. The idea for this started years ago when she had sat incognito outside the fines court in scruffy clothes. She watched and listened as defendants temporarily handed over rolls of money and items of value such as sovereign rings, watches and designer jackets to their friends. It was not unknown to hear them discuss the cost of gym membership or how much their new car had set them back. Then Circe found herself an unwilling witness to these same individuals having put on performances worthy of an Equity card, emerging from the court rooms cheering as the Bench had believed them and reduced their fines. The ushers knew the truth but weren't allowed to inform the magistrates. Circe had seen one offender making his friends laugh as the old duffer justices in court thought his new Bluetooth headset was a hearing aid and wrote off a large part of his fine on the strength of it. He had struggled to hear what was going on a couple of times, but only because he had calls coming through.

The standard procedure in fines court was for Circe to ask that the usher place a box of tissues in the witness box. This acted like a theatrical prop to set the scene and provide a clue that this was not to be a casual experience, but one likely to provoke some emotions. She preferred the first defendant to be a weaker one who might break down and cry. The sight of them leaving in such a state often encouraged those in the waiting room to get their money back off their friends who were guarding it for them and pay it to the court. It was a successful tactic which gave Circe a payment record that was the envy of the Bench.

Court Two was lined with wooden panels. The magistrates sat in front of the royal coat of arms – the Arms of Dominion. Above the words *Dieu et Mon Droit* was a rampant lion and unicorn in a stand-off position. It was a 1970's building and had almost no natural light, just two foot wide windows near the top of the ceiling which was about twenty feet high. It wasn't unusual to see herring gulls peering in and adding their raucous contributions to the proceedings. Their sense of freedom was in stark contrast to the defendants who often had theirs removed while the birds looked on. The door through which people entered and left was also wooden. Clearly visible from the Bench was a large greasy mark where sweat and fear had left an indelible print as it was pushed open. The court service was underfunded so the door remained uncleaned for the many years that Circe had been there. As the justices walked in through their own entrance and collectively bowed, Circe felt how much of a stage performance it was. She wasn't Circe Byrne any more but was a representative of an ancient tradition of local justice, a mantle that she put on and took off when she entered and left the courtroom. She was no better or worse than anyone else and she was here to dispense justice.

The first defaulter was called in and he slouched into the dock. Aaron Gunn was a weaselly-looking man though it seemed unfair to weasels to compare him in this way. His ravaged appearance belied his thirty-four years.

Unemployed Gunn took the oath by affirming. The usher had to dictate it to him as he claimed he couldn't read or write. Circe surveyed him while his numerous catalogue of offences and history of non-payments were read out by the legal advisor. They included motoring crimes, criminal damage, drunk and disorderly, possession of drugs, and assaulting police officers. The list seemed endless. He gazed disinterestedly into the middle distance whilst chewing gum so moronically that its grey putty like consistency was clearly visible. He wore the latest so-called sports fashion clothes featuring plenty of logos and designer names. This seemed pretty pointless if he couldn't read but was the recognised way of gaining credibility with his friends.

The Bench heard how he continually acquired new fines and had failed to pay the previous outstanding 'accounts', as they were euphemistically called. Circe grimaced every time she heard the legal advisor use that word – it made it sound as if it were a business rather than crime reparation. She clenched her fists under the magistrates' desk. As she looked up there was a diagonal shaft of sun making its way into the court room and she became aware of a change within her. She could almost feel tiny filaments breaking and snapping and it felt as if the part of her that was traditionally connected to law and order was breaking away, much as an ice floe might crack away from the central mass. She tried to concentrate on Aaron Gunn's income and outgoings, but something was now free inside her. It was a weird disconnected feeling.

It was the practice for every defendant to complete a means form before coming into court to provide the Bench with an idea, and it was no more than an idea, of their income and expenditure. It was accepted that it was largely a work of creative fiction, and the courts rarely bothered to check if the contents were true. 'Imagine trying to get a bank loan without any financial verification' Circe would say, 'Yet here we are giving credit with the public's money and no idea when we will ever see it again.'

Gunn had adopted an air of studied indifference. Circe interrupted the legal advisor and barked at him, 'You can start by taking your hands out of your pockets and removing that gum from your mouth!'

The weasel shrugged and put it insolently on the polished wooden bench in front of him. The usher handed him a tissue with a warning look. He picked it off the dock and placed it in the proffered tissue with leisured insouciance.

'Now tell the court why you haven't paid as ordered.' Circe's voice was loud and sharp. 'You've had seven years in the court system and we have got virtually nothing off you. You owe £3,500. You've had at least that much remitted over the years and yet you keep adding more and paying none. I ask you again, why haven't you paid?'

'Well I've had a lot on me plate – it's not like I'm trying to avoid it or nothing.'

Circe flashed with measured slowness and the practised art of a cat watching its prey.

'Mr Gunn, do you know why you are here today?'

'Yeah, love, I'm here to talk about me fines.'

The usher, unseen to the defendant, shook his head knowingly as Circe unsheathed her claws and raised her voice. 'No, Mr Gunn, you have not voluntarily asked for court time to explain why you've not paid your debt to society, have you? You've been dragged in on a warrant which has cost the state even more money and you are here to tell us why we should not send you to prison today. You came in through that door,' her fuchsia fingernails gestured towards the door he had entered by, and then she made a wide arc in the manner of an air stewardess and pointed to another door behind the dock. 'And there we have the steps to the cells. Been to prison before?'

'Nah,' his close set eyes began to look as if she'd got his attention.

'I'm sure the other prisoners would reserve a special welcome for a new boy such as yourself.'

His shoulders began to sag. 'What's with you love? Is it time of the month or something? No one has spoken to me like this before. I've got rights.'

'Yes indeed and you have exercised those at the expense of your victims. Today we are talking about responsibilities. As a court we have a responsibility to collect your many and varied fines, but when we fail, as we appear to have done with you, then we are left with the ultimate sanction. Before that, however we are intrigued to learn more about you and what you've been up to in the last few years, so using your means form, which the usher helped you to complete, let us proceed.'

The weasel narrowed his impossibly small eyes. From where the Bench sat they resembled two tiny currants.

'It says here you admit to smoking twenty to thirty cigarettes a day. Is it more likely to be forty?'

'Yeah. It's a bad habit and I'd like to quit.'

'We may be able to assist, Mr Gunn. I see you spend about £30 a week on alcohol.'

'Thereabouts, I get it cheap.'

'Indeed. Lottery and entertainment £20?'

'That's only a rough figure. It could be more or less.'

'As you say. And what about the car that so many of the offences were committed in?'

'Scrapped.' He smiled and shrugged displaying three missing teeth.

'Get anything for it?'

'Nah.'

'Of course not. So you didn't get any money that you could have usefully put towards your, fines? So may we enquire whether you have a car now?'

'Nah.'

'Mr Gunn may I remind you that you are on oath? So if I have the DVLA database checked will we find any car registered in your name?'

'Oh, now then, let me think.'

'It will only take a minute to check.'

'Yes, now, I think there may be one.'

'There we go, that didn't hurt did it? What's the make and registration number?'

'Can't recall the plate what with me learning difficulties.'

'We'll check that for you, as it is an asset that could be sold and paid to the court. What kind of car is it?'

Gunn mumbled a reply which made Circe exclaim.

'Did you say a silver Mercedes?'

'Yes. Is there a problem?'

The wingers were now in fairly deep shock, even Social Worker's caring expression had been replaced by one of complete astonishment and his eyes bulged, including the red one.

Circe answered briskly, 'There's only a problem if you haven't paid your fines and have acquired assets, the value of which should have been paid to the court. Can you tell the Bench how you have been so frugal with the housekeeping when you have only a declared income of state benefit yet managed to obtain a car of that class which is out of reach of all but a minority of people?'

'Well, it isn't brand new if that's what you're getting at.'

'It seems to us from our little chat that you are living far in excess of your means. You've been claiming benefits since you left school, which according to my calculations, was about twenty years ago.'

'Yes, love that's right. Work's hard to get.'

'Yet your lifestyle doesn't reflect your straightened circumstances of £50 pounds of state benefit a week. How do you afford the drinks, cigarettes, entertainment, designer clothes and not forgetting the Mercedes? You also managed to have four children in that time. Do you support them?'

'Not as such, their mums live off the social.'

28

'I just had a feeling you were going to say that. You had fathered no children when you first came into the court system and clearly owing society money has not acted as a contraceptive, has it?'

He smiled.

'Well, Mr Gunn, we have now reached a stage in the proceedings were things become a little more focussed.'

The curranty eyes screwed up even smaller as he feigned a lack of understanding. but made as if he was attempting to do so. It was an expression he must have used all his life and it didn't fool Circe.

She summarised. 'Well, you accept that you owe the court £3,500 having already had previous Benches remit large sums of money so that you could pay the remaining amount within twelve months. Even this didn't encourage you to pay and you committed further offences for which you were additionally fined. We tried taking the fine from your benefit directly but as the Benefits Agency are deducting the overpayment you were given following your false claim to them, that isn't possible. Yes?'

Gunn stood there looking sullen but finally paying attention. 'I'll give ya a fiver a week. How's that, love?'

'Derisory compared to what you spend on your own luxurious lifestyle. People who have been victims of your crimes have been waiting years for compensation to be paid to them. That's not fair is it?'

'OK, let's make it £6 a week.'

'You're not understanding. You are going to do the following. You're going to use your top of the range mobile phone to call your friends to see if they can lend you the money to stop you being sent to prison today. We also want your vehicle registration, as it is open to the Court to issue a distress warrant on that car and get bailiffs to sell it and pay off your fine.'

'You can't do that. I need it to…'

'To what? To go to work? I don't think so. Now get out and get phoning. We'll call your case back on shortly.'

His mouth opened and closed like an asthmatic cod. He turned twice and looked back at the Bench as he made his way out.

'Yes,' Circe said. 'We mean it.'

The morning went well for Her Majesty's Court Service and the money started rolling in. Cash Converters in Kemp Town saw a lively trade in gold jewellery and electrical items and everyone's mum seemed prepared to advance birthday presents. The only weapon Circe had was her tongue to bluff and bluster, so she wielded it as powerfully as she could, only pausing to gulp court provided tap water from white plastic cups. In the two hours up to the mid-morning break Circe managed to recover over £7,000 pounds in unpaid fines. This was a good performance in any terms, as magistrate's powers had been so diminished over the years, especially since even the right to search them had been taken away. Now all she could say to an offender was, 'If we were to have you searched what would we find?' It worked most effectively on the less experienced defaulters, and also sent a message ricocheting around the others. Friends and family turned up with surprisingly large amounts of cash to pay fines that had been outstanding for years. Suspended sentences were given out leaving a sword of Damocles over their heads. Failure to pay as ordered simply meant that they would go whistling into prison without passing go or collecting £200.

The proceedings took on a slightly biblical tone as a variety of people appeared, all claiming to be sick. They limped, wheeled and wheezed their way into court. One man in particular took nearly five minutes to inch himself in. He had the classic 'burglars breaks' – broken ankles or damaged knees brought about by leaping from someone's house that they'd been stealing from.

Since this defendant said he could no longer get out and about and was on the more lucrative incapacity benefit, Circe reasoned that he must be spending less on himself. His injuries weren't considered permanent, but whether he'd choose to work again was another matter entirely. She had heard time and again of people making long term claims for rheumatism and arthritis afterwards. By the time Circe had finished asking him questions he lost his temper and threw down his crutches with great force, leaving the court with just a respectable limp. Proceedings began to take on the appearance of an Evangelistic healing service, after the asthmatic in the wheelchair who had barely been able to whisper her name suddenly leapt from her wheelchair, knocking it over and shouting curses at the Bench. The sandwich bag of money which she'd been secreting underneath her substantial buttocks fell to the floor and was swiftly retrieved by the usher. Circe suggested that it should be counted to see that none of it had been lost. There was more than enough for the long-standing fine to be paid and the usher pushed the now empty wheelchair out of the court after its previous occupant had run out screaming abuse and profanities at the top of her voice.

Those defaulters waiting for their turn watched the difference in people exiting the courtroom and it became apparent that it would be easier to pay up than be verbally abused. One pale greasy young man with a flat monotone voice explained that he didn't work as he was depressed. He described a life where he sat in his room at the hostel watching TV that he didn't have a licence for, hence the frequent convictions, and smoking and drinking when he could get the cash. He said he had no money at all. Circe had him turn out his pockets which yielded a couple of pounds which he said was his bus fare. She looked at him hard. 'It's a nice day, and you will pay this towards your fine and walk home. The exercise will do you good and will lift your mood. You'll pass a Job Centre on the way back and you can stop off and see what's available. You've got your whole life ahead of you and you've wasted too much of it already.' He nodded and said, 'Yeah you're right.' As he left the court, he waved.

The final defaulter claimed a bad back. Circe wanted to know what the prognosis for its recovery was. He shrugged and as usual she went beyond her questioning remit and asked how he'd got the bad back. The clerk turned around to give a warning look as it should have been confidential medical information. As Circe held his on to his means form showing he received benefits, he answered her. 'I fell off my horse.'

'Horse?' Circe echoed. 'What horse?'

'I've got eight race horses and have them liveried up at Rottingdean.'

Circe could barely believe the wealth this young man had and the length of time he had failed to pay his fine. She took him through a rough guide of the costs and expenses of his equine lifestyle. It seemed there was a large amount of family money and he was a horse trainer with his own riding school and expected to return to work shortly. The fine of £900 for submitting a false benefit claim had been outstanding for three years. Circe glared at him. 'You have had the means to pay your fine. We find wilful refusal and culpable neglect. You have a prison sentence of sixty days suspended for twenty-four hours for you to pay the amount owed in full. Understand?'

'I'll have to get my boyfriend to lend it to me' he said.

'What line of work or country sport does he do?'

'He's a jeweller.'

'You really have abused the system haven't you?'

He finally was shamed enough to look down and nodded. 'You'll get your money by tomorrow.'

In the Magistrates' retiring room at the obligatory court post mortem, the clerk said that the Bench had extracted £16,000 in just one morning from laggards. The best news was that £3,500 had been paid in to the fines office on behalf of Aaron Gunn by a man claiming to be his uncle. The relationship was unlikely as the payee was a youngish Jamaican but the money was real enough. Whereas normally the court only saw a couple of hundred pounds paid at the most, today the clerk gave Circe a high five. The court books would look better balanced now, even though they were still owed twelve million pounds. Twin-set and Social Worker had clearly had their eyes opened. Well, Twin-set had, as Social Worker only had one eye working, the malfunctioning one now looked swollen and weepy enough for a touch of conjunctivitis to be setting in. Circe pulled a celebratory grapefruit from her bag and Social Worker dived for the door in his haste to escape.

Chapter Eight

GIRLS NIGHT OUT

It was Emma's seventeenth birthday and eight of the girls decided to come down from Croydon and have a big night out in Brighton. In the end only five went because some of the parents got wind of their intentions and put a stop to their daughters' plans. One girl, Charlotte, known to her mates as Charlie, told her dad that she would be home that night and he agreed to meet the train. The others concocted a story that they'd be staying in a B&B, but secretly intended to continue clubbing till late, get a mighty gut-buster breakfast in Circus Street, with their pint mugs of tea, and then get the early morning train back. They thought it'd be a right laugh and not having their parents on their backs would be the icing on the birthday cake.

When the girls arrived in Brighton it was a bright, still autumn day. The sea was like grey glass and after having had a couple of drinks in Weatherspoons they decided to go on the pier and into Horatio's bar. Their false IDs were good and they had no hassle from the security. The two bigger girls or 'biffas' as the staff called them were loud and funny, as was expected when you weren't the pretty ones. Not that it stopped them going out in short skirts, but they did have the decency to wear black leggings. These were stretched to the limit. a testimony to the strength of the Lycra fabric.

The girls happily drank alcopops then went on the ghost train and other rides squealing and laughing. As it grew dark they wandered through the noisy, flashy indoor section and played a few of the machines. The biffas were hungry so they all set off for pizzas and washed it down with bottles of Magners cider. Charlie left afterwards saying she'd better get the train or her dad would kill her. The police were already out in force in West Street so she was safe walking up there and onto the crowded pavements of Queen's Road. She was glad to see her father waiting for her at East Croydon, for as usual, she had only taken a cardigan with her and was cold and tired.

The remainder of the party had a few more drinks and then made their way down to the lower esplanade and into the Honey Club. The music was good and the DJ gave them a mention so they had a good time. A few boys made approaches, but Roxanne and Emma had boyfriends at home, though they were happy to flirt and dance, but didn't want any more than that. They were careful with their drinks and looked out for each other. Well, the bigger girls did most of the looking out as they weren't asked to dance. They got the protective lids to put on their bottles and reminded others that if they so much a put a drink down for a minute they shouldn't pick it up again in case it had been spiked.

Roxanne's new shoes were killing her feet despite the gel pad inserts. She had massive blisters on the back of her heels which were red raw. The bright lights and loud music were making everything spin. She walked unevenly to the women's toilets. The door kept moving as she tried to focus and there was a long line of girls ahead of her. Desperate she pushed past a couple of men and barged into their toilet, ignoring their shouts of 'Oi!' The stench of the room had her grab hold of the sink and throw up into it. 'Fucking hell', said one man zipping himself up. 'This is a blokes' toilet. Use the fucking girls' one, you dirty cow.' His words were lost to her next wave of liquid noise as it splattered into and around the small basin, the volley of retching drowning out other similar comments by the lavatory's patrons. One youth who clearly fancied himself as a comedian or had believed the positive image the ecstasy had given him, stood behind Roxanne's backside as she slumped over the sink simulating sex and grinning at himself in the mirror. 'Nah,' he said to his companion. 'She's too noisy for me.'

* * *

Lorcan read the serial at 06.30am. A woman reported rape during the early hours of the morning on the beach between the piers. Roxanne Stiles had been taken to the Victim Suite for support and interviewing. She didn't remember much of what happened other than talking to a young man called Ryan. Lorcan looked at the CCTV footage and nodded to himself. It was the same old pattern - spiders and flies. Local lads would hang round where clubs and pubs disgorged their customers in various stages of inebriation. Almost inevitably there would be girls who were the worse for wear and perhaps not thinking as wisely as they should. Some would make their way down to the beach with their sore feet and head to 'cool off.' Certain males, and it was predictably difficult to get proof because of the circumstances, would prey on these young women who wouldn't have given them a second glance if they had been sober.

As he watched the state of the art CCTV, Lorcan was impressed at the clarity of the pictures. He saw the victim and her friend walk down the beach and sit down. Two boys who had been lounging against the railings in thick parkas sat down on either side of them. They proffered a large bottle of water which the girls took and drank from. After all they hadn't wanted to pay club prices for it. Lorcan slammed his fist into the other hand. Not again! The GHB, or rohypnol, was in the bloody water! He carried on watching and sure enough they started cuddling like courting couples. No violence. No proof. *Shit*, he thought. *What kind of bloody mind-set makes men want to have non-consensual sex with unconscious women? Where's the thrill of the chase? Where's the compliment?* These young men were rapists of a new and low order even by the standards of rapists.

Lorcan liaised with the Victim Suite and spoke with Roxanne's friends. It seemed that the girls had been found asleep on the beach by an early morning metal detectorist, who called the police. Lorcan didn't doubt that Roxanne hadn't given her consent to sex. But he also knew the CPS wouldn't get a conviction. This happened so often. However, the same name had come up again - Ryan. Lorcan checked it. Ryan Platt, Wiston Road, Stoneleigh. A visit may well be in order.

Chapter Nine

CHILD'S PLAY IN STONELEIGH

According to her mother, six year old Chanel Jupp had been attending school on the estate regularly. However, according to the council's Educational Welfare Officer, Mrs Beeching, she only attended seventeen percent of possible sessions. Letters had been sent to Ms Denise Jupp as well as phone calls to try and encourage her to engage in the process of ensuring that Chanel was properly educated.

Denise preferred to be called DeeDee and was generally known by this nickname. It was even on her criminal record as an Also Known As. She was first given the abbreviation locally for her immensely large double D breasts which were also in part responsible for Chanel's untimely conception when only in her early teens. This was by no means a record on the estate, as the joke around Brighton went: *What do you call a fourteen year old year old girl from Stoneleigh?* Answer: *Mum.*

The hormonal and dietary havoc wreaked after the baby's birth and Chanel's sister Demi two years later by a different, but unknown father, had caused her breasts to balloon to double H, although she was still known as DeeDee, especially by men who knew she'd put out for a few drinks, fixes and fags.

DeeDee's own mother often had the kids. To say she looked after them would be an overstatement. She was a young grandmother at thirty-eight, but again this was by no means unique on the estate. They started young and more than a quarter of girls were pregnant by the time they left school. When they went around to their Nan's, Chanel and Demi would be sat in front of her oversized television that dominated one wall. Like the leather settee it was bought with Provident money at exorbitant rates of interest. The kids would eat crisps and pizza washed down with cola and other brightly-coloured fizzy drinks. Sometimes when their mum didn't come back for them the girls would fall asleep on their Nan's settee, unwashed and in their clothes. Chanel was considered old for enuresis, but she would wet herself day and night and always smelled of urine. DeeDee didn't see it as a problem, though her mum grumbled a bit when it interfered with her bingo. However, now they were six and four she could trust them on their own till elevenish. DeeDee would get her mum a bottle of something and that would usually keep her sweet. In that way DeeDee could score and if she was short of money, sell herself first. The doctor had put her on antidepressants years ago and what with her daily script for methadone she had a good base from which to top up.

Chanel's father, Gavin Slade came back into her life when she was about three. He'd sometimes come and get her, usually for an afternoon or evening. Never the morning. He didn't work, but neither did he get up. Chanel used to be glad to see her dad, partly due to sibling rivalry as Demi didn't know who her father was. But she would return to the home quiet and would get angry or tearful if her Nan or DeeDee asked her how her day had been. Sometimes she came back with new clothes which her Nan thought were inappropriate and sexualised her; crop tops, leggings and bikinis. Once there was a lot of underwear which wasn't typical little girls stuff. It was lacy and there were thongs. Demi was jealous, but Chanel seemed happy to give them to her to wear as well.

One day Mrs Beeching called in unannounced at Chanel's Nan's rather than DeeDee's, who never answered or responded. The girls were asleep on the settee and daytime TV was blaring away. The woman insisted on sitting down and looked at the overflowing ashtrays and wine bottles that littered the place. Crisp packets billowed around the floor as an overweight dog pawed at them. Her professional eye was caught by a drawing of a little girl. It was on green sugar paper so must have been done on a rare occasion when Chanel was in school. The little stick figure had a very small pink dress on and her hands were extended and the fingers long and pointed. The words 'Hep me' came from a bubble near the child's face. Most disturbingly from between the drawing's matchstick legs were what appeared to be a series of raindrops.

The official picked up the picture and went into quiet professional mode. 'This is a lovely drawing, Chanel. Is it for Nanna?'

The little girl nodded.

'Not for your Mummy then?'

'No.'

'Why is that?'

'My Mum won't help me. I've asked but she won't. She says not to bother her and make up stories. But it's true. My Nan knows and says she'll sort it out later.'

Mrs Beeching looked at the back of the grandmother making tea in the filthy kitchen, while Chanel slowly began to lift the lid on her degrading and desperate life. The children were taken into care that day. DeeDee didn't visit them.

* * *

Lorcan was assigned the case because of his experience in dealing with such issues. Gavin Slade was the self-appointed organiser of a local paedophile ring. Slade's home was raided once the police had obtained an emergency warrant and there was only one room in the house which could be described as being decent in its indecency. It was a small bedroom painted pink, with pink curtains and a pink quilted bed on which sat a unicorn with an enormous iridescent horn. Lorcan knew it would not grant any wishes of any child who clutched it. There were cameras fitted all around the walls at different angles and a mirror above the bed with a transfer of a fairy on it. Lorcan had never seen any colour as darkly as he now saw this coconut ice pink.

Slade wouldn't reveal who the rest of the circle were, but a few were picked up from films and computer images of themselves with Chanel and other children of both sexes and all ages. Fear ran round the estate that day and on the same night there were bonfires in many of the back gardens destroying evidence. DI Crook drove up the hill leading to the estate and said it looked like bonfire night as the hard drives crackled and burned. No one at the station spoke when the tears ran down Steve Tibbs face as he put the photo files together for the CPS. There was nothing that could be said when confronted with such depravity.

Chapter Ten

COMMUNITY ENGAGEMENT

DS Lorcan O'Leary understood the theory behind the ideological reasons given for the multi-agency meetings that took place between the council, police, other interested parties and the residents of Stoneleigh. This was 'community engagement.' They were intended to listen to each other's concerns regarding problems in the neighbourhood, and to share best practice on how to deal with them. There were no additional financial resources, so everyone knew it was really a pointless talking shop, and just hoped they could encourage the community to effectively censor their own antisocial behaviour and encourage better parenting. The social engineers hoped that community cohesion would be fostered in this way, and that reproval would be better coming from locals rather than the authorities.

Despite the lofty ideals and lip service to the buzzwordy multi-agency cooperation, in practice what happened was that the people who wouldn't engage with authority, employment and everything else, didn't participate. So instead of the very people who needed to become involved, it was left to a few redoubtable prematurely-aged loud matrons in cheap leisure wear. These women often sported crutches, and used Motability scooters and would dominate the meetings with their husky, smoky voices, breathless with emphysema and COPD. The police representative would sit at the panel table with either a rictus smile of feigned understanding or the furrowed brow of apparent concern, garnished with lots of nods. A couple of men with large beer bellies would sit near the back and moan loudly between chesty coughs that nothing would ever get done. Giving them credit, they were right.

There had been millions of pounds invested in West Brighton for You (WB4U), but mismanagement, in-fighting and ludicrous projects ate it all up. It was a testimony to the toxicity of Stoneleigh that the other estate in Brighton could manage to set up and run its own youth club on a voluntary basis, whereas Stoneleigh had to be given £4 million to do the same. The Safer Communities Partnership representative of the council, Arabella Whitelaw, or Whitewash as the police said privately to each other, sat at the table next to the police, a patronising smile playing around her lips. In contrast to the epauletted sharp white shirt of the local Inspector, she was an untidily dressed woman who despite being paid a massive salary by the council, couldn't find it in her heart to comb her hair or iron her floaty diaphanous clothes. When she spoke she waved her hands conducting every comment she made. Her earrings jingled and her braceletted arms clanked and rattled.

Grisly refreshments of squash and biscuits were provided at these meetings. On the whole, the real purpose could be said to give an opportunity to the locals to sound off. The Police Authority sometimes sent a member or support staff along just to be seen to be fielding a presence. Circe had responsibility for Brighton policing division, so she would occasionally attend. Tonight was one of those situations since she was required to present yet another cheque to the community from police funds. This was to pay for a new set of football shirts by way of encouraging local youth to divert their not inconsiderable energies into doing something more productive. Again, the other estate had fundraised for their own team's shirts, but Stoneleigh had to have it handed to them on a plate.

Lorcan was already there wearing a dark grey suit. It was a cheap one, but looked good on him. He hung his jacket on the back of the chair and smiled benignly at old Vera who was going on about kids kicking balls against the walls of her warden controlled flat. It was five minutes to the start of the meeting and he already had the clock on the wall of the Community Centre in his sights. The usual suspects were here. *It would be a long meeting,* he thought, as he glanced at the agenda. The council always insisted on agendas for everything. He saw that the Police Authority would be there to present a cheque. Who would that be? Councillor Keith Higginbotham, self-serving master of the free junket and whose expenses had for years, topped the league for all councillors, not only in Brighton and Hove, but for East and West Sussex as well. There wasn't a quango or other body that he wouldn't get his name on. There wasn't a 'good will visit' or reconnoitre trip to the four corners of the globe that he couldn't justify. He would return in his creased linen suits, bloated and tanned recommending large amounts of public money be spent on art projects that offered no value, certainly not to the cash strapped people of Brighton.

No, Lorcan thought, *it wouldn't be him*. No election coming up, so the political members of the Police Authority would leave public meetings to the independent members. His heart lifted when he wondered if it might be Circe. It was. She arrived with her long copper hair in a loose ponytail. As she removed her black coat Lorcan saw that she was wearing black trousers and a cashmere sweater. She was smart but also just right for the setting. Arabella strode over to her and jangled a handshake. Sensing importance, the locals slunk to their seats. Lorcan moved towards her. 'Hallo again, ma'am. Might I offer you a glass of orange squash before we start?'

Circe looked up at him, her amber eyes meeting his green ones. 'Thanks, but I'd rather drink cat's pee. However tonight I've brought a bottle of water in case there weren't any moggies around.'

Lorcan wasn't sure how to deal with this. He wasn't used to any Police Authority humour. He raised his eyebrows and Circe said, 'I don't like standing on ceremony. Please call me by my first name.'

He stared at her name badge which was pinned to her jacket. 'Thank you ma'am, I mean...' he stammered. 'Is it pronounced Sexy?'

'No, but it is not an uncommon mistake for those who aren't familiar with ancient Greek. Guess the Force diversity policy doesn't go that far. It's Circe, pronounced *sir-see?*'

Before Lorcan could practice it, she swept past and sat on the cheap plastic seat at the table next to Arabella and the leader of the Tenants Association who was wearing a rolled cigarette behind his ear in readiness. So he had to sit further away from her than he'd have liked and took a consolatory gulp of the synthetic orange squash before discarding it.

The meeting opened with the usual introductions, so if Lorcan had but waited he could have saved himself the embarrassment of calling a member of the SPA 'sexy.' As he looked at her profile while they sat there, he thought he'd got it right the first time.

He kept her under observation surreptitiously. She was very different to the usual members of the SPA. Unpretentious, yet with

41

presence. Circe handed the cheque over to the football club and posed for photographs. The Argus was pitifully keen to publicise anything positive about Stoneleigh, even if it was more handouts.

The meeting dragged on with the usual anecdotes from residents. It followed a pattern. There was always an angry feeling as the meeting started. It then moved into a kind of truce position by panel members and after the opportunity was given for locals to vent their frustrations, they ended the meeting by expressing gratitude smiling banally and shaking hands. The task for the meeting was to see how quickly the gap between the moans and smiles could be closed, nothing really changed but it ticked the box of community engagement for the statistics.

When Circe made to leave Lorcan caught up with her outside the Community Centre. She was looking up and down the narrow road.

'Looking for your car ma'am? I mean, Circe?'

'No officer, I was just looking at the estate.'

'Please call me Lorcan.'

'You're a long way from home, that's a Northern Irish accent, isn't it?'

'Yes, I'm from Dungiven.'

'And with your name you'd be a Catholic?'

'Something like that. I thought it was the police who asked the questions?' He smiled.

'The Authority are entitled to ask any officer any question that is reasonable.'

'Of course. I'm ashamed to tell you that like a lot of officers we don't really know what the Authority does, but we do fear your power.'

Circe smiled now. 'God, if only.'

Lorcan remembered. 'I was in court recently when you had one of my cases up before you. I was pleased with the result you gave him.'

'Oh, yes? Which one was that?'

'The guy in the dress holding a six foot plastic sunflower. Claimed he had mental health issues and had numerous hearings and failures to appear with warrants issued. He was up before you for £25,000 benefits fraud and a separate case of arson. His solicitor, 'Slimeball' Samuels, had droned on asking for bail and you snapped in and said it was his client who was claiming mental health issues, not you. You said you'd have to be certified to give him bail, even with conditions, when he'd abused them in the past. I was there to support the CPS in opposing it, as it's not unknown for them to have very little in the way of paperwork. Mr Rogers was there as an agency lawyer shaking an empty file, showing he had no information about him, and I was about to jump up when I heard you say to the defendant, 'Perhaps you'd like to hand your sunflower to your solicitor as bail is refused on the grounds that we have good reason to believe that you would commit further offences if released, since you have a criminal record of fifty-six to date with three outstanding, all committed while on bail.'

'Ah, yes, I remember him. He threw the massive flower it at the Bench like a javelin and called me The Whore of Babylon.'

'Yes that was him!' Lorcan offered to buy her a drink. 'Not squash of course, but I'd like to have a chance to exchange views professionally.'

'Thank you, perhaps another time.'

So he was dismissed. He watched her get into her green Nissan Figaro and swerve sharply to avoid Vera's Motability scooter which she manoeuvred unsteadily. It was well known that she added vodka to her squash from one of her many medicine bottles. Lorcan was about to retrieve his jacket from the hall when he was felled by Vera's usual words.

'Just one more thing officer.....' And there he was stuck for twenty minutes in the cold, while she sat in state on her mobile throne, fag in hand and quilted puffa jacket on her oversized body. Even Fred, the PCSO, laughed silently as he passed.

Chapter Eleven

MENTAL MOZZER

Maurice, or *Mental Mozzer* as he was known to his friends, had done well for a man in his position. He was only thirty but had managed to get on Incapacity Benefit without having had to sign on to Jobseekers first. He'd been clever and had worked it all out. He'd seen his dad pull the bad back one, but that was unreliable. They kept making him have medicals and he was on and off it according to his acting ability.

Mozzer had a low IQ, but he had even lower cunning. As a child, he'd got himself statemented as 'special needs', with ADHD, dyslexia and dyspraxia. He got computers, special support and Ritalin which he sold on the street. He even got a taxi to take him to his special school, when he bothered to go. He was brilliant at faking epileptic fits, starting with starey absences and worked up to the full *grand mal*. It was his party piece and was a great diversion for his friends to get up to all sorts while he writhed and foamed on the ground. Of course it didn't show up in medical tests, but he was still given phenytoin.

Mozzer was allocated a flat by the council with a view to encouraging and supporting him to live independently. His Disability Living Allowance enabled him to kit the place out and he'd done very nicely. He used to punch the air and chant, 'DLA, DLA,' encouraging drug dealers to use the flat for cutting and hiding their merchandise, thereby supplementing the income he received from the state. He would store knives and occasionally a gun that was hot. Every now and again he was caught for petty offences, but his solicitor's pleas regarding his vulnerability were always accepted by the police, or the courts if it ever got that far.

Today was however going to be a good day, but then Saturdays often were. There was a fair at the Old Steine in Brighton which brought lots of people into the City. Plenty of new customers to deal to. Mozzer's mate Gav called round. Mozzer's flat was always good to get pissed and stoned in before going out. Gav had fourteen year old Jim slinking along with him. He was a youth offender with a record as long as a telephone directory. Jim had spotted Gav as he waited outside the same off licence where the police had threatened the owner with prosecution if he served Jim again. Jim already had an ASBO for his drinking. So Gav took the twenty quid his mother had given the boy and got him a bottle of vodka, some tins and some fags.

They went into Mozzer's for a smoke and a drink. Jim was easily getting through two bottles of vodka a day but told his probation officer that he was in control. After an hour or so Mozzer said to Jim, 'Got any money?' The kid shook his head in response.

'Well you can earn some by giving me a blow job. Make sure you do it well. Not like last time.'

Jim got up from the settee and impassively knelt down and performed his task. When it was over Mozzer threw a ten pound note across the room. 'Go on - fetch.'

Jim did and then drank deeply from the two litre bottle of cola to take the taste away.

When they arrived in the centre of Brighton at around seven o'clock they did some deals and bought alcohol from London Road. They were swigging Jack Daniels and coke as well as Absolute vodka and lemonade. The group poured the spirits into the soft drinks bottles to get round the ban on drinking alcohol in a public place. A fight broke out near bushes by the outer edge of the fair. Gav said it was just a skirmish but he thought they should clear off as they were carrying. Mozzer suggested a kebab as they were all a bit hammered. They must have been drunker than they thought as they were refused service. Mozzer swore when he was shown the door and turned back and punched it, breaking the glass and cutting his hand. Staggering out into the street he was initially too drunk to realise the damage he'd done to himself, but even Jim knew it was bad. He led him towards an ambulance on the other side of the road, unsuccessfully trying to staunch the flow of blood with paper serviettes on the way.

When the case came to court the charge was 'wasting police time.' The police had been called by the ambulance crew and while Mozzer was being assessed by the paramedics, Gav and Jim led the police a merry dance by saying that he'd been glassed in the park and showing them the trail of blood. Dog units were called but failed to find anything other than the smears of blood leading to Kebabz takeaway. The owner didn't want to press charges. He had his own reasons for not wanting any involvement with the police. Jim and Gav were convicted and Jim got more intervention from the Social Services. Mozzer had properly trashed his hand having cut through tendons and ligaments. The damage was irreparable and he had no feeling or movement in his lower right arm. He was now properly entitled to his DLA.

Chapter Twelve

IDA DUNMORE

Circe had another message from Alice's father, on her answer phone. *'Can you call me for a chat sometime? I miss Alice as much as you do and it would help if we could be civilised and support each other. I know it's been a long time, but we're both her parents. I'm only asking to talk.'* Then he mumbled on a bit and she heard what she took to be the sound of a glass chinking in some kind of pub. She pressed the delete button.

* * *

Circe sat in court that morning and instructed the usher to hold a wastepaper bin in front of a defendant so that he could spit his chewing gum into it. He removed it with as much disdain as he could manage, smiling the while at his imagined dumb insolence. Circe then turned to his baseball cap which was on the wrong way round. She studied him for a moment then asked, 'Is there a religious or medical reason why you are wearing that hat?'

He looked blank. Many offenders showed disrespect to the court by wearing caps or inappropriate clothing. It was their way of putting two fingers up to authority as they saw it. In summer they would be wearing outfits more suited for the beach and while crop tops and bare midriffs were not uncommon for the women, the men were often shirtless. Even by Brighton's relaxed and casual standards this was not acceptable. As a result the court had an oversized T-shirt that the ushers would make defendants wear before re-admittance to the court. Only last week Circe had required an offender to turn his top inside out and put it on again. The item of clothing had sported the logo *'Fuck me. You know you want to.'*

The usher nudged the man in the dock. 'Take your hat off sir.' He obeyed slowly folding it up and then idly banging the peak into his hand, making a slapping sound.

Circe's jaw tightened as she looked at him and at his financial means form. He owed £3,400 in court fines for a great number of offences over a long period of time. Large amounts had already been remitted with the optimistic hope that he would pay what was remaining. Not only did he not pay, he continued to add further fines to his 'account.' He was unrepresented by a solicitor, as they were only used if there was a real and present danger of their client being sent to prison immediately for non-payment. On the day, the court could always refer them to the duty solicitor to supplicate, but by this time all excuses and options had been exhausted on previous court hearings. It was a mere formality in Circe's view to have legal representation, as the defaulter was going to have to pay or serve time. She always preferred them to pay what was owed since prison cost the tax payer so much and the offender wasn't usually bothered by the sentence. Compensation to victims was supposed to be paid after the sentence, but in practice rarely was. Often the prison term for non-payment was rolled in concurrently on their sentence for their most recent offence so that they could come out with a clean slate. There was a clear tariff on what the offender would serve according to how much was owed. It was a very good deal, if they weren't bothered about going to prison and didn't worry what people thought of them, as no one would earn that amount in the time spent inside. If the stigma didn't bother them then it made good financial sense to go inside, and that's exactly what they did, much to the chagrin of successive governments who tried to ensure the effectiveness of this sentence. Circe would be annoyed when they would ask, 'How much do I owe?' then when told would say, 'How long would I serve if I go to prison?' They would be given the tariff. At that point they'd often hold their hands out for the handcuffs and say, 'OK, let's go then' and the court was effectively turned over.

Circe's defendant today, Scott Riddell, now divested of his gum and cap, stood casually with his eyes playing around the public gallery. A couple of obese women gave him the thumbs up.

His means form told the usual story. On benefits, a social loan and deductions already being made so that the court was low priority in having the fine removed at source. This had been another hopeful government initiative, but which fell apart when the Benefits Agency took its own debt first. So when someone got the initial fine which was properly given, based on offence, plea, finances and response to previous sentences, they knew that if they took out a social loan they then put the court fine at the bottom of the list.

Scott was wearing heavily logoed designer clothes. The court usher had to help him sign his financial statement as he couldn't read. His hair was newly dyed and a fresh tattoo stained his arm.

'Why do you need designer clothing if you can't read? It might as well say Primark as Ralph Lauren.' Circe began.

'I like to look good.'

'What looks good is you paying your debt to society. Why haven't you paid as ordered?'

He shrugged and stifled a smile.

'How much did you pay for your clothing, hairdo and tattoos since the last court appearance? You've made no attempt to make even one payment despite us setting the rate at only £2.50 per week.'

'They were all gifts, I ain't got no money. On the dole, aren't I?'

He smirked openly now.

'Would the people who gave you these so-called gifts like to pay your fine for you, to help you out as it were?'

'Nah. They ain't got that kinda dough.'

'How is it that you have a deep suntan in November?'

'Took me kids to the Canaries. They needed a holiday.'

'These are the same children who were conceived and born in the years that you have been on the court books for non-payment?'

'Yes, as it happens.' A broad smile now

'Apparent financial penury being no contraceptive for you?'

'What?'

'You had children you couldn't support?'

'Their mums do that, alright?'

The flames of anger licked round Circe's heart as the petrol of his responses whipped up the fire.

The duty solicitor had looked round the door, seen the defendant who he knew well, and saw Circe. He looked at the Bench and made a gesture of surrender. They nodded as he backed out of the courtroom. He saw no point in defending the indefensible. He left for better chances with other clients.

'You seem to be living very well and having expensive holidays without that appearing on your means form? All gifts you say? Your

49

fines could have been paid off and we could have had a holiday from seeing you, couldn't we? I see you've taken out a Sky TV package since we last saw you in court?'

Scott nodded.

'All the channels?'

'Yes Disney and films and sport as I don't get out much.'

'But Mr Riddell. You should get out. You should get a job. You should stop offending and you should pay your debt to society. To date you have singularly failed to meet your obligations. Tell the court how much do you spend on alcohol a week?'

'Not much.'

'Well, it's enough that all your crimes are alcohol related. I can see the pack of cigarettes in your pocket, so you smoke as well?'

'Fair enough, your honour. Set the fine at £2.50 a week as usual and I'll be on my way.'

'But that is lower than your booze and fags spend isn't it? Furthermore, you haven't paid anything in eleven years.'

Silently, two uniformed jail staff emerged from the door to the cells and stood behind Scott Riddell. They knew where today's hearing was going and hadn't waited to be called up. The harpies at the back of the court started swearing and shouting at the Bench.

Scott turned round and saw his fate. He looked shocked at the reckoning.

Circe bawled to the public gallery. 'Be quiet or you'll be charged with contempt of court.'

She turned to Scott Riddell as the handcuff ratchets slid into place. 'For years you have made of a mockery of the criminal justice system. The man you glassed got no compensation and is scarred and disfigured for life. You have had the means to pay and have not done so. We find you guilty of wilful refusal and culpable neglect. You will serve ninety days in prison, which is the maximum we are able to give you. You will be inside for Christmas. Take him down.'

As the officers turned him towards the cell steps he said, 'I hope your turkey burns and all your fairy lights blow up, bitch!'

'No reason why they should, so I'll take that risk. One more word and it's contempt of court for you as well. How lucky do you feel today?'

He was shuttled out and the women left the public gallery with noisy sobs.

The following case was a managing director of a dubious antiques company. 'Diamond' as he was known, presumably as he was considered a 'diamond geezer', had numerous fines of a large value for various offences which were generally connected with 'fencing' stolen goods, or 'handling', as was the official charge. He also had more than £2000 worth of parking fines. He'd never paid anything. Checking the DVLA database it was found that he had a valuable car registered in his name. Circe promptly ordered that his Bentley be seized by bailiffs, solving two problems, getting the fine paid off and stopping him getting any more parking tickets.

The next case involved another man being sent down. He then admitted that he had left the full amount of the fine with his friend outside the court. He would now pay it. A nice eleventh hour resolution, except that after waiting in the cells for two hours it became apparent that his supposed friend had left along with the £600, leaving him to be conveyed to Lewes prison to serve his sentence. Circe's colleague predicted an ABH would be committed on his release. A lesson to pick your friends wisely.

Halfway through the afternoon's proceedings the clerk to the court looked at a message then turned to Circe. 'Madam, you may be interested to know that Mr Riddell's fine has been paid in full. It seems that there was a BMW for which he had no licence, and which his present partner has sold. She has got fed up with the life he leads and wants him to go straight apparently. We have the cash and Mr Riddell is now a free man, though we understand he is very angry with his partner. She may be staying with her mother until things settle down, as she's pregnant again.'

As there was no one else in court at the time the Bench permitted themselves a laugh and toast with the plastic cups of water.

* * *

After court finished, Circe drove to George Street in Hove, renowned for its many second hand shops. Over the years many thriving businesses had closed and become charity shops. What remained were little cafés which came and went depending on the

51

fortunes of their owners, and how often the police raided them for drugs. Coffee Republic dominated the southern quarter of the street though Circe could still remember when it had been a gentleman's outfitters of some distinction.

Circe knew the character of the different types of charity shops. Some people had favourites and if they were wealthy the clothes were more likely to be designer. Cancer and hospice shops attracted good quality donations as their profile seemed to be higher. The British Heart Foundation was a close runner up too. It was however with some trepidation that Circe would go into the stores as many of the people she had sentenced to unpaid community work would be behind the counters and she hardly felt like rummaging for clothes to wear to court in front of them.

Circe always chose her clothes with care. She used charity shops because she liked the idea of recycling. She also loved bargains. *What's wrong with that?* she'd say to herself. *I can get designer or good name clothes for a fraction of the cost.* January was usually the best time as these shops were full of clothes that were now too small for their owners after seasonal excesses. Either that, or people had cleared out their wardrobes to fit in bargains from the sales. Whatever the reason, she knew what she wanted and usually got it. She wasn't interested in underwear or shoes - that was a step too far - but suits, blouses, tops, trousers or coats, as long as they were black, represented her taste. She'd go for different textures and fabrics to enhance the black look and would make regular purchases. Sometime later she would re-donate them back to a charity shop and get new ones. In this way her wardrobe always looked varied and interesting, even with its mono colour. Her task today however, was very different.

She made her way along George Street with a carefully planned list. Circe had spent ages working out what her disguise would be. The standard attire for many on the estate was the ubiquitous hoodie with the beak of a baseball cap propping it up underneath. A sort of daffy duck meets a nun's wimple combo. It served well to disguise the face from cameras and witnesses. The rest of the ensemble would be baggy designer sportswear, which was a kind of indistinguishable uniform.

Circe wanted to be invisible so decided to work on the image of an older woman. The colour of the clothes was important and her favoured black was no good. What was neutral? Beige. No, too visible at night. Navy, that was it. She hated navy and beige with a vengeance and had vowed never to go into old age in those drab safe colours. George Street was busy and she flitted from shop to shop until she found the ingredients for her outfit. The elderly volunteer cashiers were too busy struggling with the intricacies of the tills to pass any comment on the clothing that seemed so at odds with the woman standing in front of them. There had been one incident in the Save the Children shop where a little old lady snatched hold of the jumper that Circe was proposing to buy. She was as short of manners as she was of height and hung onto the garment with surprising ferocity. Crossly Circe looked into her wrinkled old face. 'I saw this first and yet you grabbed it. Where are your manners?'

'At my age you don't have time for those.'

Circe handed her the sweater. She examined it, like it was dog's mess and threw it back down and sniffing unpleasantly moved on to the next rail. So Circe got it after all.

She took her purchases home and quickly ran up the stairs with them, narrowly avoiding being tripped up by her cat, Rupert. Before she threw it all in the washing machine she tried on the clothes. A pair of navy blue elastic waist-banded slacks, baggy enough not to define her shape. Useful when you still have a stone to lose as well. She pulled on a musty navy ribbed baggy turtleneck jumper. It added a visible two stone to her appearance. She was very pleased with the three quarter length navy coat. It was A-line with a pleat at the back, no belt and large square pockets with buttons that matched the cuffs and front fastenings. The hat was the *piece de resistance*. It was felt with a wide brim that would conceal her hair colour and face - like the beak of a baseball cap. She'd had to settle for dark brown but in a moment of sartorial inspiration added a navy nylon scarf to tie it on - a look which successfully concealed her hair and face. The one big expense were the new Clarks shoes - she emerged £50 poorer but with some very sensible navy flat lace ups which were silent and would be good for running. The shoe conscious residents of Stoneleigh would not give much attention to those.

Standing there in the smelly clothes she thought about how she'd age her face. No make-up except for pale foundation. Pencil dark rings under her eyes. She noticed that if she pushed her tongue behind her lip she looked simple and ugly. Perfect. No one would notice or recognise her. The cats stared in olfactory revulsion at their mistress. The tartan shopping trolley had been a must have. It would contain all her accoutrements and the plastic navy blue shopping bag would hold the paperwork and hand tools. She parked it next to the stack of Lakeland catalogues on her coffee table.

She pulled her tongue back long enough to smile at herself. Then she broke wind with unrestrained gusto. The boiled egg diet was living up to unpleasant expectations. The cats left the room with its heavy sulphurous odour.

Circe heaved the washing on and rolled another cold boiled egg on the counter watching its brown spotty shell crackle off. Cutting it in quarters she noted the gelatinous white which still showed the knife's ridges, and the yolk with its bluey green powder at the edge where it met the albumen. Her bowels gave out more air as she stared at it.

No, she said to herself, I need to celebrate my new alternate identity and she poured herself a substantial BSC. The mint would settle the antisocial volleys in her intestines and the juniper in the gin would be restorative. It was all coming together at last. She looked at her copper-haired self in the mirror. Moving closer she stared at her amber eyes. Contact lenses. Yes, she'd get blue lenses as she needed to have pale eyes to look older. She raised the glass to her new identity: Ida Dunmore.

Chapter Thirteen

THE RESPONSIBLE ADULT

That morning the estate wind bit through Sam's cheap but fashionable cardigan as she walked towards home. She was only fifteen but hadn't bothered with any education for a long time. She'd cleverly swerved the council's school inclusion policies and now spent her time pretty much as she wanted, which wasn't to say that time didn't hang heavily on her, like her oversized breasts and doughy abdomen.

The truanting, or unauthorised absences, as they were presently called, had started early. Sam's mother Tina was just fourteen when she gave birth to her daughter and so they lived with the grandmother. Every girl in the family was pregnant before their seventeenth birthday, but there was never any family disapprobation even when a relative was the father. In accordance with family customs, Tina wasn't interested in Sam and certainly didn't know the father's identity, so her daughter lived her life unencumbered by motherly support or any encouragement to go to school. From primary school age she'd preferred to stay indoors with excuses like tummy upsets and various phobias, and then the old tried and trusted excuse of being a victim of bullying. Tina didn't engage well with the school and didn't keep appointments to discuss the absences or respond to letters or visits. Eventually the local authority stepped in and after a lengthy period of time and non-cooperation Tina was taken to court charged with failing to send a child to school. All kinds of plans and 'back to school' programmes were set up but failed to achieve appropriate attendance. Sam's clever ploy in claiming that she was being bullied resulted in her being sent to different schools costing time and effort on the part of the authorities. As these establishments were some distance from her home. It was therefore necessary for her to be transported in taxis which were provided at the tax payer's expense, even though it was known that Sam wouldn't get into them. Sam grew overweight and began a self-fulfilling legacy of developing the health problems she'd previously claimed like asthma and eczema. Despite the court orders Tina never paid her fines and was repeatedly arrested on warrant, only to have the Magistrates believe how hard her life was and to reduce the amount owed to a 'manageable' level of £5 per week. Tina would smile as she left court as that was less than she paid out for fags each day. Result!

She did nearly lose custody of Sam on a couple of occasions. The child was fostered when her mother's drug taking and behaviour got out of control. However, it never lasted long, since it was fashionable to take the child's view into account and Sam would obviously rather have a chaotic, unsupervised lifestyle than the structured school life offered by the foster parents with their regular healthy meals. What child wouldn't prefer a bucket of KFC in front of the telly late at night with the promise of lying undisturbed in bed the next morning?

Sam liked her life and she'd got it much where she wanted it, and also had some grudging respect from other youth on the estate. Hers was a long-term troublesome family and no one wanted to mess with them. Today Sam arrived back at the home she shared with her mother and the latest drug dealing boyfriend and the two massive dogs who spent most of their time on the first floor balcony barking and intimidating passers-by with their aggressive unhappiness. Pushing the door to the flat open she flopped down on the massive settee. Tina was smoking while she watched the television, a can of Magners cider in her hand.

'Mum, you know that bitch Nikki?'

'What that dyed blonde girl who's always shoplifting? Good name Nikki, for nicking isn't it?'

Sam nodded, her colour high. 'Yes that's her. We call her 'knickerless' 'cos she's a fat slut.'

'Well - what about her?'

'She's been messing about with my Winston!'

'You're fucking joking!'

'No, I'm not, I've texted her and told her that I'm not fucking having it.'

It was a measure of the close and dysfunctional relationship that the mother and daughter had that they behaved more as sisters. The fifteen year age gap between them was levelled by shared drink, drugs, fags and men. Tina didn't approve or disapprove of Winston, he was twenty-seven, some twelve years older than Sam and two years her junior. He was reputed to have fathered at least nine kids with various baby mothers and Sam was three months gone with his latest, having put her name down on the council house waiting list on the way back from the doctor's surgery.

Sam flushed angrily. 'People have turned round and said that Nikki is pregnant with Winston's kid.'

'You're fucking joking!' Tina lit another cigarette and offered one to Sam who took and lit it, dragging hungrily on its tip.

'Nah, I'm not and if it's true, I'll kill her. I've left her some messages and I want it sorted today.'

'What's Winston got to say about all this?'

'Dunno. He's due in Bethnal Green Magistrates court today and they usually take his phone while he's in custody. He'll be alright, he's got a good brief – 'Technicality Terry' - he's called. But I'll have to deal with this myself. I'll be OK…'

She broke off while her phone gave a messaging bleep. 'Fucking slag,' Sam screeched. 'Listen to what she's written 'Yes, I'm pregnant and me and Win are going to be together so get used to it, loser.'

She shouted the last part of the message back to her mother as she went to the kitchen and took a cider for herself.

Tina screwed up her face as she inhaled her cigarette smoke. 'Whatcha gonna do, babe?'

Sam flopped heavily on the new and un-paid for white leather seven-seater settee, which although it took up a good part of the room, still allowed a good view of the television. Before she could answer her mother, her mobile bleeped again and there followed an angry stream of texts between the two pregnant girls in which dates were compared and boasts made of Winston's assurances to each of them. Finally the threats started and they agreed to sort it outside the mini-mart in fifteen minutes. Sam tried texting Winston, but there was still no reply. Tina was now asleep and snoring on the settee and didn't hear her daughter get up and leave. She also wouldn't have heard Sam go to the kitchen and grab a serrated knife from the kitchen drawer. It was part of a free set from QVC when she'd bought some jewellery. It had a black plastic handle and three silver metal circles on it and Sam pushed it into her gold sequined Primark shoulder bag. Sam felt the white rage of justified anger as she stomped the ten minutes to the mini-mart. Nikki was already there and there were a number of other young people known to both girls. Ayodele waved a hand from an oversized Lonsdale sports top. The waistband of the grey jogging bottoms were half way down his thighs as if someone had interrupted him preparing to go to the toilet. His underpants were top of the range designer boxers and the waistband proclaimed the FUBU label. 'Ya a'right shorty? Wotcha up to with yo fatty boom boom?'

Sam was glad to see him. 'Hi, Dele, you know I'm Winston's wifey and we is having a baby.'

He laughed. 'No kidding? He said there was a little problem, and that he was too fertile for his own good.' Dele laughed so genuinely that the waistband of his underpants bounced up and down. 'He's in the big City today, ain't he?'

'Yes, but I've got trouble with that bitch Nikki. She reckons she's knocked up by my Winston too and says she'd gonna take him off me. I'm gonna sort it one way or the other.'

'He was seeing you first, wasn't he?' Dele meant well, but it didn't help there was already enough paraffin on her flames.

Sam shouted and pointed at Nikki. 'Come here bitch. We'll soon see who's going to get Winston. I'm gonna kick any kid out of your body. If there ain't one there then I'll kick you so hard your bag will come out of your stinking cunt.'

Nikki waved a black and white piece of paper. Instinctively despite her blind rage Sam could see that it was an ultrasound picture. She had one herself, so Nikki must be at least three months too. How the fuck could she have let this happen to her? She was humiliated and everyone on the estate knew it. What if Winston wasn't going to stay with her? Not that he ever had actually stayed, he usually did the business and left, but she felt special as everyone liked him. He was a great guy and would do anything for anyone. When anyone needed gear or anything else they could rely on Winston. He was real East London he was and knew it all.

Sam got close enough to see the scabby scatter of acne on each of Nikki's plump cheeks. Clearly whatever makeup she'd nicked that week didn't cover the damage. The other bystanders looked interested and clearly wanted to see how this was going to turn out. Sam told them all to clear off and it was between her and 'Nickers.' Sam clearly had less of a support network than her rival. Dele hovered, sniffing rhythmically and rubbing his nose from time to time.

Sam shouted again. This time more like a wounded animal as she knew within the depths of herself that there was no happy ending. The foetus swam in the murky, dirty, alcoholic amniotic fluid and waited. Sam threw her cigarette on the floor and the door to the mini-mart was pushed open. Instinctively everyone looked round to see who was coming out of the shop. In an instant Sam pulled the knife from her bag and ran at Nikki who defensively put her hand across her abdomen. The knife went in to the centre of her hand and she fell to the ground.

* * *

Tina was woken from her drunken stupor by the police who needed her to be the nominated responsible adult with Sam when she was interviewed. It was clearly pushing the realms of credibility to give Tina this title. The duty social worker was already there when the police conveyed an unsteady Tina towards an interview room. She'd been told the story and that her daughter was going to be charged with grievous bodily harm; or in police parlance, 'A section 18 unlawful wounding with intent.'

Tina had sworn and yelled, 'the first time she ever stands up for herself, and this is what she gets. You're all bastards.'

Chapter Fourteen

SUSSEX POLICE HEADQUARTERS

ACC Anne Lancaster chaired the Community Engagement Steering Group, and the meeting was usually held at police HQ in the grandeur of seventeenth century Malling House, Lewes. It was only one step out of her wooden panelled office to the meeting room on the ground floor, whereas Lorcan and Inspector John Crook were required to make the journey from John Street police station in Brighton. It was only some seven miles away, but car parking was always an issue and spaces for lower ranking officers were at a premium. Recently the ACC had assumed more direct management functions including that of the CID team at Brighton. This was the consequence of a perfect storm with HR and senior officers off sick with stress, and one Chief Superintendent having committed suicide following a marriage breakdown. Organisational investigations were ongoing, and Ann Lancaster was thought to be a safe pair of hands at this difficult time.

When they finally sat down at the meeting, the ACC wanted to go through all the figures on the Force's meetings with different community groups. Lorcan always felt this was a complete waste of time as the police only engaged with self-styled community leaders who largely spoke for their own interests and agendas.

Anne Lancaster's steely blue eyes homed in on the DS who was twirling the free Sussex police biro that had been put with some paper before everyone's seat. It was a well-known fact that the police liked anything free and a biro could make their day. Lorcan had his own mobile on silent next to the police one. His father was in residential care and was being very challenging at present, and Lorcan dreaded the phone calls. There wasn't much he could do. His father had been 'expelled' from two already. He didn't have a formal Antisocial Behaviour Order, but he was on a kind of list of very difficult residents that were shared by different homes. There were enough people on the waiting list for them to pick and choose and if they were self-funding, as Lorcan's father was, there would be cherry picking on both sides. As a consequence of his 'issues' Lorcan had no choice but to place him in a really expensive home which was more like a top-notch hotel than a care home. The little pittance of his father's savings from the enforced sale of his house was haemorrhaging away faster than a haemophiliac with his leg cut off. However, the problem was how far the issues were due to old Mr O'Leary's cantankerous personality, or his dementia. Lorcan was very certain that it was his father's choice, rather than a medical condition, that made him go into the home's kitchen and urinate on the work tops. He had the capacity to know what he was doing right enough.

His thoughts were broken by Anne Lancaster's abrasive voice. 'Well, Detective Sergeant, how did the Stoneleigh meeting go yesterday?'

Hiding his automatic shudder he went onto autopilot. 'Well, ma'am, there were the usual suspects in attendance...' He broke off as Circe made an apologetic entry into the room. She gave a general smile to the assembled officers and civilians and sat down next to ACC Lancaster, who pushed an agenda towards her. Lorcan was surprised to feel that he was blushing.

Anne Lancaster explained that Lorcan was giving a debrief on yesterday's meeting. He resumed by asking Circe how she'd describe the attendance from the Authority's perspective.

Circe tucked an escaped strand of a red curl behind her ear. 'Well, I don't know what the Authority in general would think about it, but from my point of view it was the standard salvo we've come to expect from the estate. An ear-bending of residents, or if you prefer, a whine of service users.'

DI Crook suppressed a laugh and turned it into a sage nod as Circe continued. 'We have to have this so-called community liaison, but it's the same people who turn up whether to local action teams, LAT's, as you police like to call them, or Crime and Disorder Reduction Partnerships. We all know that it's a rather cosmetic endeavour. We have to be seen to be doing it and we never make a difference to those who really need that difference made. The antisocial types just carry on while we pay lip service to community engagement. When the police hear about cars racing through the streets at night causing a nuisance they'll put on extra patrols to catch the offenders, but we don't make much of an impact on those who don't want to ride round at a normal speed. They aren't engaged are they? Sorry Detective Seargent, I'm sure you can precis the meeting.'

Lorcan smiled. 'You've said it all. We need to see how cost effective these meetings are. If we were to do everything the public wanted then they'd insist on having a policeman stood on every street corner if they could. At basic ground roots level these meetings serve to reassure the equivalent of the worried well, as doctors describe frequent patients. We need to lift up the stone and have a look underneath at what is really going on in that estate.'

John Crook sighed reminiscently of the old days but shook his head. 'Ain't going to happen anymore. The world has moved on and you should know that from Northern Ireland, Detective Sergeant, the old ways have given way to jaw-jaw. The best thing is just to do it and try keep it as short as possible and focus on the facts.'

Anne Lancaster looked at her watch. 'We have a lot to get through and I can see we're not going to agree on this one. We have another meeting in six weeks. I suggest that we look at the crime figures of that estate alone, pinpoint the areas of concern and drill down into them to establish what is going on in a much more micro managing way. Hope that suits all the dinosaurs here? Open lines of communication need to be maintained. It is policing by consent, despite that fire engine getting rocks thrown at it on the estate last week. Everyone happy?'

No one looked up, though the staff officer was taking notes and smiling brightly. Circe wrote something on her agenda that Lorcan couldn't read despite craning his neck. He couldn't get over her writing in red ink with a fountain pen. He thought it was a real statement; nothing she wrote down could be ignored. He was left to his own thoughts as the blinds were drawn down for a PowerPoint presentation about the level of public satisfaction with the Force. He lifted up his phone and looked at the screen. Three messages. The first was indeed from the home. *Your father has just complained to a visitor that he is Jewish and that he's being denied a kosher diet. We have no note of this on our files.* Lorcan texted back. *He's a Catholic and used to eat fish on Fridays, a rule which he always disobeyed*

62

unless he could put someone out by insisting on it. Since the Church in its infinitely changeable wisdom decided that the fish stocks didn't need to be depleted every seventh day, he's eaten everything, especially if he's not paying.

The second message ran, *Also is there a need for him to be wearing Mrs Phillips' crocheted tea cosy on his head saying it's a skullcap?*

Lorcan took such a big intake of breath that Inspector Crook stared at him in the gloom, both literal and metaphorical. He texted back. *Not for religious reasons. Of course, if he's cold that's another matter.*

The third text should have been read first, it transpired. *Sorry to have troubled you. Your father has urinated into a wastepaper bin in the residents' lounge and it is very obvious to everyone that he has not been circumcised. I think the Jewish issue is now at an end.*

Chapter Fifteen

STONELEIGH ESTATE

She knew it wouldn't be long now. Tracey Wilson stood by the cigarette pockmarked UPVC window peering down the road into the increasing darkness. The original white plastic surface was stained a dirty cream from all the cigarette smoke. Where she rested her sweating hands they left whiter patches on the surface. Between the panes of double glazing the condensation glittered on a skein of cobwebs, which formed a canopy above an array of dead insects.

A large television dominated one side of the boxy room, flashing its coloured reflections on the glass, momentarily picking out her peroxided blonde hair in psychedelic shades. The room was icy. He'd left no money for the prepayment meter, but she sweated nevertheless. She could hear her two kids screaming and fighting upstairs. Pulling herself away from the window for a moment she limped the four paces to the bottom of the narrow, paint chipped stairs and yelled at them to be quiet or it would be the worse for them. A well-used threat with no currency, since things always were the worse for them. It was impossible to set a standard that would have any meaning or relevance. There was a momentary pause in the childish rumpus, then the sound of a smack and a little girl screaming and crying.

Tracey returned to her vigil at the window. The street light cast long shadows and the frost sparkled on the excrement covered grass verge. There was a cult of genderless machismo that prevented dog owners from ever bending down with a plastic bag and retrieving their beast's bowel contents and no one who knew the area would be inclined to remonstrate with them.

Tracey's head ached. She was seriously clucking. The methadone didn't deaden it. Her last fix was eight hours ago. She used an old needle to pierce the condoms next to the bed. If they had a kid together that would help. Her jaw seemed slightly misaligned this time according to the mirror in the bathroom – the only one in the house that Eddie hadn't yet smashed. She wasn't sure what was broken and what was bruised. This time her right eye was swollen shut and her lip split. He'd ripped an earring through her ear, leaving the lobe looking like a bloodied snake's tongue. She never smiled. There was no reason to, so no one noticed her four missing teeth. Right now there was a bloodstained patch of scalp where he'd pulled out a clump of her hair. She changed the parting and draped it over her blackened eye.

Where was he? Had he found someone else? Usually he was nicer to her the next day, especially if the police weren't informed. Last night that nosy old bag from across the road called them. Tracey had told them to fuck off, she didn't need help, like she always said. Their attendance made no difference. She wouldn't make a statement.

Back in the day, she sometimes did, but always retracted it before she got to court. Eddie was lovely when he said sorry, he was so loving, and he promised not to lose his temper again. It was just stress and she riled him up by not having his dinner on the table, asking him where he'd been till two in the morning, or if she had a period. 'It takes two to start a ruck,' he'd always say, and it was fifty percent her fault, she knew that. She'd just have to make more of an effort.

The court's Witness Support Team had sent a domestic violence worker round and through the letter box she tried to persuade Tracey to testify. She waited till Tracey came out to pick up the kids from school and walked along with her, she obviously didn't have enough work to do, or she wouldn't be hanging around all day. She had the cheek to tell Tracey that Eddie wouldn't stop till he'd killed her. The bitch kept going on about the time he threw her downstairs and broke her hip and thigh in four places. True, she had metal plates and walked with a limp now, and a bit of arthritis had set in, but that didn't mean he'd kill her.

The worst days were when they got the benefit money. He'd want it to go off drinking and would come back and have rough sex. It wasn't rape, just that she didn't want it and asked him not to, but he did what he wanted and then called her a slag. She knew he'd spent the money, but he was entitled to some pleasures. He'd had it hard inside when some bloke had got stabbed in Brighton and they fitted up Eddie. She gave him an alibi, but they found his DNA on the knife. The police can fake anything.

Tracey looked out of the window. The bus had disgorged its load and he wasn't on it. The tears ran down her mottled cheeks, perhaps he didn't love her as she looked so ugly now. She started crying. She saw her reflection in the window and cried harder. Who could blame him when she'd let herself go so much?

Seeing a man's shadow approach, her battered heart leapt with anticipation within her bruised ribcage. But it wasn't him, it was that dealer going to collect from next door. The street was empty, devoid of all hope.

Chapter Sixteen

IDA DUNMORE

The next day Circe had her usual challenges to face in court. It was a shoplifting trial. Two young women had been observed in various shops behaving suspiciously in and outside Churchill Square mall. Finally, they were seen in the cosmetic department of Debenhams. The security staff were alerted by the 'round robin security scheme' and turned up at once. The two girls were swiftly spotted. Girl 1, as she was referred to in court, had bright magenta red hair and very heavy make-up. So much so that initially staff were uncertain about her gender. Girl 2 was more ordinary in appearance with spiky bleached hair and more moderate make up. She had a very well-developed chest the prosecutor said, which drew attention to her. After filling their bags with a variety of expensive cosmetics they left the store without paying.

They had entered not guilty pleas and their case was booked for trial. This was despite the CCTV evidence clearly showing them stealing. As the case was about to open Circe asked their solicitor what the basis of the defence was.

'Identity, your worship.'

'How so?'

'Madam, if I may invite my clients to step into the dock?'

The door to the courtroom opened and two shrouded figures appeared. One in full burka and the other in a niqab.

The prosecutor explained that they had both apparently converted to Islam since their arrest. As if to prove the point a voice from within the burka shouted, 'Up with Allah.' The other girl shouted, 'Yeah, Mohammed is cool.'

The solicitor moved to say that identification would now be impossible, but Circe told the prosecutor that, with the greatest of reluctance, a new trial date would have to be set. She wasn't going to have a couple of silly girls making a mockery of the justice system. They would take legal and spiritual advice before proceeding. If this wasn't stopped Circe thought it would open a floodgate of manipulation.

The next case was a burglar who was profoundly deaf. When he came into court he was greeted by what was obviously his fan club of scruffy loud men and women at the back of the public gallery. Next to him was a Labrador in a red coat bearing the words *hearing dog for the deaf.* The dog looked depressed. Because of the seriousness of the case, the burglar was on his way to Crown Court for trial and it was for the magistrates to commit him. The facts were read out and the Bench stared in horror. The accused had been given this highly trained and expensive dog, which he had systematically abused and retrained so that it would act as a lookout while he burgled the properties. The dog would apparently alert him by pulling at his clothing if anyone approached so that they could make good their escape. The poor dog wasn't being prosecuted, but he was ruined as far as being reallocated to a more worthy owner. His shame filled eyes said it all.

Getting home that night Circe laid out her vigilante clothes. There was no alternative. The justice system had cratered. Had she really voted Labour all of her life for this? She wondered if she could make even a tiny difference. What had she got to lose? The part of Circe that had come adrift was now floating free. Someone had to teach these fuckers a lesson. Someone had to do something about the victims. Yes, she was ready. She put on the clothes transforming herself with every garment. *Bloody hell, I look shit.* Nevertheless, she was pleased with the reflection the mirror threw back at her.

She waited till midnight checking her paperwork and equipment. She'd decided on *Out of Court Settlement* as the name for her enterprise. Circe had taken details of convicted criminals from the court list 'statement of means' form in the fines court. This was absolutely forbidden and all court lists with offender details were to be torn up and placed in the secure official waste disposal at the end of each sitting. In doing so she knew she was breaking her judicial oath and was putting herself at risk of custody.

Her first victim was going to be Danny Garogan DOB 24/4/80. Fifty-nine previous offences. Of particular concern was four 'driving whilst disqualifieds.' He was caught in a VW Golf which he'd recently bought while on benefits and with a three year driving ban.

He was drunk and had his own and his girlfriend's kid by another partner in the car without seatbelts on. His solicitor and probation officer had pleaded that he needed one more chance to straighten out his life, so asked for him to have yet another community order. He'd had six already, which had singularly failed to engage him in any personal reformation. No, he needed to stop driving and putting other people, including the children, at risk. No probation named *'Think First'* scheme, or *'Think Last'* as Circe called it, was going to make a bit of difference to this man's lifestyle of flagrantly disobeying court orders.

She sent Alice a short email, but omitted to mention her plans. Next to the computer was a mini Maglite, spray glue, superglue, a Lakeland plastic bottle with a nozzle on intended for icing or drizzling balsamic glaze, permanent felt tip markers, a crowbar, a Stanley knife and packet of spare blades. These were in a Lakeland click and lock box. Danny Garoghan's car details and address were on a separate piece of paper. Again, information she had taken from court records, strictly against the regulations. She put her equipment in the navy blue shopping bag, as she didn't plan to use the trolley tonight on her first run.

As she got into her green Figaro she was aware of how warm she felt despite the cold November night. As she drove the four miles towards the estate, the danger of the enterprise became more obvious. What if she were caught? She'd be disgraced and certainly imprisoned. It was the worst breach of trust for a magistrate. It was unthinkable! Wiping the sweat off her brow she considered the immediate danger of being caught by the convicted criminals she was about to vandalise. *Christ! I could be beaten up, or worse. They could throw paint stripper in my eyes or stab me with my new Stanley knife. They might recognise me from court. Anything could happen.* It wasn't too late to turn back now. There was still time to change her mind. But her icy heart reminded her that there was no other option. Someone had to do something to stop the rot that undermined the criminal justice system. Offenders weren't impressed by anything the present regime threw at them, so they needed to have a taste of their own medicine.

She caught sight of her face in the mirror and shook her head. Her hands gripped the steering wheel but she didn't turn the car round. *No girl, just for once you're going to see justice done.*

She parked some way from Danny Garoghan's address. She snapped on the blue latex Lakeland gloves and covered them with the old knitted ones. She walked slowly, as befitted her alter ego, Ida Dunmore. It also gave her time to see who was about. She felt quite protected under her hat and scarf brim. Some of the upstairs windows had lights on, while others showed the bluish lights of televisions.

Circe spotted Danny's car. There were no lights on in the address she had for him. The front garden had a load of rubbish in it, just as she expected. His car was parked about fifteen metres north of his property on a road where parking was at a premium. His was within a long row of cars. She checked her watch, heart pounding, at 12.45am. A frost was forming on some of the cars. Sweating, Circe felt in her coat pocket and closed her hand round the Stanley knife. This was it. Be quick. Leave the knife till last in case of noise. She delved in her bag for the paint stripper. Having decanted it into the useful plastic bottle with a nozzle, she was able to write BANNED DRIVER on the bonnet. Good old Lakeland. A product for every job you could think of! It was easy to bend back the wipers. She squeezed superglue into the locks. Growing bolder she checked up and down the road and looked over towards the houses. Then she tentatively took the Stanley knife and slashed the side wall of the nearside front tyre. Nothing happened. How much strength was needed? She swiped again with more pressure. Under her hat's brim she was sweating profusely. Was this the start of the menopause, or just fear? Suddenly she was startled by a loud hiss. The tyre collapsed at once. She rushed round to the rear offside and stabbed it hard once. Big hiss. Yes, she'd got the hang of it.

She dropped the knife in her bag, stood up and crossed the road and made her way back to her car at what she calculated was an old lady pace. But her heart was pounding and she felt both sick and exhilarated. Circe got into her car and took the brake off and let it cruise down the hill before starting the engine and disturbing the residents. God what was that awful smell? It didn't take her long to locate the source. She'd stepped in dog's mess somewhere and it was now on her car pedals and carpet. *Great*, she thought. *That's a nice job for tomorrow.* The tree outside her house waved its branches and the streetlight glittered on the frosty pavement. But as she walked back into her own house, shoes in hand, she smiled. She'd just got a new idea.

Chapter Seventeen

ANTI SOCIAL BEHAVIOUR

Lorcan studied the morning's serials, the list of records about reported problems and crimes made to the police. He had a heavy day ahead including meeting a persistent moaner on the Stoneleigh estate, so he scanned the list, more for amusement than anything else.

There had been a call from a middle-aged woman who was concerned about a seagull which had been perched on her neighbour's roof for two hours just sitting there 'looking depressed.' The call handler, well trained in such matters, explained that seagulls often looked down in the beak and if it wasn't injured he'd probably cheer up when the weather improved. The reassurance took sixteen minutes of expensive police time, but she noted the lady did sound less worried by the end.

One serial that did attract Lorcan's attention was from Candice Tibbs, the wife of PC Tibbs. Apparently, they had themselves been the victims of a break in to the shed at the side of their house and a bike had been stolen. A smile crept across Lorcan's face and he went to make himself a celebratory cup of tea. Young Tibbs was always the practical joker, always happy to laugh at someone else's expense. So now the tables were reversed. As he fished the cheap tea bag out of the grimy cup he recalled that Tibbs used that bike to cycle to the station to get the train to work, so he'd be late today alright. He re-read the rest of the notes laughing out loud when the call centre told Mrs Tibbs that they would send a crime prevention officer round as they had forgotten to lock the shed door properly. Mrs Tibbs was keen to apportion blame saying it was down to her husband as she'd told him repeatedly to get a new padlock, but did he listen? No. She said it served him right that he'd lost his bike and had to get a taxi to the station.

The section was still laughing when Steve Tibbs arrived. He was obviously annoyed as they all started up. Lorcan's was the first, 'Has anyone shed any light on the theft...'

'Leave it out,' Tibbs growled.

'Hopefully the wheels of justice will move and find the thief.' And so it went on. Even Inspector Crooks hummed, 'A bicycle made for two.'

Tibbs was almost relieved to go up to Stoneleigh to speak to the victim of a walk-in burglary. It seemed that Nico Costello had come home drunk from the pub and consequently didn't make it as far as the upstairs of his house where his partner and her kid were asleep in bed.

When he came round the next morning a drawer of a plastic melamine shelving unit was open and all his store of cigarettes, 'bought cheap from a friend who goes to France', had gone, along with £500 in cash that he was 'looking after for another friend.'

He was clearly annoyed, but also seemed fearful. His eyes with their pinpoint pupils shifted uneasily, but the lids kept closing with longer and longer gaps each time. Lorcan and Tibbs looked round the small, dirty living room. It smelled of rank old dog, but there was no actual dog. The walls and ceiling were painted a dull aubergine. Although this masked the smoke marks, it didn't affect the stale odour of the furnishings or the stench of the overflowing foil takeaway containers that were apparently being upcycled as ashtrays. Over the mushroom-coloured tiled fireplace, Lorcan thought there was a picture, but closer inspection revealed it to be a jigsaw puzzle of some two foot by three foot which had been glued to the wall. The superglue container was on the floor half concealed by old tissues and sweet wrappers. *Whoever coined the term 'social housing'?* thought Lorcan. *There's nothing social about this.* There were a few bits of random carpet pieces with dark swirly patterns on the bare floorboards, but the surface was equally sticky on both. The officers could hear the noise their feet made as they lifted them and Lorcan even felt a slight resistance as he raised his shoes. They were his so-called smart black ones for work and he whispered to Tibbs, 'Don't forget to wipe your feet as we leave,' and nodded his head towards Nico who had fallen asleep among the drifts of empty crisp packets and kebab boxes, a slick of brownish saliva trickling from the corner of his slack mouth between the gaps where his teeth should have been.

Outside the property they shook their heads knowingly at each other. Tibbs said, 'Jesus Christ, I couldn't breathe in there.'

Lorcan leant against their car rubbing the top of his hair with both hands. The police knew that crime by criminals against each other was rife. 'Scum on scum' was more endemic than on 'innocent' victims, but such was the nature of the beast that they would rob and brutalise each other. It wasn't just about beating up old ladies, they'd take anything from anyone who'd had anything. Mostly it didn't get reported; no one had insurance so what was the point? What happened on the estate stayed on the estate, but it was surprising that this time a man like Nico phoned them for help. Lorcan speculated to Tibbs as they got into the car. 'Reckon he was holding folding, or some other stuff for someone else?'

Tibbs nodded. 'Yup, most likely there'll be another more serious crime when someone gets hold of him. We might have been a kind of insurance policy for him, poor sod, for all the good it will do him when Mr Bigger comes calling wanting his stuff.'

Lorcan added, 'You know that we've seen Nico a lot. Low level stuff, drugs normally, no violence. He doesn't usually hit anyone, if only because he's too high to manage it. Remember when he was brought in and had to have the internal search? When he bent over all these wraps of class A's fell out of his arse....'

'Oh, yeah! I heard about that one. He was the bloke who when asked to explain why that stuff was up his 'Brighton Pocket' said that the gnomes must have put it there.'

'He's a pain and a persistent problem, but not a danger, except to himself. Perhaps we'd better keep an eye out for him. Whoever owns whatever it was that got taken will probably be paying him a visit later.

They drove a couple of streets away to meet Bert, self-appointed chairman of the block's resident's association, and who was forever calling the police. He was a kind of poacher turned gamekeeper as he'd had his own colourful criminal history. Bert had finally settled down and become a balsa wood pillar of the community, when age and infirmity proved stronger adversaries than the criminal justice system.

Now sixty-six, Bert had more than earned the emphysema he was riddled with. He regularly disconnected his oxygen tank when he wanted a cigarette, a strange concession to his health and safety. Like so many of his peer group he had a mobility scooter for trips out but spent most of his time enthroned in a large padded wheelchair in his flat. He was attended by his Russian wife of eighteen months duration and eighteen years of age, Svetlana. He told everyone that she was Polish, as he was fed up being told she was trafficked or an illegal; which she was. It wasn't a good life for her, but may have been better than what she came from. Though as the officers stared into her dead green eyes it was hard to tell.

Bert beckoned them in. He said to Tibbs, 'As usual they've gone now. You're too late. You and Ian Paisley here,' he gestured in Lorcan's direction, and who answered promptly.

'Now then Bert, less of the Ian Paisley. Not every man who has himself a Northern Irish accent is Ian Paisley. You also know that we're aware of problems associated with that particular group of kids on the estate and we are doing our best to get it sorted out with the Youth Offending team and the council. We're trying for ASBO's on at least two of them. Guess it was the same crowd eh?'

Bert nodded, making himself wheeze. 'Yeah, little bastards, throwing rubbish against the windows.' He had a well-adapted flat which more than met his disabled needs. Most of these requirements were however, the long term consequences of two broken hips following a failed burglary where he fell from the first floor window when he was disturbed breaking and entering. They'd never healed right, he contended, and now he'd got arthritis in them. His immobility had caused weight gain and lack of exercise, smoking and drinking all contributed to his poor health. On the bright side he had got compensation as the owners of the property he'd been burgling had left some car parts outside the window, which had hampered his landing and contributed to the injuries.

Tibbs reluctantly took out his notebook and he and Lorcan both sat on the new brown leather settee, again supplied by a social grant. Perhaps Svetlana had made the right decision?

Lorcan asked 'So what were the kids up to this time? Tell us in your own words.'

Bert's righteous indignation caused him to wheeze more than ever and Svetlana moved towards a nebuliser on a glass topped table near the TV. These days Bert got his licence paid for him. He waved her away.

'Well it was that ginger one again, whatshisname, you know, Carl. That's it. For all the good that *Acceptable Behaviour Contract* did with his parents.'

'You know we can't discuss individual cases with you, especially youth.'

'They're bleeding terrorising this estate, especially this block where the elderly and disabled are supposed to live in peace.' He gestured piteously towards himself. 'There's that so-called asylum seeker, that Somali one, that kid, he was there, giving it all that, though I could barely understand him. No wonder his own country wouldn't have him. Then there was that Arab boy, whose father runs the kebab shop, he was there. It's like the bleeding united nations of crime here. They hunt in packs. Throwing things, shouting abuse, though I can't make out most of it, but I know what it means. Go on 'Lana, show them.'

The girl retrieved a Lidl carrier bag from the lobby and handed it to Tibbs who had an idea of the contents before he opened it.

'Svetlana cleaned up most of the mess before you got here. We gotta live. Can't keep waiting and waiting. It was human shit, well they aren't human are they? Boy's shit, which they put between burger buns and pushed through the letter box and pelted at our windows.'

Svetlana made a shrugging gesture and spoke with a gravelly accented voice. 'So much of it, how come they make so much shit? Small boys? So much trouble of the bowel.'

Bert looked over at her visibly angry, 'It doesn't matter what's wrong with their fucking arses. I don't want it through my letter box. I get enough crap through there as it is.'

Lorcan sighed. 'I'll take it as evidence, have it photographed and no doubt you'll make your usual statements.'

They both knew that the corduroy suited, softly spoken, 'client-centred' Youth Offending Team would do nothing, but Bert nodded.

Tibbs held the bag at arm's length. 'Judging by the smell they don't eat good diets.'

Bert wheezed menacingly. 'They'd eat the toe of my boot if I could get to them.' He gestured feebly with his swollen and slippered feet below his massive thirty stone body. 'If I hadn't got so big what with all this sitting around, I'd have the little bleeders. They'd shit themselves alright.' His wheezing rose to such dangerous levels that Lorcan and Tibbs rose simultaneously, and the leather settee gave a noisy retort. They reassured him by promising to alert a Police Community Support Officer and organise more patrols.

Bert was not mollified. 'Plastic policemen,' he gasped. 'They've got no powers, they always have to call for a grown up. They don't reassure me...' He went purple.

Svetlana cut in and looked at the officers. 'You want vodka?'

They shook their heads, and left, with Tibbs holding the carrier bag at arm's length, breathing through his mouth.

Chapter Eighteen

SLAUGHAM MANOR

Circe's emails to Alice omitted to mention her night time excursions to Stoneleigh, which were becoming more regular. She didn't follow a set pattern but was creative and variable in her methods. Alice was only told what she needed to know.

Hi Alice,

Still thirty-five degrees over there, is it? Well, we had a frost here last night, just to keep you up to date on the British weather. I've borrowed your black pashmina since my need is greater. It's pretty, what with those black sequins in the shape of half-moons all over it. It actually was admired by a colleague today who asked me where I got it from. I replied from my favourite store – Alice's Room!! It smells of your perfume, the one I said was a bit sweet at the time, but which has now grown on me. Vera Wang wasn't it? Your room still smells of you and your perfume. The air doesn't circulate as much as I'd like it to, as I don't really want the cats to go in there and party.

Talking of which, I'd put together a nice bowl of dead sea salts and flower petals from the garden and fragranced it with geranium, rose, lavender and black pepper oil as a concession to the old cellulite. It's really pretty and I know you'd approve. You only need one scoop in the bath and you're surrounded by petals and rosebuds and the fragrance is divine. However, cleaning the bath out is a bit of a bugger, but no matter. I try and have at least a couple of candlelit baths a week to de-stress. The cats always come in, and this week Clive was there and singed his furry trousers on one of the candles. He didn't seem to notice, but I had to leap out of the bath and put a wet sponge on him to stop the smouldering. He looked put out in every sense of the word.

It gets worse, as last night I was relaxing and listening to a nice play on Radio 4 with a substantial BSC resting on the tiles near a particularly nice soap, when my attention was drawn to a scraping sound. Unbelievably Rupert was using the dish of floral salts as a litter tray and shortly after I heard a loud squittering as he relieved himself on it with some violence. Naturally the whole batch was totally ruined and the oils did nothing to disguise the smell. I can tell you that he's back on the feline acidophilus again.

Talking of overactive bowels, since I last wrote I've been on the maple syrup, lemon juice and cayenne pepper water diet. You have to drink litres of the stuff. Apparently, the celebrities swear by it. I also swear by it when I'm in the bathroom making Rupert-like squittering noises!

It's not as bad as the Cambo stomach that told me you'd had. I don't feel sick, just starving and I have to keep taking anti-acids as the lemon juice eats into my oesophagus. I have to confess to not being 100% strict as I had a meal out with a friend, and I didn't think that a pizza and a bottle of wine would do any harm as I'd been so good. However, I'm going to have to get some new scales from Argos as we've had our ones for a couple of years and the bloody things said I'd put on three pounds. That can't be right. Must be the maple syrup retention!

I see there is some progress with the Khmer Rouge trial and convictions are happening, albeit matters are proceeding very slowly in terms of justice. Things are going from bad to worse here with regards to criminal justice, as a junior minister said that prisoners should be allowed to hold parties! I must go and freshen my drink now.

Consider yourself hugged. Sweet dreams. Love Mum xxx

Circe looked round the homely room, so empty without her vibrant daughter, then went over and stroked the cats sprawled across the velvet settee. As she went into the kitchen she pulled a sheaf of papers from the printer which had been chuntering away while she wrote to Alice. She looked at the contents. It should do the job. She used a different font from her usual - AR Carter. It was eye catching. This would be the focus of her next foray onto the estate.

Thinking back over the day, she was pleased she'd found the courage to walk out from the Criminal Justice Consultative committee meeting. The bi-annual so-called stakeholders get together where all the agencies were supposed to 'workshop solutions' to various issues. The meeting was always chaired by His Honour Judge Gittins and was held at Slaugham Manor, a police owned country house off the A23. The building was large and gracious but the main conference room was windowless with strange tartan carpet and pale blue walls. Circe had traced the lines of the pattern over the years and had mentally wished herself away from the meaningless hot air. Even the pre-meeting buffet held no charms. The police liked it, especially the lower ranks as they got very little free. They would body surf the long table like children at a tea party filling their plates with savouries and sweets alike to avoid missing out. The more restrained magistrates, solicitors, and chief executives would politely nibble at small selections. The trick was to balance their plates and plastic cups, and yet still try and shake hands while socialising with others.

Circe had arrived after the buffet lunch, as she had no intention of spoiling her diet for such processed fodder. As a consequence she struggled, as usual, to find a place to park so ended up right up in the upper car park which would delay her exiting and added to her irritation. Finding a seat fairly close to the rear of the hall Circe couldn't miss the back patting of the great and the good. She noticed yet another glossy brochure where the CPS congratulated themselves on their performance and the assurance that this was supposed to give the public so they would know criminal justice was in safe hands. By the time the Judge Gittins was inviting people's views on Restorative Justice, where criminals were encouraged to apologise to the victims of their crimes in exchange for low sentences, Circe had had enough. She quietly gathered her possessions and went through the first set of double doors and smiled at the police officer who was still guiltily taking food from the trashed buffet table.

'Missed lunch,' he mumbled through a greasy satay stick.

'Oh, I don't think you did. There was nothing to miss.' Circe responded, silently impressed at the way he juggled with three pieces of increasingly bruised fruit. Over her shoulder she added, 'Better get in there, it's all about criminals saying sorry and getting let off. I'm sure that's something you don't want to miss.'

The fruit clattered back down. 'Thanks for the warning ma'am, I'll just refuel and then go in there for a little sleep.'

Pushing through the next set of double doors to the outside she spotted Lorcan who was looking as if he was trying to talk into his mobile. It was obvious he was faking it.

Circe started to walk past him at pace but couldn't resist a barbed comment. 'Officer, we both know you can't get a mobile phone signal at Slaugham Manor. There is no escape or hope of a message.'

He furrowed his brow. 'If willing it to happen can get you a signal then surely I'd have it. I'm trying desperately to look as if I'm needed elsewhere and praying someone will call me.'

'I'm not religious, so I'm just going.'

'I'm a warranted officer and under orders.'

'Aah, there's the difference then. You also get paid for sitting there. I don't.'

Lorcan changed the subject. 'It's nice to see you Circe. Have I pronounced that right?'

'You haven't read much mythology?'

'Not too much. I went to a Jesuit school and it wasn't encouraged.'

'Yes, I can imagine. I went to a convent and you'd have thought that I'd be conditioned to all sorts of cruel and unusual torture with that kind of background, but the Criminal Justice Board does my head in.'

'I have to be here to represent the police and CJU. So.'

'How long are you out of Ireland, Lorcan?'

'Northern Ireland. Five years now. And with all that red hair, I'm guessing you've some Irish blood in you yourself?'

'Along with the myths, my rellies came from County Cork. Why did you leave?'

'It's a grand enough country - lovely scenery...'

'Yes, I've been there on a visit and saw some quite scary parts and scary people. I went to look at some standing stones and didn't check the date of my visit. As a result I got the full July marching experience. The hatred was tangible. So why did you leave, if I haven't answered my own question?'

Lorcan looked deeply uncomfortable. She saw him grip the silent phone so hard that the skin on his hand went white. There was something big here for sure.

His voice was forced and his accent made it sound almost aggressive. 'Oh, it's a long old story, let's just say in the end I just fancied a change. Swapped the RUC for Sussex Police.'

'Though now it's just become the Police Service of Northern Ireland hasn't it?'

'It was the right time to make a move. I've no regrets.' Lorcan looked at his watch. 'Anywho, I'd better get back into that conference. I may have missed something that changes my life.'

Circe stared at him, the afternoon sun catching her eyes and making them more amber than usual. 'Sounds like your life has been changed, officer.'

'See yous later,' he said, exaggerating the Irish.

'Peace be with you,' Circe gave the end of Mass blessing.

Chapter Nineteen

THE GAME

Making his way into the police station in John Street, Brighton, Lorcan's attention was drawn to the A4 poster of the Sussex Police Authority faces. It was always there prominently as part of the accessibility policy. It sat amongst all the other information notices encouraging reporting of crime, domestic abuse, details of crime stoppers and Victim Support.

As he went to press his electronic warrant card against the entrance panel he looked at Circe's tiny picture. She was the best-looking of the pack, but then there wasn't much competition. Political members, in the main, bloated self-interested councillors, with hair like grey Shredded Wheat. Others looked corpulent and monied. The females with their faded hair dyed unlikely shades, and rich husbands and indulged lifestyles. What right did these people have to set the police budget, appoint the chief officers and dictate the direction of the Force? What did they know?

Lorcan peered at Circe's image. Her picture sat in among the other independent members. To be honest, he thought, they were more intelligent and 'normal' and came from professions like head teachers or academics often working in the community and weren't interested in political aggrandisement. To be appointed these members had to be interviewed, and their competences rigorously assessed, while the political members were nodded in by their peers on a power-driven merry-go-round. The attendance record, except at the photoshoots, showed that the real sloggers were always the independents. They were the ones who pushed for more budget at the annual meeting, whereas the politicos were worried about voters, so always kept the police precept as low as possible. No, the independents knew their stuff, but the political members held the balance of power by one, and it was only rarely in the corridors outside meetings that the police and independent members could talk in secret about the 'truth' of matters. They had no axe to grind so did the best job they could, and the right job in the eyes of many of the officers. A lot of the police didn't understand the role of the Authority and the entourage of overpaid civil servants who were supposed to administer it, but knew they were expected to show deference. That never suited Lorcan. He didn't like that and had seen too much of it in Northern Ireland.

Hearing the accepting bleep of the key pad he passed through the door and into the overheated corridors. The offices suffered from terminal sick building syndrome. It wasn't just the negative people and issues they were dealing with, it made him feel bad summer or winter. Lorcan had a desk on the second floor near a window. If he opened it he would very likely get a seagull pop its head through looking for food. Last year there had been a male who was a good provider for his family, nesting on the roof of the magistrates court building next door. A previous court clerk had responded to the justices complaints about their cars being pebbled dashed by guano by installing a large plastic owl on the roof, as a deterrent. No one understood why a barrister would imagine that such highly intelligent birds would be fooled for one minute by a plastic object that wasn't even a predator in real life. The owl was clearly visible from Lorcan's window and was now covered in bird's mess too. There was a family of gulls nesting at its feet enjoying the wind break it offered. Lorcan's visitor would tap its beak on the glass whilst eyeing the officer's short-lived pyramid of mint imperials during a meeting, and he in turn would put his ear against the glass pretending to be receiving a message from his Native American spirit guide, White Gull. In the unlikely event of there being any leftover sandwiches or stale doughnuts they got tossed out to grateful recipients.

Lorcan only had a short time before his meetings began. The first of these was going to involve ACC Lancaster. Worst still it was his turn to play the game that was particularly popular with the junior members of the Force. Lorcan looked through his speech, which he'd kept as short as possible. The rules were he had to get in at least three song titles, and as Anne Lancaster was an Elvis fan his colleagues had deliberately chosen songs by the King. A nightmare scenario as she would know them all. The rewards were that if he could get in the three everyone would buy him a drink, but if she noticed then he would incur both her unbridled wrath and have to buy every gloating so-and-so in the section a drink. Great.

Lorcan wasn't due to be in the whole meeting as it was largely for senior officers and guests. He was number three on the agenda which meant he only came in to do his turn and then would leave. So, fuelled by three cups of muddy coffee his nerves were already in tatters. Going into the grand foyer of Malling House his feet clattered on the black and white marble tiles. ACC Lancaster indicated a place for him to stand at the massive oval conference table. He nodded to the staff officer to start the PowerPoint presentation. His talk was entitled *Keeping Stoneleigh Safe From Itself.* Lorcan had his carefully prepared statistics and pie-charts. His dialogue was serious, but because of the strength of his accent and his natural speed of talking people often leant forward to catch what he said.

'Sussex police have a large area to cover and we do have a few particularly challenging places within it. One of these is the Stoneleigh estate which is continually on our radar and *always on my mind* in particular.' He saw DI Crook smirk and rub his face with one finger. 'It seems to the outsider to be a place that *only the strong survive.*' The DI placed two fingers against his cheek. Lorcan went on to describe the demography and types of crime committed by those who lived on the estate and also those residents who were victims. Anne Lancaster looked at him intensely and took copious notes.

'Only last week, at the public consultation meeting, one older lady with mobility issues understandably became very emotional and her comments struck a chord when she asked how we would like living *in the ghetto?*' Crook put two fingers in front of his left ear and one behind. 'She was right when she said we went home to nice houses in safe areas. And I personally *just can't help believing* that she and her fellow residents do indeed live with *suspicious minds* about how much the police can do to keep them safe.'

Crook was openly smiling at the notes he was making with five fingers now against his cheek. Lorcan had done it! A few more clicks of the mouse, coloured slides with a ubiquitous photo of an ethnically diverse group of people smiling at two officers in HiVis jackets and it was over. The standard promotional image. Well, they weren't going to show angry motorists being stopped with a speed gun were they?

Lorcan summarised. 'Thank you, ladies and gentlemen, for your time. We need a concerted, joined-up effort to turn this estate around. I don't want to keep seeing people like Maria Griffiths who, as you probably know, has lost two of her children to drug overdoses. When you go into her flat, it's a kind of shrine, with all the photos of the kids before they went downhill and she has at least another kid in prison at any one time. When I was last there she said "This isn't a home, not even a halfway house. It's a bloody *heartbreak hotel,* I tell you." So as a Force we need to work out a strategy to engage the community and keep them safe and that means tough love.'

ACC Lancaster looked up as the lights went on. Her cold blue eyes revealed nothing. Lorcan had got away with it. As he picked up his papers he saw DI Crook smiling to himself and shaking his head spreading the six bony fingers across it like chipolatas. Lorcan's eyes briefly travelled round the table and locked onto Circe's. *God!* He was actually blushing. Jesus, Mary and Joseph. What was wrong with him? He'd just put his career on the line with a speech, most of which was for a bet, and he was stupid enough to blush because a copper-haired woman was looking at him. Her expression betrayed nothing either.

He left the room as the next act was being called on, sweating slightly and glad to be free. 'It's a jungle in there,' he said by way of increasing the anxiety of the next officer due to go in. His airwave pinged. A text message. He stopped walking and stared at the screen. It was from the Chief Constable who had been at the meeting in an observational capacity. SAME OLD GAME I SEE. GOOD TO SEE YOU HAVE A SENSE OF HUMOUR AT LAST. YOU MAY HAVE GOT PAST ACC LANCASTER, BUT NOT ME. BEHAVE.

Now Lorcan seriously blushed. *The Chief? Oh, God!* Well, that was his shaky career in tatters. Predictably DI Crook had texted colleagues saying he was a lucky Irish bastard so he returned to a hero's welcome, but he felt as joyous as a man with a guillotine hanging above his neck. A greasy cupcake with vermillion icing from the box by the kettle didn't make him feel any better.

On his desk was a series of reports of serious antisocial behaviour on the estate. For all his fine words something was going off. Vandalised cars and hate campaigns. What was going on? Wearily he got his jacket and set off for Stoneleigh again.

Chapter Twenty

BUSY NIGHT IN STONELEIGH

She'd nearly been caught! It was a very close thing and her plans may now be in jeopardy. Even thinking about it made her sweat and shake. Circe went to her notebook to record the events and evaluate her mistakes.

She was a natural writer, preferring her Lamy fountain pen with its pure chilli red ink to her computer screen. Even if she changed the font to be as close to her convent educated italic writing as possible, it still didn't bring her physically in contact with her true self in the way that feeling the pen glide over virgin paper did. Usually she wrote in a black and red spiral bound notebook, but she had a fetish for the pretty notebooks in *Paperchase*, so it might be one of those occasionally. Alice had bought her a lovely notebook before she left.

'Write your thoughts down and things you'd say to me if I was here,' she'd said, kissing her mother. After she'd left, Circe couldn't bring herself to even start it. She didn't feel anything would be good enough to put in it.

However, when she conceived her revenge plans, the 1960's style black and pink flowered pad seemed perfect. No particular reason why, it just did. Also there was a plastic keyring of a sun attached to the top of its spine accompanied by a selection of bright ribbons which added to its attraction. Just looking at the cover and its accessories made her smile, as Alice had intended. She knew how bereft her mother would feel.

What she wrote in the interior was indisputably darker. The first page was simply labelled *Out of Court Settlement*. It was real judicial payback. A kind of play on the words of the Community Payback HiVis vests supposed to be worn by those doing community service or unpaid work. However, the liberal minded Probation Service didn't welcome this initiative. They didn't see it as reassuring the public that something was being done to punish offenders. No, instead they saw it as infringing the offender's human rights and humiliating them in public. This was part of an ongoing debate in the City. Over the years there had been discussions about the local press naming and shaming miscreants. Local papers used to have pages devoted to snapshots and summaries of offenders and their activities together with court outcomes. It was a useful public information service. Now it was now considered politically incorrect and draconian, so people didn't find out what their neighbours did and it no longer served as a brake on behaviour. As more became hidden and private there was less peer group opprobrium. No one behaved themselves out of fear of what the neighbours would think. It was almost *de rigeur* for Stoners to boast of their crimes. They wore their outsider status in their oversized designer sportswear, Burberry fabrics, baseball caps and cheap, ostentatious gold jewellery. The tattoos and piercings told their own stories.

Circe sighed and suppressed a shudder as she thought about last night's adventure. She'd had three on her special list. All very deserving cases.

The first was Sarah Cowell. She wouldn't send her kids to school. So Skye and Courtney were absent most of the time. There had been many court listings and adjournments. The council's prosecutor politely and laboriously outlined the herculean efforts made by the council, teachers, social workers and others to encourage Ms Cowell to engage and send the girls to school. Their mother wouldn't answer the letters or respond to the phone calls. Every now and again, as the court date loomed closer, she would write a scrappy note saying that either she or the kids were ill. No medical corroboration of this was ever received by the authorities despite frequent requests. The years were ticking by and the older girl, Skye, had not attended her GCSE courses and looked destined to leave the school she was barely at with no qualifications. The same as her mother, who had been on benefits all her life.

Circe needed to find a way to encourage Ms Cowell to leave the safety of her home and for the authorities to be equally aware of the opportunity her plan of action was going to provide them with, for an 'intervention.'

That morning she had pulled her car up outside Lagoon Bait in Hove; an emporium of male fishing accoutrements - a secret world. Making her way towards the back of the shop she approached the man behind the glass counter which revealed boxes and bottles of unimaginable items.

'Can I help you, madam?' She didn't look as if she was going fishing.

Circe handed him the containers. 'Would you be good enough to fill each of these with maggots, please?'

'They'd hold about a pint each. Don't you want them in our tubs though?'

'No thanks. Mine are just right.'

Soon she had three tubs set on the counter and asked for a plastic bag to put them in and for it to be taped closed.

'They ain't going anywhere, those maggots, especially not with those lockable tubs you've got them in.'

Circe felt some explanation was required. 'Fine. I understand, but they are a present for some fishing friends and I don't want them escaping too soon.'

'Keep 'em cool - just in the fridge will do till you need them.'

Circe put them in the icy boot of her car in a large plastic Lakeland picnic box. She had a phobia about maggots and couldn't bear to look at one as a rule; they weren't going in her fridge. *God bless Lakeland plastics,* she said to herself.

When she arrived at the dead of night at the address on Haybourne Road she crept out and using a green flexible chopping board, again courtesy of Lakeland, she made a cone shaped funnel and pushed the narrow end through the letter box where the maggots skittered and cascaded onto the shag pile carpet.

Circe had the letter ready for the council. It was going to be posted from the post box on the edge of the estate. It was forensically prepared and was addressed to the council's prosecuting lawyer. *You may feel that the authorities are in a position to intervene in the case of Sarah Cowell currently living at 12 Haybourne Road. Her home has become infested with maggots and she will be unlikely to want to remain there until the matter is remedied. Signed - a concerned citizen.*

Still shaking from her instinctive revulsion at maggots, Circe's next task was to go for a male offender. Sayed Ahmed was a repeat offender who continually drove his white Mercedes while over the drink limit. The court was told that this car was a present from his parents so that they could be given lifts to hospital by their son. Circe had already banned him for another five years and until he passed a driving test. Since he'd been claiming benefits for the last twenty seven years, the fine was effectively derisory. He had never obtained a licence and swore he never drank except for cough medicine. To illustrate this assertion he cleared his throat loudly and often. He usually blew at least three times the legal drink drive limit, and no amount of Benylin or other linctus would make the reading that high. He always went 'not guilty' as he was legally-aided and had the state pay for legal experts on top, who would do various calculations on how his different cold medicines might affect his ability to drive. Never mind that he had never passed a test and had run this defence for twelve years. On the latest occasion when the police stopped him because of his erratic driving, he nearly fell out of the car. Only as the car began to roll down the road did the police spot the plaster cast on his foot and ankle. One officer threw himself across Ahmed's lap to use the handbrake and luckily got the car to glide into the kerb. He was very drunk and shouting abuse that the police were picking on him like the racist scum they were.

Circe made her way to his home in Stoneleigh Way. There was the distinctive Mercedes across the untidy front garden. Using her trusty Lakeland flexible chopping board again she funnelled a bottle of Galloways into his hall floor carpet. The sticky brown viscous liquid would leave a challenging stain and its fragrance should make him think. Moving over to the car she superglued his locks and bent back the wipers and aerial. Her knees cracked loudly as she crouched down and squirted expanding foam up the exhaust pipe. *The noisy explosions of old age*, she thought. She was too close to his house to stab his tyres as she couldn't risk the hissing waking him up so she finished the job in what she felt was becoming her signature. She wrote *Drunk driver, no licence* in brake fluid on the bonnet and left a teabag soaked in paint stripper on the roof, its rivulets fizzling down the paintwork. Circe had put a lot of attention and detail into the enterprise as the teabag was a herbal one and its fluttering tag said *For colds, coughs and sore throats.* She hoped he'd get the message this time.

As she left his garden she heard a dog barking further up the road in the direction she needed to go for her final visit of the night. She had her shopping trolley with her and was dressed in her usual disguise. She smelled the smoke from the man's cigarette before he reached her. The massive dog panted close to him, its legs were at each corner of a very large body.

'Evening, grandma' he said quietly, his mean unshaven face lit up by the streetlight. 'You're out late ain't ya? Bingo having a lock in, is it?'

Circe didn't know how to deal with this. Her mouth was dry and her heart beat loudly. She could feel the pulse in her throat against the woollen scarf. She was worried that her voice would sound too young so she accelerated her walk and attempted to pass him on the outside of the narrow pavement.

He sidestepped and moved in front of her. 'What's your hurry old lady? Got your pension money, or your savings in that trolley? Let's take a look see, shall we?'

He leant towards her and she could smell the stale skunk cannabis stench of his jacket. His breath was foetid and hung almost like a solid cloud in the air. Kebabs and beer. He was within six inches of her and the dog growled low.

Circe had no time. Her right hand was already in her pocket, the nice roomy one in the coat. She felt the mace spray and clenched it with her gloved hand. This was going to be a problem as sensitivity was less than it should be. The thick gloves made it hard for her to feel, but once she had it lined up she pulled out the phial in one sweeping arm movement and sprayed her assailant full in the face.

The brim of his face-concealing baseball cap had the effect of concentrating the stinging mist. He screamed so loudly she feared her eardrums would burst. Her position of power was returned and she swiftly sidestepped him and noticed the dog whimpering as it had obviously picked up some of the pepper spray. It was growling and crouching as if to spring. 'Shut up you bastard,' his owner shouted causing the dog to leap at him and bite hard into his arm. Circe loved animals and would never hurt them, but this poor creature was a weapon and not a pet anymore. She did nothing to pull the dog off his owner. The two were rolling and wailing. Characteristically of the indigenous population of Stoners it was some time before anyone looked out of their windows to see what was wrong.

Convinced that he was blinded, Wayne Smith ended up in the casualty department of the Royal Sussex County Hospital, in the same building where Circe volunteered to sit with the dying on a regular basis. The dog went to the emergency vet conveniently three streets away on the end of a dog warden's noose. The police were called as Wayne would not comment on how he had come to have this substance sprayed in his eyes or how the dog got his collateral damage. The police took the silence for a drug dealing row.

As a man with seventy-eight previous convictions, most of them for violence, there was a certain *schadenfreude* among the police and private jokes about what might have happened did the rounds. Wayne didn't want the case investigated so they just charged him with possession of the serrated hunting knife that he had in his pocket.

The vet thought it a kindness to castrate Butcher, the dog. He was also found to be a banned breed of dog with fighting scars so his ultimate fate was going to be decided by the authorities.

Circe meanwhile had scampered back to her car and made her escape without doing her third hit. She justified it by saying to herself that probably her attacker counted as the final item on the evening's agenda. The temperature was just about freezing and the bagged up dog excrement would keep fresh, so she put it outside her back door.

Her nerves were shot to pieces though and when she got in the cats' sleepy blue eyes watched her as she swigged direct from the turquoise bottle of Bombay Sapphire. 'Shit, that was really close.'

She caught sight of herself, the old face in her twisty ornate dark wooden Victorian over mantel. She loved that piece and had bought it when she was about twenty from a junk shop. She never had it re-silvered as it would have taken away the impressions of all the faces who ever looked into it. The old face it now reflected back had a hat and scarf on at an odd angle as its owner continued gulping the gin.

Chapter Twenty-One

THE MORNING AFTER

As Lorcan arrived on the estate he noticed the Golf with its tyres clearly slashed and paint stripper all over the bodywork. Pulling up ahead of the car he called in the registration. The owner was a known disqualified driver, but curiously no one had reported the damage. Getting out he walked round the car. The eyes of the neighbourhood were clearly on him. Curtains twitched and a couple of small boys who should have been at school came over, pulling their hooded tops onto their baseball caps.

'What are you looking at?' The taller boy asked Lorcan directly. This engendered a fierce debate within his head. This little tyke had no right to start questioning him, most likely he was a truant, who perhaps was responsible for the damage. Who was he to ask what he was doing? Then again Lorcan needed to build up the trust of the community, to engage them in useful dialogue so he might as well start here.

'Hallo, son,' he began, with an attempt at his best smile.

'I'm not your son, copper, I'm sure my mum would never have fucked you. She ain't choosy, but she ain't desperate.' The shorter boy sniggered at his friend's rudeness.

This was not a promising start. 'And what makes you think I'm a police officer?' Lorcan asked still trying to keep things positive.

'That's simple. You stink. You all stink, can smell you a mile off.'

'Well, according to my book shouldn't you be a mile off in school right now?'

The shorter boy had a brand new bike, impossibly expensive for families living off benefits. Lorcan wondered if it was stolen.

'And where did you get that bike from, young man?'

The boy's thin upper lip curled revealing teeth that were already rotten and nicotine stained.

'Mind your own fucking business, copper. It was a present, alright?'

'Mind if I take a look?' Lorcan wanted to check its serial number. The boy jammed the tyre aggressively against Lorcan's foot. 'Fuck off,' was the clear answer. 'You got any questions ask the Youth Offending Team, cunt-stable. And we've been excluded from school so don't have to go no more.' They grinned broadly at their sub-educational cunning.

Lorcan knew that there was no point continuing any dialogue with them. Better people than him would have failed at the task. He moved away fearing for his car's safety, but it was police property, not personal, so he didn't move it.

He went round the corner under the jeering gaze of the boys and knocked on Charlene Dunkley's door. It was opened by a short, stout woman with thinning hair and bottle bottom glasses, through which she peered at Lorcan. He held up his warrant card and she sniffed acceptance. He was ushered into the living room. Lorcan never ceased to be amazed at the differences in how people could decorate a property. This was a massive patterned wallpaper and equally swirling patterned carpet. Lorcan moved past the cluttered tables and yapping Shi Tzu dogs who she called Ricky and Bianca.

When their noisy protests subsided Lorcan began, 'Mrs Dunkley I'm here to investigate some reports of antisocial behaviour. Can you tell me what's been happening?'

Charlene Dunkley was fishing about in the bottom of a glass of what appeared to be Coca Cola. She produced a set of dentures and inserted them into her mouth, giving her palpy face slightly more structure as she did so. Lorcan hid his revulsion as the brown liquid ran down her chin and onto a crochet style sweater which already poorly concealed her massive stomach.

Finally finding some sense of social decorum she snapped at Lorcan, 'The coke gets 'em cleaner than the denture stuff.'

'Oh, sure,' said Lorcan quickly as he didn't want her to think that he thought it odd behaviour. She ran a white coated tongue round the plastic teeth and coughed, rattling the phlegm in her chest and throat. 'Want tea?' she asked.

Lorcan shook his head decisively. 'No thank you, Mrs Dunkley, if I could just take a few details? You've phoned the police on a number of occasions...'

As he went to take his pen out of his pocket he became aware that his left leg was shaking. Looking down, he was horrified to see that one of her ghastly tatty dogs was dry humping his shin. Its lipstick penis rubbed frantically at his trouser leg and it wasn't as dry as it should have been. He tried to shake the dog off.

Mrs Dunkley was having none of it. 'Don't worry darling, he doesn't take long, he likes men and I've got a cloth here to clean it off your leg.' She held up a crusty tea towel that had Lorcan's stomach flip over. He shook his head. She was right, the dog was quickly finished and he started to take notes with slime running down his leg while the other dog sniffed it appreciatively.

Charlene Dunkley outlined a series of problems with 'kids.' This was a generic complaint used by many people who felt intimidated by young people who were hanging about, gathering, kicking balls, talking loudly, and so on.

Mrs Dunkley's complaints were higher on the scale; dustbins tipped up and rubbish scattered, kids having sex in her garden, condoms thrown at windows. *At least they're practising safe sex,* thought Lorcan. What with the dog's behaviour it wasn't as if she was a stranger to nature taking its course.

'They should be castrated', she shouted, while Lorcan stared at the oversized testicles wobbling on the back of Ricky's furry behind.

Mrs Dunkley had a point. She and a couple of the neighbours were being bothered, 'terrorised', she called it, and she was afraid to go out in the evening for fear of being shouted at, or her property being damaged. Getting descriptions proved hard.

'They all look the same' she said, and her glasses were indeed very thick. Lorcan guessed it probably involved the dynamic duo with the bike outside, as he could see the baseball cap beaks behind the hedge. All kids wore hoodies according to old Charlene and the girls were all slags. *Not much to go on,* Lorcan thought. *Same old stereotypes.* The kids weren't as bad as all that, it was poor parenting that was responsible for failing to control them. Like those two boys in the street. They had very little hope of a decent life whilst being allowed to roam and become part of a feral pack. Trying to reconcile

96

Mrs Dunkley's needs as well as theirs wasn't easy. Keeping the peace was every police officer's duty. He sighed and said he'd write it up as a report and come back to her with a plan. He left quickly as the dog was looking like it had refilled, and he wanted to get back to the station. Once both his legs were safely on the unkempt path among the empty tins he remembered the damaged car outside. 'Know anything about that vehicle?'

Charlene Dunkley shook her head. 'Nah, probably kids.'

'Do you know the owner?' The words were barely out of Lorcan's mouth when she slammed the door closed.

Lorcan took it that she did.

It was raw and cold outside and the north easterly wind cut into him, but he was still glad to be on the street. It had really been a job for a PCSO, or a junior officer, but things were so bad he needed to put it together as part of the picture of the estate. You wouldn't get Anne Lancaster taking a look at the sharp end of anything other than a statistics chart.

Lorcan looked up and down the bleak road. He was checking the vandalised car as he passed, then caught sight of another one with a cracked windscreen. He frowned and made a note of the registration. That hadn't been rung in either. Odd.

He made his way towards his car and as he was pulling the door open, he noticed what looked like two separate sprays of a familiar looking white gelatinous substance stuck to the cold bodywork. 'Fucking little wankers,' he muttered reaching for a wet wipe from the car. Twice in one day, brilliant.

Chapter Twenty-Two

DIVISIONAL CONGRATULATIONS

Domestic violence always presented Circe with one of her greatest challenges. It was a prevalent offence, it was insidious and had massive impact on the victim and the children. The police had made progress in that 'policing the personal' had moved to the forefront and inter-agency work meant that a coordinated response was expected. Teachers and social workers could liaise in confidence and healthcare professionals all had the appropriate training to recognise the signs so they could try and offer the victim help.

It took lots of attempts and injuries before women would come forward, the average being twenty-eight. There were also many male victims who would suffer in silence, humiliated at how they could be bullied emotionally and physically by the partners they loved. They too became broken. The world was secret and hard for the police to penetrate. There were a lot of hidden victims, and a lot of brutal people.

Circe despaired when domestic violence cases came to court. They were always fast tracked in the hope of getting the offender to face justice and the injured party to be safe as soon as possible. To some extent the speedy listing was achieved. At Brighton, the victim would be assigned a Witness Support Officer. They worked hard with victims, assuring them and engaging them in the process. They would also provide a comprehensive history of call outs to the address to help build up a picture of the situation. Often the perpetrators were surprised to find this evidence raised. They would object and say, 'It's not like I've been charged or convicted of anything.' But it would indicate a pattern. Curfews were often part of community sentences but it made no sense to confine a perpetrator to their victim's home. So they might find the tariff for a community sentence upped instead. A curfew would be setting everyone up for failure and further endangering the victim.

Last time Circe was hearing DV cases, the first one involved a man spitting at his wife in the street. It was witnessed by a female parking attendant who at first thought it was for her since she was accustomed to such abuse in the course of her job. She called up the police on her radio and when they arrived and spoke to the man he'd answered, 'She's my wife and as a Muslim I can do what I want with her.' It transpired that they were returning from the family court where the children had been placed in care because of the father's violence and the wife's inability to protect them. He pleaded not guilty to the spitting charge as he said it was within his cultural rights. The court had no choice but to set a date for the trial, which no one thought his poor wife would attend.

The next defendant was Mark Thompson, who failed to appear in the case against him for assault by beating his partner Sharon Wilson. She also didn't turn up. The prosecutor read out the facts of the case and said that it would be difficult to prove in the absence of the main witness. The neighbour across the road who'd phoned the police was in attendance, as was the police officer with statements regarding the victim's injuries. Circe took the view that if a defendant didn't show up on the day it demonstrated their contempt for the legal system and they had made a choice not to participate in their own trial. They'd been warned of this when first given court bail. 'I must warn you that if you fail to attend on the time and date we have set, then your trial may take place in your absence.' They were asked to acknowledge that they understood. So Circe would always hear cases in absentia. The lawyers often withdrew as they hadn't obtained instructions. This was a practice generally carried out in the precincts of the court and in court time after they had, of course, obtained their legal aid funding. On this occasion though, Circe hesitated. If she heard the case, and found him guilty in his absence, albeit without the victim, then a warrant would be issued so he could be brought in for sentencing, but then he'd have no reason not to batter Sharon senseless. The court had heard the catalogue of offences he'd committed against her, as well as his general activity on the crime scene; supply of Class A drugs, assaulting a PC, obtaining by property/cash by deception. They knew him to be a danger and the police DV worker sat in court and briefed the prosecutor on how imperative it was that Sharon Wilson and her kids be protected. Their eyes looked pleadingly at the Bench. They had no automatic right of audience, and the harassed agency prosecutor for the CPS was not the most interested or persuasive of intercessors.

Circe felt on the horns of a dilemma. She and the Bench would be damned if they did and damned if they didn't. Her fountain pen drew a mass of red swirls on the court list as she thought. She felt that other part of herself step forward from the depths. *'You sort it out'* she heard it whisper. Finally she took the line of least resistance in the court and suggested that they issue a warrant for Mark and the CPS said they would summons Sharon to appear. 'For her own good.'

Great, thought Circe. *A hostile witness.* But she could see a slight advantage to Sharon in that Mark would know it wasn't her choice. Circe knew she had to do something quickly. It wasn't just antisocial behaviour like some of the others; it was life and death.

It would be necessary for Ida Dunmore to target him from that point on. His car would be marked 'I beat my partner' in acid. The DSS would get a letter informing them that he was working and they would stop his benefit while they investigated. A letter was swiftly sent to Lewes prison where Sharon's brother was serving time informing him of the danger his sister was in. He'd had absolutely no idea of what was happening to her as his sojourns in prison meant they didn't see that much of each other. He went into full brotherly fury and put out a GBH contract on Mark which would be executed by some of his associates on the outside.

* * *

In the afternoon Circe had to present the Divisional Congratulation awards to police and staff for outstanding work and bravery. It was always a moving occasion where the families would proudly attend and there would be refreshments afterwards, which would be well received. Circe was to make a speech as the Brighton member of the SPA, and then listen to each citation as they were read out by the commander. The awards went to people who had achieved above and beyond the expectations of the job, often demonstrating tremendous bravery and quick thinking. Others got it by dogged determination and not giving up on challenging investigations. Regardless of the circumstances Circe always got a lump in her throat at such triumph of the human spirit in adversity.

The first officer had talked a suicidal man off the top of a car park. He'd spent a considerable amount of time trust-building and just when the officer thought he'd calmed down he made a dive. He only just managed to grab him by the legs and hang on fifty feet up. The man he was trying to save kept calling him a bastard, which didn't help. Afterwards the officer told Circe that playing for Brighton Rugby Club really helped.

'Just a case of taking him up and not down, I've always been told to grab his legs, so it's second nature.' He grinned placing four large rolls on his paper plate to which Circe thought he was more than entitled. During the ceremony lots of other citations had followed, including investigative work by undercover detectives including drug test purchases, which necessitated anonymity for their own protection.

Then she looked up as she heard the commander read out DS Lorcan O'Leary's name. As if in a blur she and the assembly heard how he'd been first on the scene following a stabbing. He had the presence of mind to place a credit card over the man's chest to stem the flow of blood until the ambulance arrived. Matters became complicated as the ambulance went to the wrong address and then got badly caught up in traffic. Lorcan had ended up having to press the card down for forty minutes whilst reassuring the victim. When the crew finally arrived they were impressed with Lorcan's efforts. Moving the credit card to inspect the wound a geyser of blood covered them all, resulting in a universal HIV blood test.

Later as she circulated the buffet area, a stick of celery in one hand and glass of water in the other, Circe saw Lorcan with a crowd of uniformed officers and stopped to congratulate him again. 'What happened in the end to the guy you helped?'

Lorcan shrugged. 'He followed the man he'd stabbed first, through the pearly or bloodstained gates.'

'I see. Still, you did a great job with your credit card in stemming the blood flow. I never knew that. I thought it was all about tourniquets.'

'Oh, it's changed now right enough. But you need to know that it wasn't my credit card. God, I wasn't going to have that covered with blood and waiting forever to get a replacement from the bank. So I commandeered one from a passer-by.'

'No! Really?' Circe was shocked.

'Yes, there's always someone standing about in a crisis, so we may as well make use of them. At first she was happy to help. She hovered around for some time then started saying that she needed the card. I told her that she'd have to get a new one from the bank. This was now evidence. She was pretty pissed off for an older lady and said I had no right asking for it if I knew that would happen. I was on my hands and knees and my arm was numb with the pressure I was applying to the bloke on the ground who was thrashing around as well and to be honest I didn't give a shite about her card. In the end a colleague took her details and the last I heard was her saying she hoped he lived and I died. Nice eh?'

She smiled 'Fair enough, you knew you'd inconvenience her!'

Circe only spoke to him once more on his own, and this time it was as they both circulated. She was expected to work the room. It was odd seeing him in dress uniform when he usually wore what she thought of as detective shabby chic. His green eyes met hers above a violent pink French fancy that was disappearing into his mouth. He could see ACC Anne Lancaster looking worried as if he might disgrace himself in front of a Police Authority member. He turned his back to avoid her face. Circe looked at his overfilled plate, 'Takes a lot to put you off your food, Detective Sergeant.'

'Yes Ma'am. Where I come from you still need to eat, whatever you've seen, or had to do.'

Circe did up the button of her black boucle suit, which was eight pounds from the British Heart Foundation shop and was garnished with the MBE brooch that seemed to be required wearing for these sorts of occasions. Her amber eyes showed her interest. 'It was a wonderful act of bravery.'

He shrugged, 'The English have lower standards to judge these things by. It's horses for courses in Northern Ireland. I'd have to pick up bits of children's bodies at the worst times.'

'God how dreadful. Did you ever have treatment for post-traumatic stress?'

He wiped the last of the icing off his fingers. 'You ever had that yourself?'

'No.'

'People say it's a waste of time. An indulgence - keeping on reliving it. Half my mates had it and half didn't. I couldn't tell which of the bastards had or hadn't had it. For sure we were all a bit mad. You only had to listen to the craic in the pub. Your experiences make you what you are and you have to get on with it. Therapy works for some, but me? I don't need it.'

Lorcan then hesitated as if he was going to ask her something, but his phone rang and he had to take the call. His father. What had he done now? When he raised his head a moment later the room, despite the heat and people, felt colder. Circe had gone.

Chapter Twenty-Three

BIRTHDAY PARTY

Circe had much to do as she headed for home in her Figaro. Clive, Nigel and Rupert were glad to see her. It wasn't just the food, she was sure, and she sat down and petted them in turn while reading and answering her emails. She eyed the turquoise bottle of Bombay Sapphire with its list of life giving healthy herbs on its glass exterior. But she couldn't have any until she got home again. Instead she had a Slimfast. Shuddering at the sweetness, she made her way up to her bedroom and changed into Ida Dunmore.

As she finished and talcumed her copper hair she wondered what Lorcan would think if he could see the so-called esteemed member of the Police Authority dressed like a little old lady and just about to leave to commit offences. Blackening one of her front upper teeth and two lower ones with Halloween tooth wax, she set off for Stoneleigh. So far, every time she went to the estate she parked in a different spot, and tonight was no exception. She didn't park near The Dog as it was to be the target. She slowly made her way into the pub and sat down in a dark corner near the doorway to the toilets with half a Guinness. No one looked at her. On the greasy, drink circled table in front of her she had a copy of 'The People's Friend' and was, to all intents and purposes, totally absorbed in its contents.

Circe had done her research and she knew that there was going to be a birthday party celebrated there tonight. She'd seen the poster welcoming all comers to Billy 'Tombstone' Tiernan's thirtieth birthday. It was a good name for him. Circe had seen photos of his tattoos in court pictures. His body was literally a pallid, flabby tombstone. He had two massive praying hands then 'Dad' with their birth and death dates and the same for his Mum and Nan. There were spaces there that could be added to. At every opportunity he would take his shirt off, so everyone could see the testament to his grief and affection for his family.

Tombstone's party was due to kick off at 8pm. Circe suspected that they'd be getting drunk on cheap booze and drugs before turning up to the party proper. The usual pre-load. A lot of the estate was expected as Tombstone was due for trial in two weeks and they were using this as a chance to say goodbye, as even his brief had said things didn't look good for him.

Circe looked under the brim of her hat as people started arriving; Smirnoff ices, vodkas and lagers were ordered along with JD's and coke. Not much sign of people on benefit here. Circe was waiting and hoping that Eddie would get there. She had really struggled to think of a plan as to how he was going get his comeuppance. She didn't think she'd get a better opportunity than this. There were some girls who were already drunk. Some rake thin and weaselly with hair scraped back into ponytails and others plumper with dyed blonde hair. Big cheap earrings, large amounts of make-up. Fat bodies squeezed in to tarty leggings, stomachs bare, trashy mini-skirts, laughing loudly and displaying their tongue studs. *The tattoos, God the tattoos.* Tombstone had some competition here, but not like his, the favourites being around calves with a fair number on backs and over-pierced ears.

Circe spotted one girl, with oversized breasts who came in behind a pierced and tattooed gorilla. His hairline was low, leaving him with a short forehead and his number two haircut seamlessly blended into his stubble. He went straight off with his male friends to play pool in the adjacent room where the dealing was going on. His tipsy girlfriend was left balancing unsteadily on a grubby velvet bar stool, drinking double house spirits like there was no tomorrow. By the time she'd necked the fourth she was wondering where the next would come from.

Circe watched her. She'd noticed Eddie come in ten minutes earlier. He was now on his second pint. It was all about timing. Tottering over to the bar Circe queued up near him to get a packet of crisps. Although it was crowded there was a strange kind of chivalry towards the old girl they saw trying to get served. Someone got the barman's fragile attention. 'Here mate, this Nan wants serving.'

Circe quietly thanked him and asked for her crisps. She was close to the light now and kept her head down. They shouted in turn,

'Wanna port and lemon, love? I'll treat ya if you promise to take your teeth out for me later?'

'Ta, but no thanks.'

Then the rest chorused, 'Want some weed grandma? Something to pick you up? E's or K's?'

She was in the lion's den and felt the sweat running down the inside of her arms. This was really dangerous. *Give it up now* she said to herself. The gods were with her though, as two girls pushed in and the tormentors lost interest in her and tried to grab them instead. Circe tapped on Eddie's arm and whispered, 'Thought you might like to know that that young lady over there must fancy you. She's been eyeing you up and down.' Circe gestured to the drunk girl at the bar. As she made her way, in what she imagined was an old lady style gait, back to her seat she pushed a scrap of paper towards the drunk girl from behind.

Circe was already seated again by the time the girl picked up the beer stained paper. It contained two words, 'Wanna Drink?' Puzzled she looked right and left swivelling on the bar stool. Looking along the bar for anyone who might have sent it, she noticed Eddie looking at her. Characteristically he smiled and winked following it up by snaking along the bar and automatically used his tried and tested opener. 'What are you drinking, darling?'

'Lots' she answered back truthfully.

Circe watched him get the attention of the bar staff. She knew he was on jobseekers allowance, but you'd never know it to watch the drinks flowing. Perhaps it was Tracey's child benefit money? She wasn't here tonight. Eddie slipped his arms round the girl's shoulders with the practised ease of the seasoned adulterer. She was drunk and was flirting with him openly, laughing at what he said, her breasts jiggling.

The sound of male laughter competed. A loud guffawing as the girl's boyfriend came out of the pool room. He'd won and had taken money off his opponent. The smile died on his face when he saw her leaning up against Eddie. His face contorted, and he snarled, 'What the fuck is going on?'

The answer Eddie made was entirely in character but was unfortunate. 'What's it got to do with you, fat boy?'

Gorilla grabbed his girl and pulled her behind him with his left hand while the right, the one with a tattoo of a skull with worms protruding from its socket, caught Eddie with a blinding crash on his jaw and ear. Now partially deaf, with a burst ear drum, and concussed, he feebly attempted to strike back, but Gorilla had the better of him. Despite the noise of the band, people realised that Eddie had tried it on with the Gorilla's girlfriend. Several of Tombstone's friends came over. Swearing and shouting, they also joined in the fracas. When Circe saw him glassed she should have winced, but she'd seen too many police photos of what he'd done to Tracey.

The pub staff were trying to break it up. Big men wearing black barked and swaggered. One called the police while the others punched and kicked Eddie long after he'd hit the floor. The CCTV had been disabled and it was a measure of local stoicism that very few left the premises. So engrossed were they in the spectacle, that Circe had an easy passage to the door even though a piece of wood from a chair broken over Eddie's head whistled past her. She turned before closing the door and saw the Gorilla take a flying kick which landed between Eddie's battered legs. He was already unconscious and did not flinch. Nevertheless, the Gorilla screamed, 'Keep yourself and your stinking cock away from my woman', at his prostrate body.

Circe was driving back down Stoneleigh Way towards Brighton when she saw the blue lights of the police car screaming towards the pub. *Job done,* she said to herself as she thought of her Bombay Sapphire waiting for her at home.

Chapter Twenty-Four

COUNCIL OF WAR

Anne Lancaster called a crisis meeting in her office. She was enjoying micro-managing and was in no hurry to help the inexperienced Superintendent skill up. It was attended by Inspector Crook, Steve Tibbs and Lorcan. They went there with the depressed appearance of condemned men.

'So, what it's all about?' she asked, her usual non-specific opening approach. Were her eyes not the angry Tanzanite blue that they were, Lorcan might have cracked the, 'Is that a philosophical question ma'am?' joke. But even he knew from the pit of his stomach that there was a problem.

Crook tried to diffuse the silence. 'Ma'am is this about last night's disturbance in Stoneleigh?'

The ACC wheeled on him. 'Disturbance? Is that what you call a near riot? Your standards and ideas of disturbance are very different to my own, I can tell you! And you, DS O'Leary, weren't you up there this week? What intelligence did you obtain about the mood on the estate?'

'Well, right enough, I was there investigating reports of antisocial behaviour by children on some of the older members of the estate. I spoke to victims and possible perpetrators, but there was no particular evidence to connect the two...'

'You got some DNA on your car, though.' Tibbs forgot himself.

'What was this?' Anne Lancaster pressed her fingers together making a steeple like shape that could have fitted around any of their necks.

Lorcan gave Tibbs a look that should have felled him. 'Ma'am, we only had a slight problem with a couple of young boys who masturbated on the car.'

She looked directly at him. 'And?'

'And unfortunately keyed the words, 'jerk off' next to it.'

Tibbs suppressed a guffaw at hearing the story again. It was his anecdote of the week.

'Constable,' she turned on him. 'I've been looking at your arrest record and performance. I am very worried about you, and your role in this police force.'

Tibbs paled and looked very unsettled. But Anne Lancaster having wounded him carried on to the bigger prey. 'I have an Inspector and Sergeant who are part of a dedicated interdisciplinary team, and we have a major situation on the estate. It wasn't even a weekend night, it was a Wednesday! We get a man kicked half to death in The Black Dog for chatting up a girl and no witnesses it seems. Then all the windows of a flat are smashed with rocks and the resident is accused of being a paedophile. According to our records he is just about everything else, but not that. So how did that happen?'

Lorcan felt the buzz in his pocket. *Bet it was the care home.* That was all he needed.

Crook answered. 'Ma'am, we know about the paedo, sorry paedophile allegations. It seems that someone is posting notices around the estate making accusations, even phone numbers are being listed. It's a strange kind of naming and shaming, except that the victim of the broken windows wasn't a paedophile!'

Anne Lancaster stared hard at him. 'What was he then?'

'A very well-known drug dealer as it happens. For some reason he was falsely accused on a notice outside the shop. It seems some of the residents took exception.'

'Had he ever been attacked before?'

'No ma'am. As a drug dealer he was officially a pillar of the community, despite being on a charge of ABH for breaking a client's arm who owed him money. Paedophilia wasn't his line of business, as far as we know.

Lorcan cut in. 'The interesting thing is that no one lifted a finger against him until he was accused of child molestation. Now he is so frightened he's requested the council give him emergency housing and he's looking to leave the area.'

'Is he now?' The ACC released her gaze slightly. 'Now what am I going to tell the Leader of the Council and the Community Safety

Team? That we can't keep residents safe? That we drive them out of the city with scurrilous rumours?'

All three men looked pensive. They hadn't looked at the situation in this way. They knew that they were responsible in an oblique way for not protecting the drug dealer, but silently rejoiced at his impending departure.

The ACC continued. 'We have a duty to keep everyone safe, do you understand? Not just those who abide by the law. You need to come up with an urgent action plan. You've got twenty-four hours. See you in here tomorrow, at the same time.'

She waved the back of her hand at them as if they were irritating wasps. Thus released from her hateful glare they backed out of her office. Looking at each other as they stood in the deep pile carpet of the upper landing in Malling House they silently raised fists of triumph and smiled. So Norman Moody was going, was he?

At that moment the Chief Constable emerged from his massive office, catching sight of them he stopped short. 'Everything alright boys? Good news is it?'

They quickly scuttled off down the stairs murmuring, 'Yes, sir.'

When they returned to the dingy open plan office they shared in John Street CID they instructed Tibbs to make tea, which he did very badly, barely washing the cups. Thoughtfully they worked their way through a packet of Jaffa cakes which clearly belonged to a staff member, as it had his name and the words *Keep off* clearly written on the side. He was notoriously proprietorial and never put into the tea fund or bought a round of drinks. Tibbs went to the trouble of putting some used teabags in an evidence bag, inserting it into the empty cardboard box and gluing the lid closed before replacing it in the cupboard. 'That feels about right and should buy us some time.'

Crook nodded in agreement, 'We are saving him from himself. He's a bit of a porker, that one.' He puffed out and patted his belly to illustrate the point and said, 'OK, team, you heard the lady, now what's to do?'

Lorcan was busy texting the care home: *I appreciate that it doesn't look good when you have an inspection, but if my father wishes to wear a colander on his head, surely they will understand his circumstances? It is also your staff's job to make him put his*

110

clothes on. That's what they're paid for. I'm at work so I'll call you later.

Crook looked at him. 'Any chance of you joining us?'

'Yeah. Problems with my old man again. Mind you he may have the right idea. What about us all putting metal colanders on our heads? It'll protect us from the flak and we can claim mental health issues. Or Tibbs can wear his cycle helmet as he hasn't got any other use for it.'

Tibbs glared. 'I'm still hopeful of an arrest on that one.' Any further observations were drowned out by his colleague's gales of laughter.

Finally Crook sighed. 'This bloody estate. Most towns and cities have a problem area, but this is getting out of hand. We know drug dealing goes on, but it's relatively contained. A bad problem, but if Norman Moody goes then that leaves a vacuum perhaps for some Londoners to break into the market. Remember that Somali group last year? We clamped down on it quickly, but it's an ever present threat.'

Lorcan rubbed his hair. 'What I don't understand is why people aren't reporting the crimes. Obviously they don't generally have insurance policies they can claim off of and they hate us right enough.'

Tibbs said, 'Well, that's a start isn't it? We don't usually have much contact with them as victims.'

Crook took over. 'Not true. The kid who was killed, Luke Marchant; we did a lot of community work there. Reassurance and the like. Same as when there's a DV call or any request for help. We always get up there asap. We aren't always welcomed, it has to be said, by some people there, but we try not to lose the opportunity to make a positive impression.'

'So who's doing all this then? One person, or the usual kids?' Tibbs drummed a biro against his knees.

Crook brushed the Jaffa cake crumbs from his shirt and slurped his nearly cold tea. 'The notice left outside the shop was a bit creative for them. They weren't any spelling mistakes and to be honest Norman Moody probably was their supplier. I think we've got several issues here. The usual ones with kids and residents are scum on scum, but we may have a new person in the mix that is pitting them against each other and creating a climate of fear. Perhaps he's some loner, some freak who lives with his mother, plays around with his computer and maybe is doing some kind of experiment.' His eyes shone. 'It could even be some lunatic sociology student at the university setting this up as a social engineering project. Wouldn't surprise me.'

Lorcan nodded. 'Yeah, I've seen this back home in the Troubles where all kinds of mischief was set up. It only took one person to finger another and it was as good as curtains for them. Hard to know what the truth was and if you survived a kneecapping for instance, you'd not be chatting to anyone now, would you?'

Crook and Tibbs looked at him. No doubt Lorcan had the experience. He was the man for the job, and this time religion didn't come into it. Seeing them looking at him he knew what they were thinking. 'No,' he said. 'You're not lumbering me with this one. I'm telling you, no!'

The council of war concluded. They hadn't got much to offer the ACC tomorrow except Lorcan's experience. To deflect attention away from himself, he said he'd talk with Victim Support and canvass their views. What he really meant was he'd use it as an excuse to call Circe.

No one else picked up on this as they now had to move on to the report of the rape of a seventy-year old widow in Hove. It seemed that the perpetrator had lain in wait in shrubbery by her front door and pushed her through and assaulted her. The night duty CID and crime scene investigators had done a good job with the victim and it was now down to Crook's team to do the footwork on the fairly poor description, which wasn't surprising in the circumstances. The rapist was thick set and shaven headed. Crook read out the description. 'Could be anyone, including a couple of officers I can think of. But it's not funny. He knocked her around quite a bit and it has a number of similarities to the one in Lancing three months ago. Strangely he used a condom, so there's a bit more work for the DNA. Victim said his genitals were shaved and there was some writing on his penis.'

'Jesus, not a tattoo, surely? How painful!' Tibbs was diversifying as usual.

'Her glasses were knocked off, but that's what she thought.'

Lorcan got up to go. 'That'll make the identification parade interesting won't it?'

Chapter Twenty-Five

A FREE LUNCH

Circe spent the morning doing her Victim Support work. She was quite tired from her evening outings and had to stifle a few yawns. She had an appointment booked in with a man who looked like he had a few problems.

Just before he was due, she took a call from Lorcan. She was a little surprised to hear from him, but then again, she wasn't.

'Hallo, Lorcan. What can I do for you? Need some new Elvis playlists?'

'Morning, Circe. It concerns some issues on the estate, so it does.'

Her heart sunk. God, they'd found out. She'd be arrested, humiliated and destroyed professionally and personally. Why the hell had she done it? Waves of regret and fear crashed over her head. How much did they know? More to the point how did they find out? She hadn't told anyone and she was always so careful.

Lorcan's voice cut into her thoughts and the silence. 'Am I ringing at a bad time? Is it OK to talk?'

She pulled herself together and said with artificial brightness, 'No it's fine, go on.' She held her breath waiting and regretting her campaign. If her prayers were answered would she give it up? Would she? Would she trade safety for justice?

Lorcan spoke before she could answer herself.

'There are a number of things happening up there right now and as the Police Authority member for the area we would welcome and value your input if you could spare the time.'

Her heart pounded, she was surprised he couldn't hear it. She sighed audibly.

Lorcan said again, 'Are you sure this isn't a bad time?'

Swiftly the fire rose within in her and she swept to attack. 'No, I'm just waiting for you to get to the point Detective Sergeant.'

Her rudeness was wasted on him, he'd had it worse back home. He also wanted to press home an advantage, a rare chance to liaise with her. 'Could we meet? It would be easier, if that's ok? What about a quick lunch?'

How little he knows, she thought, but answered despite herself. 'Yes that would work. How about Hangleton Manor. They have a log fire.'

'Sure. See you at 13.00 hours.'

Circe smiled to herself at his police precision. Scarcely having time to push the strand of copper hair off her slightly perspiring forehead she sighed with relief and looked up as a smartly dressed middle-aged man was shown into the office. Simon Peterson looked strained and upset as many people contacting Victim Support did. He wore smart mustard-coloured corduroy trousers and a navy blazer.

Nervously he told her his story. She maintained the calm professional mask of her outer self.

Simon, who gave his age as a believable sixty-five, had been in his property when he heard someone climb over the back gate and then saw them break into his garden shed. He hurried outside and the thief, some thirty years his junior, turned and began to run off.

Simon picked up a discarded Spear and Jackson spade and threw it like a javelin at his retreating back. The apex of the blade caught him just above the coccyx felling him instantly. Simon was still standing with one foot on him like a colonial big game hunter when the police arrived, having been summoned by his wife Vanessa who had broken off from her Pilates practice upstairs on hearing the commotion. Although in better condition than many for her age there was still a way to go and the green leotard was voted worst outfit of the week at the station. Simon was devastated to learn that the CPS said there was insufficient evidence to prosecute. His unhappiness and that of West Hove Golf Club's committee who heard it in the 19th hole was worsened when they learned that the putative burglar had got legal aid to pursue him for an assault occasioning actual bodily harm. Never mind that he couldn't feel anything because of the opiates in his body and hadn't ever worked in his life.

Circe's face did not betray what she thought. She could only offer tea and sympathy. It was desperately unfair. The only consolation, and one which she didn't comment on, was that the police were privately supportive of him. Two officers came round to his house with so-called crime prevention advice. Looking Simon squarely in the eyes they said, 'You've got foxes and cats coming over your gate, haven't you sir?' He'd looked puzzled, so they'd said, 'The best way to stop vermin breaking in, as it were, is to nail up some gripper rod on the top of the back gate. We are animal lovers ourselves and we can tell you they won't go near it or get hurt, but the less intelligent vermin, like the one you have been troubled with, may put hands on it and find them damaged whilst also leaving DNA for future reference. We trust this is helpful to you? We know Carpetright has a special offer on gripper rod right now. Just trying to be helpful. Also to suggest that it is put in place sooner rather than later, as properties often get revisited. However, in this climate I think it best that you didn't hear that from us.' The other officer nodded. 'Good evening, sir.'

Simon took some comfort from that as he waited for his case to be processed.

* * *

Circe got to the pub and sat on the settee nearest the fire. It was a grey day and nearly dark, but she wasn't going to have any food as today was her alternate day fast. She had fizzy water with ice and not even a citrus slice in case of temptation. Looking up she saw Lorcan on the other side of the bar with a pint of Murphy's in his hand. He waved and came over.

'Drinking on duty, Lorcan?'

'Yes. Can I get you another? What are you having to eat?'

'Nothing, water's just fine for me. I'm having a big meal later on,' she lied, scarcely convincing herself.

'Really?'

Coming as he did, from a family with five sisters, Lorcan knew some of the ways of women. The girls had large appetites, but would be seen to put virtually nothing on their plates as they grew up. However, being observant he knew they grazed, their hands absently reaching into biscuit barrels, larders and fridges on a continual basis. Their cars would be full of sweet wrappers and their handbags likewise. When they bemoaned their figures, 'I can't see how I can

115

be this big when I hardly eat anything,' he would point out where their logic failed them. A couple of thumps from his oldest sister Maeve soon had him shut up and if he so much as met their eyes during their discussions he'd get threatened. Saoirse would yell at him, 'And you can turn your big old green eyes away and stop looking at us critically. Who do you think you are to judge?'

The time he answered her truthfully brought back painful memories. She nearly burst his tympanic membrane with the slap. As a result he had to go round with a wodge of cotton wool sticking out of his ear for the next few weeks and looked like a toy with stuffing coming out of it. When he joined the RUC, as one of the few Catholics they managed to recruit, he warned his sisters that he'd take his truncheon to them now if there was any trouble. The balance of power shifted though the weight on their hips never did.

Lorcan went to the bar and ordered a pizza. He also paid for a side order of fries, some olives and dough balls. When he sat down again Circe was illuminated by the firelight and seemed to glow. The reflected brightness flickered orange and red on her face and hair.

Lorcan explained about the recent issues on the estate and she nodded thoughtfully as she listened. Lorcan's lunch was delivered promptly and Circe looked at it hungrily. He cut the pizza into wedges.

'Go on have one,' he offered.

She shook her head resolutely.

Fresh ciabatta bread nestled against the shiny green olives in herbed oil. The dough balls glistened with garlic butter and the beautifully arranged fries had a frosting of sea salt adorning their golden brown crispy lengths. Lorcan waved a fork in their general direction Again Circe declined raising a fuchsia pink nail varnished hand in a final stop sign.

'OK.' He spoke with his mouth still half full, washing the food down with his second pint. 'The problem is that I'm having my bollocks squeezed by Anne Lancaster.'

Circe stared at the dough balls, not noticing that he'd clearly overlooked the considerable differences in their status. The food smelled wonderful. She hadn't eaten since last night and was not only hungry, but extremely worried. She always used eating as a way of self-soothing when anxious.

Lorcan was happy to have her ear and ate voraciously while talking. 'What's really biting her is the increase in antisocial behaviour and crime. Cars vandalised and notices being put up fingering people as sex offenders.' He paused and considered what he said. 'No, that doesn't sound nice, but you know what I mean.' He threw an olive up into the air catching it in his mouth. He was too engrossed to notice that Circe had paled. Surely he had some lead on her?

Automatically she reached out and took a fat, moist olive and nibbled its flesh delicately. As she put the stone in the white china saucer next to them she retrieved a dough ball and absently ate it. She didn't bother to wipe the buttery garlic sauce from her fingers as it would only get greasy again when she took the spare wedge of pizza that Lorcan had deliberately placed on a side plate together with a handful of fries. Wisely profiting from his painful female sibling training he said nothing and kept talking. He wanted her to feel comfortable with him, though he hadn't yet asked himself why.

'So I'm to be hung out to dry if I don't get any answers. Now yous know the estate and go to the meetings up there and half your court cases must come from there. What in the name of all that's sacred is going on there right now?'

Circe coughed, her face reddening. She'd finished her water so Lorcan handed her his Murphy's and she took a great swig. 'Thanks, Lorcan. I don't know what's going on in Stoneleigh. I've heard nothing, but since you say it isn't being reported that's not surprising. If, as you say, they're attacking their own, perhaps they're dealing with grudges as a form of summary justice?'

'Oh, that's always happened, but not like this. No one will talk, not even a whisper.'

Circe felt safer now and scooped the last salted chip. Lorcan knew that no woman could resist stealing a man's fries. The psychology degree he'd done taught him a lot, but the French fries test worked a treat every time.

She said slowly, 'It may be too early to see a pattern, but you should have daily or weekly crime records. What do you normally get at this time of year? Are there more offences committed on the estate, as opposed to off the estate? It may be worth checking arrests of people from Stoneleigh and making some comparisons. Shouldn't be hard. Obviously you'll control for things like weather and so on. We all know that when it's cold people seem to stay in. As I say it might be a bit early to spot any trends, but you could get the data set up. I'm guessing you aren't a statistics whizz kid?'

'Jesus no! We've got a department for that and I find keying in the simplest numbers a nightmare. There's a story about a massive mistake I made, which I'll tell you about one day when you're drinking.'

Circe got up to go. 'Don't let the ACC bully you. She should know well enough by now that there is always trouble on that estate. It comes in peaks and troughs. I'd be interested to know if you get anything off those figures. I'll probably see you at the meeting soon, so we can catch up.'

Lorcan played it cool. 'Sure. Or I'll email you if anything looks useful.'

Circe thought for a moment and then said, 'Look, I'll give you my home email address as the Authority ones get routed through the administrative staff. I know the Chief Executive likes to know what goes on and we aren't supposed to fraternise with lower-ranking officers. It's nothing personal to you,' she added quickly, as he looked crushed and she scribbled down her email in her notebook and tore out the sheet and handed it to him. 'Anyway, thanks for letting me eat half your lunch.'

'I'd not noticed. I'm used to my big sisters spearing a chop or roasties off my plate, so I am. I'm hardly likely to miss a couple of chips.' His gallant reply worked, and Circe smiled. 'Thanks. I've a long day still to run.'

'I'm off duty at six, officially. No budget for overtime so I'll get the estate figures sorted in my own time and will look forward to the meeting with my nemesis tomorrow.'

Buttoning up her long black coat with a faux fur collar Circe made to leave. 'A piece of advice, on the house, as payment for lunch.'

He looked up and the flames of the fire were behind her leaving a flickering glowing aura about her. As he didn't answer she said again. 'Lorcan, do you want the advice?'

He nodded stifling an oregano flavoured belch.

Circe frowned. 'Don't bring in the Elvis shit. It's not big and it's not clever, especially if you want a career rather than to be popular with the lads. Anne Lancaster must be special needs not to have seen through you.'

'You may have a point,' he said as the logs in the grate shifted. The sparks cascaded upwards and she was gone.

Chapter Twenty-Six

STONELEIGH ESTATE

Circe hurried back to her Figaro, there was much to be done before evening. First she drove along to Hove Lagoon. Parking outside Lagoon Bait again, she considered the plans that she had made so meticulously. With the police sniffing around Stoneleigh were these now compromised more than ever? Circe wasn't sure. She sat still weighing the pros and cons. She'd been desperate when she thought she might be picked up and arrested. She remembered how panic struck she had felt only that morning when Lorcan rang. It may be that she wasn't on the police radar and she should be grateful and go back to being a 'normal' member of society. There had been some near misses and she'd probably made a few offenders stop and think. What with old Eddie being in plaster still, he wouldn't be knocking Tracey around for some time at least. The respite might give her a chance to see him in his true light.

It was cold sitting there. The condensation was building up on the car's windows and she looked at her own amber eyes in the rear view mirror. Was this enough, should she just call it a day? What was she doing this for? The bloody Human Rights Act that became a charter for feckless criminals and left victims to an existence of loss and unfairness. If she was caught, and she sincerely hoped to the core of her being that she wouldn't be, she would publicise her cause and hopefully then someone else would take up the baton and run with it. Others had gone before her - some even served prison sentences, but in her position while she was able, she was well placed to do as much damage to offenders as she could. Decision made. Shivering she got out of the car taking three Lakeland food storage containers with her for the maggots. This was becoming a habit.

When she got home she made a fuss of the cats. Nigel, Clive and Rupert loved her and were so pleased to see her. Clive had nearly turned to liquid since he had developed a habit of sleeping under the electric heat pad in their basket. The others would then lie on top of him so he was pressed down and overheated by their body weight too. Once overcome with warmth he would lie half-baked and comatose until Circe would drag him out and give him some water. She'd threatened him with turning it off but was too soft hearted to do so as they all loved its warmth so much.

Going through her notebook she reviewed tonight's targets. They were three women, Sherene Gillbank, Rosario Demanio and Keeley Jupp. While she did this she drank another Slimfast, grimacing at its slimy sickliness.

Sherene had been pregnant for most of her life since she was fourteen. She now had nine children all of whom were in care or adopted. There had been massive interventions by the state, with a social worker even living on the premises at one stage. Despite that, the child had to be removed and yet again Sherene became pregnant once more. She never attended to the children or met their needs in any way. She would shut them in another room so she could hear the TV better. She liked the maternity grant and spent it on drink and drugs in the main. The fathers were generally unknown except for the last two kids. They were by William Bryant who had fathered more than twelve himself with different women in Brighton, and again most of which were in care or fostered.

When she wasn't on her back, Sherene shoplifted prolifically for herself and to feed her drug habit. She had been banned from most of the shops in Brighton as a condition of her ASBO, but she breached that continually.

The Probation Service always said that she had emotional issues due to her children being taken away. When Sherene would appear in court and these excuses got trotted out, Circe would point out that the offending behaviour occurred before, during and after her obstetric history and was therefore independent of this. Sherene routinely went to prison and came out and carried on just the same as before. Nothing ever stopped her and despite all the drink and drugs in her body it still seemed supremely capable of producing babies.

Again it was a cold night, for which Circe was pleased. She knew the maggots would lie still until they hit the warmth of the houses. She set off on the now familiar route to the estate. It was about 12.45am when she arrived at Sherene's house. It was largely in darkness but with what looked like a television on in an upstairs bedroom.

Creeping up the path in her soft soled shoes Circe removed the Lakeland thin and flexible chopping board and made a funnel shape. Crouching down she placed it through the battered letter box. Her knees protested at the cold and crouched position. She carefully unlocked the plastic container barely glancing at the maggots, who much to her relief were unmoving. She tipped the contents carefully down her home-made chute. She heard the rush as they went through like beads and then silence.

In response to her general questions about the lifecycle of maggots Lagoon Bait advised her that maggots moved surprisingly quickly secreting themselves in carpets and skirting boards if dropped at home. Circe knew that laminate floors were a contemporary preference, so hoped they would indeed move at the smart pace she was promised. The interiors of the houses and flats weren't large, so a pint of the creatures should make quite an impact. They would be in warm enough conditions to metamorphize into ugly black flies. Circe was amazed when the shop owner had described how a friend of his had left some maggots in his car in summer. They had swiftly gravitated below the floor mats and when he opened the car door a couple of days later it was evidently like a scene from a horror film with a swarm of fat bluebottles flying at him.

Circe had selected her first case relatively easily, and the second was also a clear candidate. Rosaria Demario was thirty-nine and had four children by four different men. Her latest conviction was for benefit fraud of £15,000. She had secured a job as a care worker and left various friends in her flat at night to keep an eye on the children. This had ended up being a regular meet for druggies and alcoholics to doss while she wiped the bottoms of the elderly who were too vulnerable to object to her diffident style and careless cruelties.

Rosaria systematically failed to declare to the Benefits Agency that she had been working and the care home owners were typically slack about running checks knowing that the infrastructure of inspections was cratering under the limited budgets. Rosaria was only found out because an elderly neighbour, sick of the nuisance from the night time guests, grassed her up anonymously. Despite that

Rosaria guessed the identity of the informant and, equally anonymously, threw a brick through her neighbour's window. But it couldn't be proved.

Circe checked the address she had for Rosaria. It was a flat, so getting in to the shared entrance might be a problem. However, she was banking on it being vandalised and on creeping up to the door, was pleased to see that the security light was smashed and the shattered glass was below its protective metal cage. Her guess was that it had been shot out by a BB gun.

There were sporadic lights on the landing, and Circe counted along till she got to the flat. She could hear noise from within. *Oh, God*, she thought, *I'll be discovered doing this*. She rummaged in her bag and found the superglue. Quickly squirting it into the lock she waited for what seemed an eternity, though it was in actual fact only five minutes. She was just about to get out the flexible Lakeland chopping board and pour the maggots through the letter box when the communal door opened and a fat young couple wearing tracksuits appeared. The girl was the larger of the two and she had a nearly finished portion of fish and chips in a greasy paper wrapping. The male was whining for some. 'Come on, girl, give us a chip. You've eaten all yours and now you've taken mine, you greedy, fat bitch.'

Circe put her head down. Her hat obscured her face and hair though there were drifts of talcum powder on the shoulders of her navy blue coat.

The couple caught sight of Circe who continued rummaging in her bag as if looking for her key. They clearly thought it unusual that she should be out at such a late hour. The behaviour of the residents on the estate meant that there was a kind of institutionalised curfew for anyone over sixty, especially women.

It resulted in a strange night time population. Many of the troublemakers were subject to an official curfew and were tagged. So they were indoors and with the elderly not being about it made for a diluted population. Some people were awaiting trial and possible future tagging while others were luckier for not being caught yet. The male spoke as they approached Circe. 'What you doing old lady? Ain't it past yer bedtime?'

Circe tried to answer in a kind of croak to disguise her voice. She didn't look up just muttered, 'Keys.'

'Want the door shouldered in, love? These frames give in easy.'

'No thanks, my grandson's coming any minute.'

'Ok, suit yourself.' He sneered.

The girl walked on reaching the next communal door then she turned back and shouted, 'I hate old ladies, you all stink of fish.' With that she threw a piece of cod at Circe. Despite her fat arms she was still quite fit and Circe dodged quickly to avoid the greasy missile. Her swift reflexes could have proved her downfall except that the male grabbed the paper bag from his companion and stuffed the chips into his own mouth and so, jostling and shouting, they went on their way at last.

In many ways it had been a gift. No one tended to open their doors to see what the shouting was about as you would never know what you'd get, so Circe took the opportunity and funnelled the chopping board through the corroded letter box and deposited the maggots into the flat. She was sweating with fear and her hands were slippery. She could still hear noise inside and hoped the maggots would land quietly. There must have been a mat or carpet as she couldn't hear anything. She was not sure if the superglue would have made any difference to the flat door. But fearful now, she hastened away back along the urine smelling darkened corridor and out into the night.

Regaining the relative safety of the cold air, Circe had to choose whether or not to continue her plan. God, she really needed a drink and could almost taste the BSC. The fragrant hit of the Bombay Sapphire and the refreshing coldness of the soda water and the unforgettable flavours of the lime and mint. She stopped under a street light. The last plastic container of maggots protruded from her shopping bag's sides. Circe sighed deeply. She was also very hungry. It seemed a long time ago that she'd had that Slimfast.

Her last case was Keeley Jupp who had a lengthy record that took in a selection of everything. Nothing ever made any impact with her and she never paid her fines. When finally brought into court on a 'no bail' warrant she would chew gum and agree to pay the minimum amount towards her massive and increasing fines. But she never did. All attempts to make deductions at source failed as she took out one crisis loan after another and the DSS always recovered debts to themselves before making payments to the court. She well deserved some maggots.

Wearily Circe trudged up the road wondering how residents on the estate got so fat since it was such a workout just getting up and down the hills. A lone dog barked unhappily. Circe jumped. Was it an omen? Keeley's small house was soon in sight and she stood looking up and down the cul-de-sac. It felt a bad place to be and she could be trapped if she was caught. From a distance she could hear loud voices. Sound carried a long way on the night air. God how she'd changed and knew she was becoming a real creature of the night. As she turned the corner to approach Jupp's property she heard a car approaching up Stoneleigh Way. It moved at a steady pace, not like the drunks or youths who revved and braked.

Circe pressed herself into a segment of dirty hedging just as the lights of a police car flashed, lighting up the night with its blue strobes.

She saw a face studying a phone. She couldn't be sure, but if she had to bet money she would have said it was Lorcan's profile. She had no choice but to abort her last mission.

Circe didn't sleep that night. She kept replaying events in her mind. This was also the mind that was clouded by nearly half a bottle of Bombay Sapphire and all this on an empty stomach. At 4.30am she disturbed the furry weight of the cats and went downstairs to her computer.

She wrote a short email to Alice saying nothing in particular. Then she made a cheese and cucumber sandwich with extra mayonnaise. *Fuck the diet,* she said to herself, and washed it down with a strong coffee. As she stared at the half-full cafetiere she thought *what if the game is well and truly up now?*

Chapter Twenty-Seven

A FIGHTING CHANCE

Lorcan had been summoned to the estate when a fight had developed that was more than the response team usually dealt with.

He was shattered, and his evening had been spent on the phone to his father's care home trying to work out how much of the old man's behaviour was deliberate and how much the genuine results of cognitive decline. Lorcan was coming to the reluctant conclusion that Patrick was definitely playing up. Sure he'd been through a lot in the Troubles, as everyone had, and he wouldn't say much about what, if any, his involvement had been. Lorcan could only speculate on what he may, or may not, have done. In truth he really didn't want to know one way or the other. He suspected that his father had very strong Republican sympathies, but the less said then the less could be tortured out of you if it ever got to that. Their home town of Dungiven was a quiet place and in many ways more cosmopolitan than most. However, when Lorcan, unusually for a Catholic, joined the RUC things with his father began to get more difficult. Lorcan's mother had been killed many years back in a terrorist incident and Patrick went crazy for a time. Well who wouldn't? He always liked a drink and wasn't sober then at all.

Lorcan's sisters ran the home and their own lives. They grew up, married and somehow Lorcan ended up caring for his dad. He was the youngest of the litter and didn't make his escape quickly enough. By the time he wanted to make his move it was too late. Like so many men of his age, Patrick became manipulative and difficult. They had a legendary Uncle Fearghal who had displayed eccentric behaviour of a kind that even the benevolent Irish struggled to rationalise. It was like a timebomb miasm. No one actually came out and said that Patrick was going that way, as they all knew he'd been through a lot already, but he started behaving very oddly. As a result, it was decided, that when Lorcan transferred police forces, Patrick should go with him to England. Old man O'Leary didn't object, after all the new Ireland was a compromised failure to him. It should have been thirty-two counties, or nothing. So he allowed himself to be moved to the land of the oppressor. Eventually though, his behaviour was so challenging that Lorcan had no choice but to put him in residential care as his assessment by Social Services had been one long unfortunate litany of 'feck offs' and 'feck yous'. Lorcan's father had savings of more than £20,000 from the proceeds of his wife's insurance policy, so he would have to pay for his own care. This rankled on every level.

Patrick was difficult and his booming voice was bound to get him noticed. But so was treating baskets of washing as if they were cats or dogs, petting the clothing and trying to walk the basket by threading a tie through it and dragging it along, barking if they passed anyone. The least he did was put his trouser legs over the taps in the bathroom and rearrange other people's shoes into odd pairs yet wearing matching shoes himself.

Technically, as Patrick was a self-funder, he could choose which home he went into, but in reality his choices were becoming increasingly limited by his record of behaviour that was building up into a substantial dossier. The care home managers were entitled to assess whether individuals would be suitable and that their needs could be met. It was reaching a point where old Mr O'Leary was not going to be offered a place regardless of however much he paid. Lorcan was determined that he should stay at his present home, which was a good one. However, Patrick was hanging by a thread at Seahaven House, or 'See-Heaven House' as he called it. The manager was a woman who didn't like to admit defeat and so Lorcan worked tirelessly with her to help his father settle in. They both knew it wasn't working, but neither wanted to be the first to say it. Lorcan had been informed that today's antics included his father's misbehaviour in the arts and crafts room. It had been difficult to see what could go wrong there. Was it spilled paint? Apparently not. It was more artistic and crafty than that. Lorcan didn't know whether to laugh or cry when he heard that his father had made a collage of his toenail clippings and pubic hair. A lady trustee had been visiting, and on inspecting the art room was appalled. Matters didn't improve when Patrick snarled at the woman, 'What yous looking at? Haven't you seen a man's pubes before? No, looking at you with yer old

127

mouth all pursed up like a cat's arse, I don't think you have, so make the most of mine. All you'll be getting is a look at the garnish. The meat and two veg would run a mile from the likes of yous.'

Councillor Mrs Walker was, despite her age and experience, shocked by this. The manager who had been showing her round was hoping to avoid Mr O'Leary senior and had scouted around earlier to avoid any difficulties. He never normally went near the arts and crafts room but clearly, having his own materials, he felt motivated to use them.

His articulate reasoning, albeit abusive, showed how much in control he was of his own mind. Lorcan was now in a quandary. Should his father be in a home at all, just because he was angry and difficult? If the answer was no, then in God's name where was he going to go and how would Lorcan cope? He needed to consult the sisters, for all the help they'd be.

DC Tibbs drove the pool car up to Stoneleigh while Lorcan sat catatonic beside him. Tibbs swore all the time they drove and Lorcan let him rattle on as he welcomed the break from this own thoughts. It wasn't hard to see where the fight was. There were people spilling out of houses onto the street and others standing about with mobile phones. Most of them just seemed to be shouting and swearing. Lorcan thought how well his father would do on this estate with his own foul mouth.

Pulling up they both got out and Lorcan immediately called for back-up. One large male was circling a smaller man. They both held knives at arm's length. Lorcan and Tibbs approached. Both protagonists and many of the onlookers/supporters were fairly well known to the police, and when they shouted at the men the knives miraculously disappeared and they stopped squaring up to each other. The officers took them separately to one side to hear their versions. There was quite a lot of similarity in their stories. They had both received texts from an unknown number which claimed that one had firstly slept with a neighbour's daughter and the other had given drugs to his son.

Emotions were clearly still running very high. The two men got taken in for questioning, and the spectators were told to go home as there was nothing to see. One older woman shouted at the officers, 'You're bloody blind, then. There's a fucking lot to see, if you know where to look.' The group of bystanders quickly told her to shut up and, still clutching a massive bottle of half-drunk cider, she was hauled back into a nearby property.

Both the perpetrators were later cautioned for the fight. It was the easiest way to resolve things. The police were under increasing pressure to try and deal with issues themselves and there was precious little money for the time spent processing the offences, and then the inevitable 'not guilty' trial. They always went not guilty as there was a very good chance the victims and witnesses wouldn't turn up in the months it would take for the trial to take place. This was without the inevitable adjournments. Justice delayed, was really and truly, justice denied.

* * *

Inspector John Crooks summoned Lorcan and Steve Tibbs to his office. His face was haggard from all the marathons he ran and the continuous preparatory training. He looked at least fifteen years older than his forty-five years, and rarely snacked on the junk that formed the refuelling of the majority of the force. There was never any explanation for the china cup-cake on his window sill. On the glazed frosting was a label *Use it or lose it*. It was regularly the subject of admiring attention from seagulls on the ledge outside.

Crooks gestured for Lorcan to sit down on a chair adjacent to a small round table. Not getting his nod to sit down Tibbs hovered, then sat himself down on a hard, un-matching chair near the door. He was fully included in the official bollocking though. Crooks cleared his throat and pressed the tips of his fingers together in a spire. To the untutored eye it almost seemed a peaceful and relaxed gesture. It wasn't. Lorcan and Tibbs stared sightlessly at the neat spiral bound notebook he had with him at all times. He admired Anne Lancaster's style and was endeavouring to copy her questioning approach. He began, 'Any idea why I've called you both here?'

Neither answered; they knew the old self-incrimination game too well.

'I'll tell you why. Because there is an almighty fuck up going on at Stoneleigh. You know what I'm saying?'

129

They pressed their lips together and nodded sagely in a kind of knowing acknowledgement. It didn't mollify Crooks who raised his voice. 'It's a shower of shite up there, and we all know it always will be. But right now there seems to be a new innovation. It's become a scum on scum scenario and they aren't as kind and gentle to each other as they could be. There just isn't the community spirit these days.' He emphasised the word spirit so that it almost sounded like 'spit.' Tibbs tried to meet Lorcan's eyes but he was having none of it. You didn't corpse during one of Crook's bollockings. They'd be spit-roasted if they did. There it was again 'spit.' Lorcan bit his lip. He felt his mobile vibrate in his pocket. *Oh, God, not See-Heaven House again?* The very thought removed his desire to laugh. He couldn't check who'd called for sure until JC had finished chewing them over.

He was in full flow. 'So what the fuck's going on up there? Isn't it enough that they provide the core business for the courts? That our appalling crime figures are dictated by their criminogenic activity? You bloody go to enough fucking community meetings, what does your so-called finger on the pulse of the monster say?'

Lorcan studied the pulse above the inspector's carotid artery on the right side of his neck, as it visibly pumped dangerously fast beneath the skin. A seagull looked in through the window, pacing hopefully on the guano covered sill. Its yellow eye seemed drawn to the china cupcake. It pecked the glass repeatedly.

'We're supposed to have multi-agency partnership support for this estate; the council, the Police Authority, Social Services and all the other bloody agencies you can think of. So what's going on? Can someone tell me? I've got complaint after complaint about neighbours feeling intimidated as if other residents are watching them. The typical climate of indifference has vanished. Yes, I know that statistically scrotes like the Stoners can expect to be victims of crime, but this phenomenon of shitting on your own doorstep with such spite and intention is new, and I don't like new things I don't understand. Get it?'

He spoke to them very differently from the artificial veneer of pleasantry that he adopted at meetings with the great and the good. This was the true man and it was pretty obnoxious. Lorcan and Steve worked hard and didn't need this bullshit. Lorcan's eyes closed for a second as he recalled Circe's description of her favourite drink, the BSC, designed to cope with the bullshit in life, to a degree. He came back into reality when he felt JC's eyes boring into him.

'Well, Detective Sergeant? Well?'

It must be something serious for his rank to be mentioned. Crook wasn't necessarily informal, but he did usually call him Lorcan. He blustered, 'Yes, Inspector it is serious, and yes there is a change in the pattern of offending.' He looked nervously to see if JC's face clouded more than usual. It wasn't, so he must be approximating the right answer.

'As I see it we should organise yet another crisis meeting bringing in key players to see what's going wrong and why things have changed.....'

He trailed off as Crook was shaking his head slowly with his thin lips pursed in a silent 'no.'

Lorcan didn't feel he had any choice but to try and continue justifying his thoughts. 'But, sir, that's the agreed policy. Involve the community in dealing with issues on their estate...'

JC's roar was so loud that the seagull outside leapt backwards, its normal confidence rocked by the human tirade. Steve Tibbs writhed uncomfortably on his hard chair.

Pointing a bony finger with an over loose ring on it at the officers Crooks bellowed, 'I've had it with you two and your cosying up to the fat old bags who litter the estate and who claim to represent that motley menagerie who masquerade as 'the community'. Not forgetting that old bearded git on his motorised scooter.'

'Mr Knowles?' Lorcan interjected in what he imagined was a helpful way.

'Oh, yes Mr Know-All. Though if he did know it all, he'd get his great old fat track suit bottomed arse out of that state paid motorised tricycle and do something with his fucking life. Same as that old cow with the fucking oxygen tank she drags round with her. Emphysema is it? No. It's fucking speaking too much on behalf of other people that she has no business or mandate to do. She needs more oxygen than the rest of us because she won't shut the fuck up. The only time she buttons it is when she's dragging on a fag. What possible understanding does she have of the drug issues, violence and feral kids in Stoneleigh, other than breeding five of them, all of which ended up in care? In my book that doesn't make her an expert, it makes her a slack-fannied breeding sow...'

The tirade was one of JC's worst ones. Steve and Lorcan looked down. It wasn't that what the Inspector was bellowing wasn't true, but it was one thing to think something in the darkest hours and quite another to screech a politically incorrect tirade at the top of your voice to junior staff. There was a sharp knock on the door and unannounced ACC Lancaster swept into the room. Inspector Crooks stopped mid-sentence.

She sat in the chair Lorcan immediately vacated for her without thanks. 'I didn't know you bred pigs Inspector, for I assume your rather loud remark related to an issue with your porcine charges?'

He coloured unhealthily. 'Er, not exactly.'

'We can discuss the content of your comments later. I'm glad you are all together in such a friendly cabal. I have certain important people with louder and more insistent voices than yours, Inspector, who want to have quick answers to what is happening in Stoneleigh. As I was over here this morning, prior to our scheduled meeting later, I wanted to know that I am going to have some solutions that I can look forward to passing on.'

Lorcan involuntarily dragged a weary left hand down over his face.

'Ah, I see you are discussing the very issue in your livestock chat.' Her cold blue eyes had the power to chill the room down in response to the overheating that John Crooks had given it.

The Inspector treacherously indicated in Lorcan's direction. 'Detective Sergeant O'Leary was just about to give us the benefit of his professional opinion as he works so closely with the key personnel on the estate'

With false expectancy they all turned to Lorcan who was now leaning against the doorway, every cell of his body wishing it could dematerialize and find itself on the other side. Since that failed to happen, he decided to opt for honesty. Tibbs stared at the seagull who offered no inspiration.

Clearing his throat and looking directly at ACC Lancaster. 'Ma'am, as I was just about to brief Inspector Crook, I can now categorically say that we have absolutely no idea at all why there is what seems to be a campaign amongst the residents of the estate against each other. No one is saying that these Stoners have always got on well together, but they've always been united against the police. Now they are attacking each other and typically we are marginalized and, to a large extent, helpless to help them, so to speak. There are a lot of secrets up there and they don't want them shared. However much they hate their neighbours they won't give any evidence against them. They'll sort it out in their own way. To give you an example, Ma'am, remember the way in which the so-called Stoner community dealt with the travellers who parked up on a field near the estate? Christ we'd have to have gone through weeks of tip toeing around getting proper notices of eviction, working with the Council's designated Traveller Liaison Officer following procedures. Not so the Stoners - on the second night they stomped over to the illegal encampment and we can only guess what methods of persuasion they used, but it worked all right. The travellers moved straight on, so they did, though they did pitch up at Brighton Rugby Club, who seemed uncharacteristically genteel about the invasion. It took us all of sixteen weeks to get them off and local tax payers had to stump up the £26,000 bill to clean the site and pay the lawyers. Great believers in summary justice, the Stoners. They don't go by the rule of law in any of their dealings. Which is why it will be difficult to get access to whoever is doing this. It may be a group rather than an individual. We have no intelligence until someone talks. I do realise, Ma'am, that you are under *political* pressure ...' He emphasized the word as contemptuously as if he was trying to clear a slug from his lips. 'But if I can speak frankly?'

Anne Lancaster nodded, but her eyes narrowed dangerously.

'As long as they are picking on each other it may mean that they don't have so much time to cause a problem for the rest of Brighton and Hove. It would be for senior officers to find a way of marketing the 'improvement' in the crime figures, if there is any.'

The officers stared at Lorcan as he delivered this heretical statement. The ACC's eyes looked like pools of sulphuric acid, the seagull sat fatly and silently at his post. She waved the back of her hand dismissively towards him and Tibbs to leave.

'Get out,' she hissed, turning to Inspector Crook.

Chapter Twenty-Eight

SALAD DAYS

The bus into town had a tough route. It started in Stoneleigh and then picked up residents of Portslade – 'the Sladers' – taking them into Brighton. The journey took in the Royal Sussex County Hospital after it passed the Churchill Square shopping mall and the fast food outlets. Oversized and indifferent mothers took up a lot of space with massive designer pushchairs, though they ignored both their offspring and their wailings. The bus drivers seemed to relish the opportunity to stamp on their air brakes and have passengers stumbling and grabbling at each other to regain balance. One might be at the back of the bus one moment and then hurtled to the front the next. Complaining was pointless.

The other useful drop off point was outside Brighton Magistrates Court. Cigarettes could be conveniently smoked on the steps, or nerves could be soothed by visiting any of the nearby pubs. 'The Jury's Out' was just across the road from the court and there was an array of other pubs five minutes away via George Street or Dorset Gardens in Kemptown. Many of these were characteristic of the LBGT community that they served, and whose own lives were generally very unlike the Stoners in court.

The court service users were a challenging group. If it wasn't the alcohol, it was more likely to be drugs they'd taken. The courthouse toilets were a dumping ground for used syringes and other drug paraphernalia. The court security search team at the front of the building were no match for the creativity of the defendants who would routinely store their gear in their 'Brighton pockets.'

Circe often regaled people with the story a Welsh solicitor, Mr Evans, who routinely harangued the Bench in long-winded sonorous tones. On this occasion he was defending a scrawny, pale ratty-faced man who was on trial accused of walking out of the Currys store on London Road with a boxed microwave that he hadn't paid for.

He was arrested one hundred yards away waiting for a bus to take him into Brighton. The large box was balanced unsteadily on his lap. In defending his client, Kyle Brown, Mr Evans exercised his right to take up the whole of the morning's precious allotted trial time by alleging that there wasn't a case to answer. No one had seen Kyle take the microwave and he was asked to look after it by a friend called John, about whom he had no more details, and which was why he made the 'no comment' interview to the police. Mr Evans vehemently contended at lyrical length that it wasn't his client's fault. Kyle was just helping out a mate.

Circe and her magistrate colleagues were obliged to listen to his representations at the start of the trial and then adjourn to determine if the evidence presented indicated that there was a case to answer. They took five minutes to agree that there certainly was. One magistrate had said that the evidence was so overwhelming that they didn't need to retire and they could just turn on their heels and go back in to court. But it was agreed that for the sake of appearing to discuss it they should stay out for fifteen minutes.

In that time the defendant had taken the opportunity to take a comfort break.

The cast reassembled in the court room. Kyle Higgins was now seen to be swaying, his eyes rolled and closed as if there were lead weights on them. He attempted to force them open again. Mr Evans sat in front of the dock so didn't have sight of his client's struggle with consciousness. Circe began to explain their findings. 'The Bench has been asked to consider an application from the defence that there is no case to answer...'

The defendant shouted from the semi-prone position where he'd slid in the dock. 'Come on Mr Evans, boyo. You know I done it, she knows I done it, let's stop pissing about and get on with the sentence.'

Mr Evan's mask like face turned the colour of putty. He uttered four words, 'I rest my case,' before angrily slumping back into his seat.

Circe glared at them both. 'Mr Evans, whatever form of refreshment your client took during the break seems to have acted as a kind of truth drug on him.'

Kyle Brown slurred, 'Come on, love, it was only a bit of H. I'd have gone guilty at the start, but my brief said to run with it. Not that I can run much with these thromboses I've got from shooting up. Me veins have collapsed and as it happens I've got an appointment with the doctor today, he's going to put me on Incapacity Benefit, on account of me health.'

Mr Evans wheeled round on Kyle, all camaraderie between them gone. 'Let me do the talking, you're incriminating yourself further.'

There was a soft thud in answer, as Kyle's legs gave way and he drifted to the carpet in the dock. His case was adjourned for the Probation Service to prepare pre-sentence reports, looking particularly at his history of drug abuse and previous enforced detoxes, five drug rehabilitation orders and his failure to respond to all previous sentences. Mr Evans still got paid his fees through legal aid though.

It was one of Circe's favourite moments. From that day on whenever she had Mr Evans in front of her, she would always interrupt him and ask if his client needed a break. They both knew what she meant, and he would glower darkly. Her reward, to everyone's benefit and relief, was that he kept his representation a great deal briefer than before.

Circe got out of court at lunchtime and, as she crossed the road between the court and Kemptown, her phone rang. It was Lorcan. She'd saved his number. For what reasons though she'd asked herself?

'Hi, it's Lorcan O'Leary.'

'Hi, yourself. I'd know those Northern Irish tones anywhere.'

'Oh, yes, I suppose you would. How's yous?'

'Did you phone to ask after my health?'

'No, not just that. We've had some major problems going on in Stoneleigh and as you are a key player I wondered if we could meet up and share ideas?'

'I thought we'd already done that?' A cold hand crept round her heart. Was he finally on to her? Had anyone else seen her, or was there any evidence that connected her?

'Yes, but things are getting worse and I'm getting my arse kicked all over the place. I'll take you to dinner. You choose.'

Better play along, Circe thought. *Keep it nice.* 'OK, I'm free tonight, but only want something light.' She was on raw food this week.

Lorcan recalled with some irony the last time they met in Hangleton Manor, and how she'd nicked his food. He smiled silently at the memory. Who did women think they fooled? Certainly not the scales.

'There's a new place, a salad bar in St James's Street.'

'Not sure I know that one, sounds a bit healthy for the police.'

'It's not long opened. Does fresh juices and a big choice of salads. It's called Tossers.'

'Of course it is,' Lorcan guffawed.

'No, seriously. You can have a choice of tossed salads, or the soup of the day; the so-called tosspot.'

'I can't wait.' He pulled a face to himself.

'It's not licensed.'

'Gets better and better.'

Lorcan met her there at 7pm. Tossers closed at 9pm as there obviously wasn't a great call for late night salad munching. It wasn't going to challenge the market currently occupied by the chippie or kebab shop. The establishment was like a minimalist wooden-floored Ikea café with slow moving, brightly-clad, woolly, knotty-heads serving. Lorcan's heart sank.

They sat down with their plates mounded high with greenery. They looked at each other over the top of the mountain of lettuce, past the table decoration of a vase with pebbles and two large alliums in water. Lorcan's vivid orange carrot juice, which was served to him by a man with the same colour hair, was opaque and foamy. Its grubby bubbles advertised the 'no peeling' policy chalked onto the specials board. Circe had treated him to a shot of wheatgrass. 'Don't want you looking like an Orangeman, so you need some green,' she smiled.

As they started eating it seemed to Lorcan that the more they ate the more there was on the plate. The sprouting alfalfa and chickpeas, the seven types of lettuce, three of cabbage, shredded carrots, the staining grated raw beetroot and not forgetting the 'energy bombs' which were in fact uncooked Brussel sprouts. Lorcan asked himself several times what he was doing here. The crunching made it almost impossible for him to hear anything, never mind make conversation. It was impossible to talk anyway, because bits of vegetation and detritus kept springing apart as he got it to his mouth and bits dropped down his shirt. What with the topping of assorted nuts and linseeds ricocheting like shrapnel across the table, it truly was an unfulfilling and socially embarrassing meal. He knew his teeth would be full of it, just by the fact that Circe's were, and she had bits of linseed stuck in her auburn curls too.

After twenty minutes chewing he put his knife and fork together, but since the compost heap of a meal still didn't appear to have diminished, he had to rest them against one of the slopes.

'You've hardly eaten anything.' Circe said.

'It's not for lack of trying I can tell you. Anyhow, I was saving myself for a piece of what looks deceptively like chocolate cheesecake, but the handwritten italics tell me is made of ground raw almonds, cacao, agave syrup and crushed black olives to create the illusion of chocolate. I don't want to spoil it for myself, but I know the fact that they have put the words 'chocolate surprise' in inverted commas tells me that it has no relationship to it. Anywhere else they would be done under the trades description act. I can imagine lots of kids crying their eyes out when they have got that bitter black goo in their cakehole.'

'You've not enjoyed it have you?' Circe asked with a long piece of raw spinach trailing out of her mouth. She gestured to his untouched shot of luminescent wheatgrass. *At least it's liquid*, thought Lorcan. He'd already partly drunk the carrot juice if only to wash down some of the salad and had an orange smile as proof. There was a hand painted banner above the juice bar section exhorting customers to *toss a shot*. So he did.

Circe had also put down her cutlery, though he didn't know it was to watch him. The smell of the fluid didn't hit him until it was at the back of his throat by which time it was too late as his swallow reflex had started. He later described it to Tibbs as the texture of pond slime and the taste of liquidised grass cuttings. To him it was green alien putridity, an eye watering, and stomach churning fifty millilitres of baby's mecum.

Lorcan's green eyes paled beside the vivid greenness of the drink, which was now just a viscous slick in the bottom of the glass. He'd had some experiences in his time and consumed some wild drinks as all young men do. To date the worst thing in his mouth had been some tramp's spittle. He'd been reading him his rights for urinating through an open window and the tramp gobbed phlegm into his mouth. Lorcan had been secretly impressed at how strong the old boy's urinary flow was and wondering if the pressure was enhanced by the fizzy chemical soup that was White Lightning. Subsequently he'd had to have a battery of tests for HIV and hepatitis with all its attendant uncertainty, while the tramp got off with just a fine from the magistrates, which he never paid.

All this passed through Lorcan's brain in an instant as the wheatgrass shot started to descend his oesophagus. He looked appealingly at Circe, after all he'd drunk it to please her. She must have known it was an acquired taste. He coughed as his stomach revolted and the odious, but super healthy liquid reappeared spraying the table and catching the ruffle on Circe's black cardigan. She leapt back, her chair scraping noisily on the wooden floorboards.

'For God's sake Lorcan, it's only a tiny health drink.' She brushed herself down while he continued coughing and semi-retching. It was a full five minutes before order was restored, the table wiped down and plates cleared. Lorcan's eyes were now bright red and he was blowing his nose vigorously, trying to expel the last of it. He swilled the carrot juice down in a failed attempt to take the taste away, re-enforcing the bright orange smile on his cheeks as he did so. When he could at last speak he croaked at Circe. 'Jesus, Mary and Joseph, don't you EVER suggest something like that again. You must have known it was going to taste like toad's shite.'

'Lorcan, it's really good for you and will give you a good dose of vitamins to counteract your dreadful police diet. They wouldn't sell the drink in such quantities if it was so bad.'

Lorcan looked accusingly at Circe through brimming eyes. 'That was assault on a police officer and you have a very strange sense of humour if you think half killing someone is funny. The evidence is clearly there as you didn't have a shot of wheatgrass yourself, did you now? However, I'm a good man, so I am, and I'm prepared to accept a beer now to wash away the taste and by way of an apology from yourself.'

Circe knew she'd pushed it. They were colleagues and she sat on the Police Authority and certainly shouldn't abuse a DS in this way! She felt her cheeks flush with chagrin.

Soon they were seated on the pink velvet chairs in the Queens Arms. It was a testimony to the progress made in LBGT community relations when a police officer and magistrate could sit together in a boudoir of a gay pub and not bat an eyelid except when a feather boa, or sequined stole from the drag act brushed across their faces. They sat in a plush 'cornerette', as the barman called it when he brought over their drinks. Lorcan's Guinness had taken some time to settle allowing his stomach to do the same.

Lorcan drank deeply allowing the cold dark liquid to caress the back of his throat. 'Circe, we've got a real crisis now at Stoneleigh. The animals are ripping each other's throats out. Anne Lancaster is going ballistic and thinks there's some kind of campaign going on there and wants to know who's behind it. Worse in a way, if you can believe it, because the grand likes of yourself doesn't get to see him, is our Inspector, John Crooks. You might catch a glimpse of him in passing, but he's as much plankton as we are in the eyes of the ACPO officers, though he sucks up to authority smiling falsely and all. I can tell you that he gave Tibbs and me a right fucking bollocking - 'scuse my language.'

Circe shrugged. It didn't bother her, and she used far worse herself. She felt the heat a little at what he was saying though.

'I'll paraphrase to avoid offence, but he considers we are liaising with the wrong key players on the estate. He expressed a forcible opinion that the obese and wheelchair users don't reflect the estate's population.'

'Course they do.' Circe put down her empty BSC glass with a thump of finality.

'Another?' he asked, impressed at her speed of drinking. Not to appear weak he finished his while a drag queen freshened their drinks.

Circe chewed on the mint leaves. 'If the indigenous population aren't complaining about the largely unreported crime wave, who's worried then?'

As she bent forward to pick up her glass, Lorcan's professional nose could detect the fragrant eau de cologne smell of the Bombay

140

Sapphire and the sharp spearmint tang on her breath. 'What's that you say? Oh, yes, it's not enough that we have to try and sort out crimes that we get told about, now we're being ordered to use our valuable resources chasing unreported incidents. The truth is that they don't want our involvement and certainly won't be witnesses. There's going to be a crisis meeting shortly. No doubt you'll be on the party list, so I'll be grateful if this chat is off the record.'

Circe nodded. Her hair was swept off her face but she left loose flowing curls behind her. Lorcan watched the flashing fairy lights of the Queens Arms illuminate her hair. He liked that style and always thought of it as business at the front, party at the back. It suited all occasions.

Circe moved to leave. Lorcan turned on his Irish charm. 'Surely you'll stay for one more, we've not yet discussed what we can do about the problem, have we?'

Circe went to sit down again, but his Airwave police handset rang calling for his attention. She raised a palm in farewell and mouthed, 'Bye' as she wove out past the evening's drag acts. The moment was lost and a boy of no more than fifteen sat in her place and winked at Lorcan over the top of his vodka and Red Bull. Lorcan's bladder was full of carrot juice, wheatgrass and Guinness, but he was certain that it wasn't going to be relieved in these toilets.

Chapter Twenty-Nine

OPEN AND CLOSED

The shadows from the trees outside Circe's house were long, and the branches waved menacingly as if in warning. She was tired and not sure if she'd completely thrown DS Lorcan O'Leary off the scent. When she opened her black front door she felt that the house was colder than usual. In fact an icy wind hit her, and unusually no cat came to greet her.

Flicking on the hall light Circe went towards the radiator and grabbed its metal spine. She pulled her hand back at once as it was red hot. Her hair was moving in a draught and she went straight through to the dining room. Her heart hit the back of her throat, she couldn't believe it! One of the French doors was open! Her mind raced through all the reasons that this could have happened. Had she forgotten to lock it? She'd gone outside last night to pick a few mint leaves that were still growing in a sheltered corner for her BSC. Had she forgotten to turn the key again? God this was a bad sign and meant her memory was not all it should be. A break in? No sign of broken glass or any damage and at first glance it didn't look like anything had been moved.

What if someone had taken her computer with Alice's emails on? She realised that this was her prized possession and held her most important messages along with the photograph albums. Circe stopped and listened. Where were the cats? Normally they'd be shouting and mithering for affection and food. Why was the door open for God's sake? She couldn't hear anything. She used the edge of the curtain to close the door to preserve any fingerprints, and in the silence listened again. She didn't need to be on her own, she could call a friend to come over and check for intruders with her. It was still only 10pm and not indecently late, but she'd stopped socialising when Alice left and friends eventually stopped calling. There're only so many excuses people can take.

Standing in the hall with the absence of the cats made her more worried. They weren't allowed out at night because of the many dangers of traffic, foxes and thieves. What if someone knew what she'd been doing on the estate and had come to attack her? She got Lorcan's number up on her phone. At least he was the police. She would press the button if she needed it, but she didn't want anyone poking around her house. Slowly she crept from room to room. The light from the streetlamps cast yellowy shadows in the hall and kitchen, while the glass lantern ceiling gave an eerie hue to the black and white floor tiles. Circe's was a typical Victorian house and it creaked ominously as she made her way upstairs. She had taken off her shoes and now held one stiletto in her left hand and the phone in the right. The doors to the rooms were usually kept open so the cats could have free rein. All except Alice's bedroom. She objected to cat's hairs on everything and while she loved the creatures, Circe wanted her possessions to remain as Alice had left them. There was the incident of the chewed and ripped rosy fairy lights - a gift from Alice's boyfriend before she left the country. This was a reminder of the logic of the request and Circe honoured her daughter's wishes after that.

The rooms and cupboards downstairs were empty of intruders and Circe turned on her computer and then went upstairs with her heart pounding. She really needed a drink. Really needed one. The upstairs rooms and wardrobes were clean of any uninvited visitors. She looked under her own bed and there, curled up against the cold were three bleary eyed cats. She could have shrieked with joy and relief. They were safe! They were intelligent creatures and she'd trained them to use the toilet, though of course they didn't flush it and people would be very unnerved to see cat turds in the bowl. Looking at Nigel she recalled how he could also stand on his hind legs and open doors. Perhaps he'd done this on the French door then realised how cold and unpleasant it was. He had never learned to close them though.

Circe sank gratefully on to her bed. She'd had a near miss and her home had been open not only to the elements but to any old burglar or junkie who cared to break in. Someone was certainly looking after her. After she'd secured the house again she poured herself what would be a quadruple strength BSC. She hoped the Guardian Angel of livers would also protect her. Standing in the kitchen as she mixed it she raised her eyes to heaven and to the glass lantern ceiling where the waving shadows seemed friendlier now. She sat down at her desk as the now thawed cats draped languidly round her feet and wrote a long email to Alice.

That night, before she went to sleep, Circe carefully packed all her revenge kits and disguises away in a large pine blanket box. Best to have the whole lot concealed in one place, she thought. She closed the lid and placed a large pot of aspidistra on the top. She had surprised herself by thinking about anyone coming into her bedroom in *that* way and told herself that it was just in case she had a real break in and the police had to search. She'd been quite casual about where she left things, and she'd had a wake-up call thanks to the cats. As she lay in a rather alcoholic stupor, she thought that she had been lucky, and then she turned over hoping for sleep. The effort made her burp an eau-de-cologne flavoured pocket of air. Clive lifted his head and sniffed. He knew his mistresses' smell. Circe wondered if she was subliminally thinking of bringing a man back. Perhaps one Lorcan O'Leary?

She stared into the darkness suddenly sober. No, he wasn't her type, though she wasn't sure what that was any more. He was certainly cute in a green eyed sort of gay way. Surely he wasn't straight and he hadn't been married. He had a lot of sisters and looked after his father, so was every bit the stereotype. Had he noticed her as a woman? On a couple of occasions she thought he might have, but then her instincts told her that he was just being polite as any other officer, and a junior one at that, had to be to a member of the Police Authority. Besides, Circe wasn't interested in a man in that way, or any other way. She lay on her back and pulled in her stomach. She was self-sufficient and had everything as she liked it. Didn't she?

Circe stared at the ornate coving and plasterwork on her ceiling and felt the tears stream down both sides of her face past her ears, soaking her hair and drenching the 400 thread percale pillowcases.

Chapter Thirty

SEAHAVEN HOUSE

Anne Lancaster summoned her council of war and invited all the usual suspects. John Crook and his team were very anxious.

Earlier that day Lorcan had texted Circe and invited her to accompany him on a visit to Seahaven House. He needed an unbiased second opinion on his father's true mental state before making yet another decision on the home that he should go to. He trusted her experience in judging situations. She'd agreed to his request since she knew how difficult the situation was, and from what Lorcan had said, the old boy seemed such a character. As Circe had court in the afternoon, following the meeting, they arranged to go in the early evening.

Anne Lancaster chaired the meeting in the conference room in Pevensey Block at police headquarters. It was a low-ceilinged, long room with little character and an equally long arrangement of tables which allowed twenty or more people to sit in relative discomfort. There was a large whiteboard and screen at one end of the room where many long-suffering delegates would stare as they were held ransom to PowerPoint presentations.

The halcyon days of the tea lady were long past, so in a corner near the door was an open cardboard box with a selection of individually wrapped twin biscuits along with a tea and coffee pot, paper cups and little packets of milk. Cost cutting in action. As usual, most of the police grabbed the refreshments as if their lives depended on it. Lorcan was different though and didn't like to be seen as dependent on a few scraps. Instead he'd take puritanical pulls from the water bottle he brought with him.

Before the meeting began, drifts of paperwork were circulated and statistical charts were brandished. There was no mistaking the figures, crime was down in Stoneleigh and in all other areas where Stoners would normally have been involved. There were undoubtedly a number of offences taking place on the estate itself, but it wasn't making it into the official statistics. The council leader, who had a predictable preoccupation with his own career and political safety, voiced the unthinkable.

'Ladies and gentlemen, although there are clearly some statistical anomalies in the crime figures, I think we need to recognise that in such a challenging environment, we have seen success in making the lives of the residents of Brighton and Hove safer.'

The police exchanged glances with each other. Lorcan caught the eye of John Crook who clenched his jaw in suppressed annoyance. Lorcan knew the look well. Keith Higginbotham continued. 'It is therefore our public duty to share the good news with the City's population and I propose we organise a press conference with The Argus. I'm prepared to make myself available for a photo shoot around the estate with yourself, ma'am.' He inclined his head towards the subject of his political validation, Anne Lancaster. She had a face on that Madame Tussaud's would have been proud of by way of pallor and immobility.

Entirely unaware of the effect he was having, Keith Higginbotham smarmed on. 'It is rare in the world today that there is good news about crime in an estate like Stoneleigh, and the reasons that this has come about will surely emerge in due course. Until then we have a duty to inform the people that they can feel safer.' He so warmed to his theme that he emphasised the points with a flat palmed thump on the table with his fat, liver-spotted hands. Creamy, viscous triangles of spittle coagulated at the sides of his smoker's lined mouth as he bared his discoloured teeth in a rictus and insincere smile. 'So I take it that's sorted then? Another glowing tribute to the efforts in community cohesion made by the council that I am proud to lead.'

There was a queasy silence. Circe stared at the slatted blinds and on to the lawn beyond. She was unable to see Lorcan's expression as he was on the same side of the table concealed by Keith Higginbotham's ample belly. Anne Lancaster tried to dissent without offending him.

'I think it would be better if we waited a little longer to see what the nature of this phenomenon is. Spikes of any kind on our graphics are usually explicable within a short time. For example only six months ago....'

She was cut off with a phlegmy throat clearing from the councillor who was clearly keen to have a cigarette break. 'Thank you, Assistant Chief Constable.' *He's great on quoting titles*, thought Circe. *They're so predictable.* He carried on. 'But I think we should make this public. Fear of crime is the bane of people's lives.'

Circe heard a voice which she later recognised as her own. 'I wonder if I might put in a word here as a Magistrate and member of the Police Authority.'

ACC Lancaster nodded and raised her arms slightly in acknowledgment of the seemingly inevitable.

Circe pushed a copper curl back from her forehead. 'Thank you, Chair. I think we've all heard comprehensively what the council think about this apparent improvement on the estate. However, in my opinion we need to be very cautious about claiming success for what might only be a temporary improvement. If matters weren't to continue in the same vein then popular opinion could turn against the council.' She turned and looked hard at Keith Higginbotham who was wresting something unpleasant from the back of his teeth with the end of his biro. He resolutely stared in the opposite direction, his crumpled linen suit rising and falling with his laboured breathing. Circe carried on. 'I think we should wait until we can confidently attribute the reasons for this change in patterns, checking they are properly collated from police and court records, and then accurately assign cause and credit.'

The police looked both pleased and relieved. They didn't need the flak if things didn't keep improving and there was always the displacement effect where crime just moved down the road whenever they had a crackdown on a hotspot. Things were dynamic and always moving.

Keith Higginbotham didn't look happy, this wasn't going to plan. He drummed his fingers, tapped his biro and cleared his throat while Circe spoke. At the end of his calculatedly restless display he butted in to thank her ostentatiously, even though he wasn't chairing the meeting.

'We are of course most grateful to *Ms* Byrne.' He exaggerated her lack of councillor status. 'But I think we're all agreed that we need to capitalise on any improvement, however small and for however short a time.' Here Circe clearly watched him nail his political colours to the mast.

Lorcan was leaning back in his chair with an air of leisured insouciance and said quietly but with his distinctive accent. 'I agree with the Police Authority's views, and Ms Byrne has been sitting in our local court for many years and knows what she is talking about I'm sure. Do we need a vote or will common sense prevail?' He knew that his comments were metaphorically pouring petrol on the glowing embers of Keith Higginbotham's anger and, as the white heat blasted from him, the rest of the group clearly said, 'Yes, let's wait.'

Anne Lancaster delicately made a note on the agenda. 'For review in, say, three months' time?'

'Eight weeks,' growled the Councillor, having wanted four which the ACC knew.

'Very well, eight weeks and trusting we have some clear figures by then. I hereby announce the end of the meeting.'

* * *

Early evening saw Circe and Lorcan arrive at Seahaven House in separate cars. He got there a bit earlier than she did, so checked his phone messages till he saw her Figaro pull in. Despite the cold weather she had let the roof down, but with the heater blasting to keep her feet warm. She needed to let off steam.

'Hi, Lorcan,' she called. 'Thanks for the support at the meeting.'

'I could say the same for you. There didn't seem to be a voice of reason, just the windy trumpeting of pompous self-interest. Talking of which that so-called meal at Tossers had me up all night with a stomach so distended that it resembled a barrage balloon, so it did.'

'That would be the kidney bean pate´, no doubt. It can take some getting used to.'

'Jesus Christ, I was that full of air that you could have tied a string to me leg and flown me, right enough.'

'What a lovely picture you conjure up.'

'And what with that green snot shot you had me toss back, that was assaulting a police officer.'

'Yes, I recall you saying something to that effect at the time when you got your voice back. Well, I'm sorry you didn't like it, but I'm here to give you a second opinion on your dad. Patrick is that right?'

'Yes, fair play to yous, and much appreciated. I don't know if he's really gone doolally or just playing them up. I know you're not a psychiatrist, but you do seem to have a knack of seeing the truth and cutting through the bullshit.'

'I'm happy to give you my very best opinion, and it is definitely an unprofessional one.'

'Good enough for me.' Lorcan led the way into the home. Circe thought that his walk may have been a little less masculine than his colleagues perhaps. She relaxed, so he was gay. Big deal.

Lorcan keyed in the security numbers on the door pad. Circe's heart fell. Poor bastards condemned to a prison that only death would release them from. Nothing like the soft sentences that the scrotes in court got. Her thoughts were interrupted as the smell hit her; old people, urine, cabbage... Why always cabbage? Egg sandwiches were set out on Formica tables, but there was no sign of cooked food. So why the smell of cabbage then? Circe could hear a voice booming in an unmistakable Northern Irish accent.

'I want to feck you... you never said that last night ...you were happy enough then, you little tease...'

Circe's heels sank noiselessly into the thick carpet with the stain minimising patterns. Her first sight of Lorcan's father was of a very tall man; he had to be all of six foot three, leaning on the reception desk. His tie was knotted around his head, schoolboy style, otherwise he looked the perfect picture of a well-dressed older man. He had on a hound's tooth sports jacket and cavalry twill trousers, though they did ride a little high for him.

He caught sight of Lorcan and bellowed, 'There's the fecker who's imprisoned me in this hell hole. Come on you little shite, put up your dukes.'

Patrick boxed his way over to Lorcan and Circe. 'Hallo, Da,' his son said. 'How are you doing?'

'How the feck do you think I'm doing? They're all fecking mad here except her.' He pointed at the pretty Jamaican girl in shiny, skinny jeans who had been the subject of his amorous advances.

She smiled understandingly at Lorcan. 'Mr O'Leary is having one of his days. He doesn't mean no harm and we've cleaned up the sandwiches he pelted at the windows. He's got a good overarm, he should have played cricket.'

Lorcan sighed, 'He did, but there were some anger management issues and the club banned him. Never lost the bowling skill though. I can still see one stuck to the French door, shall I pick it off?'

'No, Mrs Roberts thinks it's a bird and I suppose she's nearly right as it is egg mayonnaise, so we're leaving it there till she goes to bed.'

'With its wings of sliced wholemeal,' Lorcan replied.

'We do our best.'

'Of course you do.'

Circe smiled at Patrick who snapped at Lorcan and jerked his head towards Circe. 'What's *she* doing here? Thinks it's a circus, does she? Come to stare at the ferrets, has she?'

Lorcan rested his hand on his father's sleeve. 'Da, this is Circe, a friend who's come to say hello.'

'And what kind of a name is that?' Patrick asked.

'Some people might think that of Irish names.'

'Yes, and we know what they are, don't we?'

Circe cut in and held his hands with both of hers. She looked into his unfaded green eyes. He met her gaze and held it for a second.

'You'd be the first girl he brought home to see me, and about time. Always thought he was a faggot.'

Lorcan raised his eyes to the ceiling as Circe smiled at the old man. 'Let's sit down and you can tell me what's making you so cross.'

Patrick was angry at the question. 'Jesus, Mary and Joseph can't you see, woman?' He sat down heavily in a plastic covered upright armchair, the support of which his lithe body did not yet require. The smell of the chair Circe sat on was so overpowering that she knew she'd have to clean all her clothes; even her suede shoes would need treating. It seeped under her skin and even though she took little shallow breaths she still felt it absorbed into her. This was hell, no question of it, and if you had an ounce of wit or realisation it would be the most frustrating thing to be here.

'Tell me,' she said, simply.

'Well if I do tell you, perhaps you can tell that steaming pile of manure,' he gestured at Lorcan. 'That I don't belong here and set me free.'

'Just tell me,' Circe's amber eyes held the old man's gaze.

By way of illustration old man O'Leary pointed at the other residents. 'Look at that daft fecker. Thinks the radiator is a fish tank. There's another one,' he pointed at a man in his late sixties doing Bench presses with invisible barbells. 'I'm coaching him, he'll be in the next Olympics, but I'm worried about his medication routine. Is it OK to compete if you are on the old chemical cosh Quetiapine, I wonder? What will the committee have to say about that? I'm feeding him up and he always gets the protein pellets the staff give to the resident guinea pig. He loves them so much he puts them in his ears. I've told him not to conceal them about his person, but he won't always listen. Well, he can't with those in his lugholes. It took a lot of effort getting one out of his Jap's eye, but he don't feel pain, that's the beauty of Quetiapine. He drinks his own wee too and rolls his turds up and lines them along the edge of the sink. I thought they were cigars when I first saw them.'

Circe didn't know what to say, and while she paused another old man came and sat down with the group. 'There's a boy in my room,' he whispered conspiratorially to Lorcan.

He answered the elderly man reassuringly, 'I'm sure he'll be gone now, and it's OK for you to go back.'

His mood visibly darkened and the old man glared at Lorcan baring his denture-less gums. 'They always tell me that, but I know he's in there, I keep him in my bum.' He pointed at his backside and tapped his nose knowingly as he shuffled off.

A pale plump woman beckoned to Circe and then came over to her. She could have passed as a middle-aged secretary, she had such an air of competence about her and looked so proper and permed. 'I'm eighty-three, my mother is eighty-three and my grandmother is eighty-three and so is my daughter. Isn't that funny?'

The home's manager came over to them. 'Hallo, Patrick, how are you?'

He sighed. 'I'm OK, but I still can't fly,' and flapped his arms sarcastically.

She turned to Lorcan. 'We had the nose blowing and wiping it along the reception desk again this morning.'

Circe looked at him and saw him looking intently at her. A small smile flittered across his stubbly face.

The manager carried on listing his crimes. 'Your father also has a habit of swapping the other residents' medications and hands them squash with his laxative in.'

'Nothing wrong with my arse except that you are up it,' he barked.

Circe couldn't help noticing how much bottoms and orifices featured in the conversations. It was like little children saying what they imagined was the rudest things.

The manager continued. 'We are doing our best for Mr O'Leary, but he doesn't seem to be settling, I'm afraid.' She made this comment as an elderly lady in an oversized ballet dress wheeled a doll's pram past with two plastic dolls in it.

Lorcan could only say 'mmm,' as he was unusually lost for words.

'We try, Mr O'Leary, we really try.'

'I'm sure you do.'

'Oh, feck off, you mad cow,' Patrick growled, unhelpfully.

'Would you like tea and biscuits?' she asked Circe and Lorcan. Circe was fastidious at the best of times, so shook her head.

Patrick boomed again, 'She'll not be wanting that shite. She doesn't look like she needs the bromide, does she now? She'd rather have a drop of the hard stuff.'

The manager smiled professionally and went into her office. Lorcan followed her to discuss how serious she was about discharging Patrick and to persuade her to accept next month's fee. As a self-funder, it was costing Patrick £2,400 every four weeks.

Circe and Patrick were left alone, except for the woman saying, 'eighty-three, eighty-three, eighty-three…'

Patrick grabbed Circe's arm and hissed, 'You think like me. I can see it in your eyes. You look like a fox. You and me; we know, don't we?'

Circe wasn't entirely sure where he was going with this one. Her sense of reality had curved since arriving and she wanted to get out.

He continued, 'You've got it, so make sure they don't send you to a place like this. I can tell you've got it.'

Circe didn't dare patronise him. How much did he know? Had he got some special knowledge? Now that was crazy.

He looked so soulfully at her. 'Please help to get me out. I won't tell on you or what you've done. I'm the seventh son of a seventh son and I know things I do.' He began singing Rolf Harris's 'Wimoweh' using a plastic notice as a wobble board.

When they left, Circe asked Lorcan if his father was a seventh son and learned that he was the third of eight children, five of whom were girls. A truly uneventful and unspiritual arrangement.

'Aah,' she smiled.

Chapter Thirty-One

GRASSING UP

Circe was still working the estate. She used her mobile phone to call the DSS and leave messages regarding those individuals that she suspected, but couldn't prove, were working or making money on the black. She gave details of cars being driven by people too incapacitated to get out of bed and she gave the CSA an up to date, but anonymous, list of the addresses of some sexually incontinent fathers. The results of this campaign could take some time but it ought to create a climate of fear and suspicion amongst the estate dwellers.

Circe had information from the court papers and she also had the mobile numbers of those who appeared before her in court. She could only imagine the surprise on the faces of the slack jawed, gum chewing offenders as they looked at her anonymous messages.

Told the DSS on you. Better get yourself a proper job now.

Told the CSA where you live and about the other babies. Better start saving and using condoms.

Her personal favourite was the non-specific but unsettling, *I'm watching you and know what you are up to. If you don't like it then don't do it or move on.*

There's bigger boys than you and if you hit women you're going to find out how much it hurts. Pack it up.

Circe also now considered herself an accomplished method actor and would even get into costume when she sent the texts. She found inspiration in being Ida Dunmore.

The effects of her messages were varied. When there was domestic violence it went one of two ways. The perpetrator would confront his partner with the message and demand that she tell him who she'd told about their private life. The woman would naturally deny it and he might subsequently threaten or abuse her even more. Sometimes this became a catalyst for her having the courage to leave him and make a better life for herself and sometimes not. On other occasions the men might be fearful of a brother or even a father coming for him. Men who were violent to their partners or kids were cowards at heart, and they just might make an effort to change. Alternatively, they might move on to abuse the next woman who'd have him, which would at least afford the present partner and her kids some respite.

There began to be a churn on the estate. Some of the known big drug dealers backed off while things cooled down. It gave some unprofessional minnows a chance and they soon got picked off in a variety of ways. They were certainly easier prey for the police and the test purchasing officers were surprised at the shift and happy with the easy arrests. Unsurprisingly though, the sentencing was often subject to political pressure, and was less severe than Circe or some of the others thought it should be, but there were still changes. The mood of the estate was different as if there was a collective holding of breath. Some of those who had been on the receiving end of the maggots learned they were not alone in their infestation, as the council had to send a pest control operative round to other households. He said he'd only seen this kind of situation when there were anglers who were sloppy about taking care of their bait. Estate residents were surprised to hear that there was an infestation of this sort in Stoneleigh. It didn't make sense and it disrupted the torpor of their existences.

Circe phoned Lorcan later that night. 'Hi Lorcan, you wanted my opinion on your father?'

He sighed in response. 'There's been another incident involving some toilet rolls - I won't bore you with the details. Have you come to any conclusions? Is he mad? Frankly at this rate I'll very likely end up in Seahaven House meself, right enough.'

Circe smiled, but her voice didn't betray it. 'There's a thin line between us all - the mad and the sane; though it's politically incorrect to use that word I'm guessing. Look, Lorcan, I think your father is some distance away from mentally needing to be there, despite the diagnosis of dementia. I think he's angry and confused and is just a bright man who needs some support. After all he's not even in Northern Ireland anymore. He's lost his wife and he feels imprisoned. I do think he needs an eye kept on him. Now what I'm going to suggest sounds crazy but stay with me. What about putting him in a little bungalow on the Stoneleigh estate? His moods and behaviour parallel a lot of the residents and they might calm down next to someone whose anger management issues are worse than theirs. It will also be an opportunity for you to visit him and he can be the eyes and ears for you?'

Circe stopped as Lorcan's laughter was so loud she had to hold the phone away from her ear. She stared crossly at it. 'Well thanks, Lorcan, kindly remember that you did ask for my help.'

'Hey, I'm sorry, the idea is brilliant! Absolutely fucking brilliant. You're a genius. Who would ever have thought of anything like that? Our very own weapon of mass destruction! Dropping old Patrick O'Leary on the unsuspecting, but very worthy recipients of Stoneleigh! Sure to God they'd all be asking for a transfer themselves. Seriously, we could try it on a temporary basis and give him back his freedom, and if it worked we could find another more appropriate place of independent living. We could get in the old care package of home help, Meals on Wheels and so on. Me Da would keep the bloody squatters at bay that's for sure. Him and that broom handle of his. I'll get on to it today, it'll assuage my guilt. You're a lifesaver Circe; he's every reason to be grateful to you.'

'No he doesn't. You've a lot of responsibility with him and I'm just trying to think of a way to create some options that might make him happier and would take the strain off you. I could see the very real sadness in his eyes. He's just expressing himself like a powerless naughty child. He may need some help readjusting to an independent life, but I imagine he is still housetrained and that his high jinks are a coping strategy.'

'Let's hope so! If this crazy idea works, and the rational part of me thinks it won't, at least we can say we've given it our best shot. Though what I'll say to the sisters, I've no idea.'

Circe noted the word 'our.' 'Lorcan, he's your father, not mine.'

'Sure, but some of the organisation will need a woman's touch.'

'Then contact the local Catholic church, there are bound to be a whole load of good bodies who'll sort him out and be happy to help.'

'He doesn't go to Mass anymore, as far as I know.'

'Perfect time for him to reconnect if he wants, but even if he doesn't, he's still of the Holy Apostolic Church and one true faith.'

'He'll test their Christianity, no doubt about that.' Lorcan felt the weight of responsibility lifted though.

So calling in all the favours he could from the housing department things started to progress. There was one little bungalow that was down to be refurbished and he asked if Patrick could stay there until the work was due to begin. He accepted full responsibility and they agreed to the plan. Social Services were a bit concerned and thought the unusual experiment was destined to fail. When Patrick threw the Meals on Wheels food back down the path after the volunteer yelling, 'take yer fecking slop with you,' it looked as if the doubters were going to be right. Patrick spotted a neighbour with luminescent bleached hair and several sets of gold creole earrings watching him with her fat arms crossed over her fleecy chest. He wheeled round and shouted, 'And you can put yer fecking starey eyes back into the holes in yer ugly fat face. Mind yer own fecking business.'

His Northern Irish accent had a novelty value that seemed to carry with it an implied threat of violence to Stoners, whose only contact with the province had been delivered by the TV news appearances of Gerry Adams and Ian Paisley. Everyone knew what the pecking order was however high or low they ranked. It was quite a contrast to the Brighton/London combo that generally characterised the volley of insults and exchanges.

When Circe learned that Patrick had not taken gladly to the care package, she visited him with a bag of groceries, suspecting that he just wanted his independence. It felt odd to park her Figaro in full view in daylight and she almost expected to be accosted. Approaching the shabby front door it was flung open by Patrick before she had a chance to knock.

'It's yerself with the red hair I see.'

'Hallo, Patrick. How are you doing? Can I come in?'

Circe stepped carefully into the house. It needed work doing to it, but it was surprisingly tidy.

'I wondered if you fancied preparing your own food rather than having it brought round? Lorcan said you were a master chef with a stew.'

'That's what I was trying to get that old bag to understand. I'm a reasonable cook if it's not too fancy, and I want to eat what I want to eat. At my age I've got a right to choose.'

'Sure, Patrick, I hope you don't mind, but I bought you some bits and I hope they might be of use.' She unpacked potatoes, onions, carrots and lamb.

The old man smiled broadly. 'I'm famous for me Irish stews and it'll last for a few days. I always put Guinness in my mashed potato along with the butter. It gives it more flavour. It's a family secret.'

Circe could imagine the grey tinge that this would give the dish, but if he wanted to do it and would eat it, then fine. She sat with a cup of tea while he deftly prepared the vegetables, carefully peeling and stacking the skins for his new compost heap that he had already marked out among the junk and rubbish in the rear garden. When it was nearly ready she politely declined his offer to join him and got up to go. He insisted on paying her for the groceries, 'I don't take charity from anyone.' So she had no choice but to accede to his request. She told him how to get to the local shops. He seemed keenest on fresh food which was something of a challenge as the local mini-mart catered for the majority taste of processed food, particularly specialising in microwaved kebabs, burgers and hotdogs.

Circe knew Lorcan would need to get in some healthy provisions for his father and made a note to tell him. 'Well Patrick, I'll be off now. Enjoy your stew. It smells lovely.'

'Mind how you go; the woman next door has some funny visitors.'

'Does she now? Funny in what way exactly?'

'Men coming and going at all hours of the day and night. Her son sees them at the door and then they go. Can't hear the radio sometimes for the knocking and door slamming.'

Circe smiled inwardly, that was just what they'd been hoping from the old man, an observant spy in the nest. She'd pass that on to Lorcan as intel and see if they also needed any of Ida Dunmore's special treatment.

She watched him spooning a large portion of his meal into the centre of a ring of grey mashed potato. He turned to her, 'Oh, Circe, one more thing.'

'Yes?' she stopped and turned back.

158

'There's something about you that's familiar. I can't put a finger on it, but it will come to me.'

A thousand thoughts went through Circe's head crackling like blue lightning. 'Let me know when it does,' she said neutrally.

As she closed the front door she wasn't surprised to see two scruffy boys circling her car. 'Alright lads?' she said loudly hoping to scare them off.

'Ginger bitch,' they snarled menacingly. Automatically she looked carefully round the car as they sauntered off. No sign of keying, that was something, but there were two broken beer bottles under the rear wheels. That could have been nasty. Using gloves, she carefully removed them and dropped them in Patrick's recycling bin. She smiled. They were amateurs, but still the idea was worth having.

Chapter Thirty-Two

A NUMBERS GAME

Circe's next time in court included two men who had been arguing drunkenly in a Brighton street. Such was the ferocity of their disagreement that the police had advised them to leave the area and told them that if they were seen anywhere between the two piers again that night, they risked being arrested for being drunk and disorderly. The officers were dismayed when a couple of hours later they heard their loud voices and the occasional thump on West Street. The police approached them and asked what they were doing there and to leave the area again. They were now even drunker than previously. Since they were causing such a nuisance to themselves and harassment, alarm and distress to any other passers-by, it was clear that they needed arresting. As they were being loaded into the police van the Sergeant said, 'So what was all that fuss about then gentlemen?'

The fighting started once again, and the shorter, balder and more toothless of the two blurted out, 'He started telling people about me fucking a mermaid, and it wasn't his secret to tell. She's my mermaid and I don't want him telling people I'm fucking her right?'

The defence solicitor later said to the Bench in mitigation, that they might recognise the severity of the drink problem that his client was suffering from by the very nature of the claim that he was making. At this point his client jumped up in the dock and yelled, 'Shut up you scabby young prick! You know nothing about my mermaid and I'm not having her talked about in front of these stuck up bastards. Send me to prison. I know that I'll have Oceania waiting for me.'

The Bench had no intention of wasting public money and sending him to prison on this occasion, preferring instead to address his alcoholism. He was given a probation order in the faint hope that he would engage with the Drink Awareness Course. When his mate got a similar penalty he shouted, 'I'm fucking aware of drink. I'm an expert. I'll show them how it's done. I drink like a fish and he fucks a mermaid. Understand?'

* * *

The council were the hosts of the next Community Safety Forum and it was going to be a challenging meeting. The police had the statistics relating to the crime patterns on the estate, a factor which Councillor Keith Higginbotham considered a mere formality. He was going to make this an election winner. His party had finally solved the running sore that was Stoneleigh. Anne Lancaster was white-faced and thin lipped. Circe had a look of studied composure while Lorcan looked concerned. The statistics were circulated by one of the police staff, and John Crook stood up to talk everyone through it.

'We have gathered information in two ways. Not just official crime figures and views of officers called to the scene, but we have obtained informal victim statements from the residents of Stoneleigh.'

Circe's heart beat so loudly that she was certain someone must hear it. How could they have got information like that? Stoners wouldn't talk to the police and they weren't usually insured, so why would they discuss it with the authorities? This could be the most public exposure it would be possible to have. Everyone was there, the Council Leader, Assistant Chief Constable, police press officer, council press officer and a whole lot more. The vein at the right hand side of her neck throbbed visibly and she knew she was pale. Lorcan looked over at her and mouthed, 'You alright?'

She nodded briefly. It was apparent she wasn't. What were the options? Leave the room? Go to the toilet and leave? Yes, that was it. Let them reveal the truth of her campaign to each other, then come for her later. She couldn't face being arrested in front of everyone, as she surely would be. What she'd done were criminal offences and quite serious ones at that. No point claiming it was for the greater good. She'd set herself up as judge and jury when she unilaterally decided that the criminal justice system wasn't up to the job. Who the hell was she? Who did she think she was? What right did she have to do what she'd done?

A blinding moment of pure clarity hit her. What had she been thinking? She, Circe Byrne JP, MBE was going to lose everything, because she felt she could teach some scrotal lowlife a lesson. She must have had some kind of breakdown. Yes, that was it. The strain of it all. She wasn't coping. All those victims and no one to help. But the truth was they all lived in a democratic society and if they didn't like it they could vote the politicians out. The fact that they had the system they did though, meant that people were accepting of the status quo and here was she, a one woman vigilante, persecuting people that the authorities didn't think worth prosecuting.

Sure, the lives of those people would be better by any objective test if they didn't hit each other, take drugs, get drunk, and abuse women and children. However, the law was there to make those decisions, not her.

In the time it took John Crook to signal for the blinds to be drawn and the Police Authority researcher to start the PowerPoint presentation, Circe had to decide what to do. She'd reached the stage in her life where she couldn't stand by and watch victims failed and powerless time after time. No, her campaign was necessary by everything that was right, just and decent. She'd stand by it and take what was coming. Maybe she'd be a martyr? Maybe the Daily Mail would start a campaign of common sense for people to be given a voice? Or perhaps she'd just be shamed and disgraced and serve her sentence? For sure she would be jailed in her position, in solitary to protect her from the other criminals who'd just love to get their hands on a magistrate. Two small spots of colour appeared on her cheekbones. Fuck it. It's show time!

John Crook was not a natural person to be handling technology. He wasn't comfortable with the computer. He was an old fashioned coppers' copper. Having been told to do the presentation, which he knew would count towards his personal development review, he decided to read the words he had, rather than try and match them to the screen. No one liked PowerPoint anyway, he reasoned. He was wrong though, since the senior officers lived and breathed it and politicians used statistics to justify every decision they took.

Circe took a sip of water which went down the wrong way as her throat was so dry. She started coughing and tears streamed down her face turning it from translucent white to a suffusion of magenta. Her nearest colleagues patted her helpfully on the back as she coughed and spluttered. John Crook was privately pleased at the diversion and tried to crack on under the cover of her choking. Anne Lancaster was having none of it and signalled to him to pause.

So, Circe regrettably found herself the centre of attention as she gasped for breath and finally gestured to the Inspector to start, even though she had not yet regained the power of speech. Crook explained that the research was done by the Department of Criminology at the local university as part of the degree assignment. The police provided access and permission and in exchange were given the statistics and information. It was an arrangement that worked well for both sides. The students had knocked on doors, talked to people in the shop, pub, at bus stops and at the community centre. He said that there was a real difference between the reported crime and the unreported. The reported was fairly low level.

Older people had burglaries, neighbours called the police when domestic violence got too out of hand. Schools reported failure of parents to send kids to school, but it was mostly crimes by residents of Stoneleigh, against the other residents of Brighton and Hove. Normally they were hugely over-represented on the court lists as perpetrators, rather than victims. However, in the last few months even those crimes had dropped. There was a significant statistical difference in crime being committed by the estate residents. Less acquisitive crime, less violent crime and less property and car crime had been reported. It was a complete change from previous crime records.

There were conspicuous exchanges of glances around the room, which Circe joined in by raising her left eyebrow a fraction. No need to go too mad, as all heads could turn to look at her at any minute, so she felt it best to preserve some fragile decorum. People were looking surprised at the figures as copies were passed around the table, but Councillor Higginbotham leant back thumbs in his waistcoat grinning like a hyena. 'Well thank you Inspector, it seems to me that this is good news then. We'll release the press statement, which the council has taken the liberty of pre-emptively preparing. The community needs to hear some positive news.'

Anne Lancaster held up a ringless left hand. 'Just a moment, Councillor Higginbotham, I mean Keith...' as he feigned dismay at

163

the formality of the title, but which he openly loved. 'We need to hear the second half of the story.'

He made an ostentatious display of looking at his Rolex, picking up his BlackBerry phone and then shrugging as if helpless to the press officer. 'I'm sure it's just detail, icing on this delightful cupcake, so to speak.' He smiled, baring his smoky brown teeth.

Anne Lancaster's icy blue eyes fixed on him in the way a cat would stare at a rodent. 'Without wishing to spoil the surprise, I think it may be helpful if you forget the cake stand and visualise a dry piece of Melba toast that has been left in the sun on a bird table for the best part of a week.' She spoke tartly, stroking the crown on her shirt epaulette that indicated her rank. She had his attention and Circe's, who was now swallowing hard. No one would understand why she'd done her campaign, not even her daughter Alice, and her probably least of all.

John Crook's over exercised face already had fat free furrows running its length and breadth. His eyes were now so narrowed Circe thought that a teaspoon would be required to prise them open. 'Well, the qualitative research done by the student researchers showed that the experience of the people on the estate is at significant variance with the official records of them as service users of the criminal justice system.'

Councillor Higginbotham cleared his throat. 'Yes, Inspector, please come to the point.' He swallowed the phlegm. All eyes turned to John Crook expectantly, as Circe felt as if the air stilled and the flecks of dust on a lone sunbeam hovered. She looked at her hands. The fuchsia nail varnish looked even deeper pink in comparison to her whitening fingers.

Crook sighed and then began. 'Ladies and gentlemen. There is some kind of phenomena. A wave of offences on the estate that is not easily explained. The victims gave this information in confidence and we don't have their names, so I am unable to categorically verify that they are known to us. If we make an assumption.... Please, Councillor Higginbotham...' he pleaded with the bored council leader whose eyes were skywards and viewing the world through his bushy grey eyebrows. 'That assumption may be that the reason these events haven't been reported is because the victims suspect that they may not receive the usual standard of sympathy and service that they have a right to expect from the police. So it appears they have been suffering in silence, and that a culture of fear has grown up among residents of all ages. This has disrupted the lives of a sector of Brighton and Hove residents. We on the Community Safety Forum ignore this at our peril.' Arabella Whitelaw rattled one of her seven chunky necklaces thoughtfully, and crossed her legs displaying her colourful Clarks T-bar sandals.

'I'll give you some examples of what people have told us. Maggots being put through their letter boxes; front door furniture being superglued. Dog faeces being placed where people would inadvertently touch it. Cars targeted and vandalised with chemicals and spray paints, as well as being scratched often with messages. Particularly sinister is a letter and text campaign. In the old days this would have been called poisoned pen letters. But this is a contemporary, insidious and toxic campaign. People told the researchers in confidence that they were receiving texts of a threatening nature. These took the form of a making a variety of allegations including benefit fraud, infidelity, informing various agencies such as the DSS and CSA, together with a variety of unsavoury accusations.'

Circe couldn't help but feel that the way the Inspector delivered the information didn't make it sound very nice. But it wasn't like that. It hadn't been that way. It had been to help people. She noted the tense of her internal monologue. Had? Was the campaign over then? Clearly it had been successful. Even if she wasn't found out, and it seemed unlikely as they were clearly on the case, she'd better stop. That was it. She promised to the 'powers that be' that it wouldn't continue. At that point she made her bargain with the Universe, wondering why she had ever thought she could get away with it.

The Community Safety Officer asked the dreaded question. 'Who do we think is responsible? Is it one or more people? Do you know if they live on the estate, since you imply that they seem to have inside knowledge of Stoneleigh and its inhabitants?'

'We are working on a number of leads...' he answered, and Circe swallowed hard. 'And we are confident that we will uncover the identity of the perpetrator.'

Circe decided that the game was up. She looked down and saw her hands were shaking and the pen wobbled in her nerveless fingers.

Arabella carried on verbalising her line of thought. 'You don't think it is a group of people then?' Circe waited, holding her breath for the big reveal.

John Crook ran a scrawny hand down his equally scrawny face. 'At this stage of the investigations we don't want to say anything that might prejudice our enquiries...' Circe could have sworn he looked over at her. 'As soon as we have something to say, you'll be the first to know.'

Anne Lancaster cut in. 'So ladies and gentlemen, in the meantime you can see why there should be no trumpeting of crime reduction initiatives, not if we have a so-called vigilante responsible. I must also say to this meeting that the information you've heard is absolutely in confidence, and any suggestion of vigilantism in Stoneleigh will be considered to be a breach of that confidentiality. I can't make that any plainer. I hope you all understand and appreciate that.' She scanned every face in the room, her eyes managing to bore into everyone there.

Keith Higginbotham's face turned puce. 'Are you telling me that you are holding up sharing this good news? You've no proof of this so-called campaign.'

She continued. 'I'm asking you all to be patient until the person responsible is brought to justice. If after that time the estate continues to improve, we can trumpet this achievement at that stage.' Staring at the popping veins on the Council Leader's face she said bravely, 'Self-congratulation is a little premature in this case, Councillor. We may have cause for concern as it appears that security and data protection have been so comprehensively breached.'

He looked in imminent danger of apoplexy. 'Are you seriously implying that one of us could have undertaken this series of incidents?'

The ACC stared at the point between the two long windows in the room. 'Anything is possible and, as I said, we'll let you know. This matter is given the strictest security rating. Remember the riots last August? Well we don't want a repeat of that do we? I call the meeting to a close and will email you all with details of the next one.'

Circe found her legs so weak that she was unable to push her chair back to stand, so pretended to be gathering her notes and rummaging in her briefcase. Lorcan moved towards her. 'Are you ok? If you don't mind me saying so, you look a bit peaky, as me old mother used to say.'

He was observant and correct as Circe answered him by getting to her feet and promptly fainting.

Chapter Thirty-Three

IDA DUNMORE'S DEPARTURE

Living on his nerves for so many years was useful for Lorcan, as it gave him the speed to catch Circe before she hit the table and he promptly put her head between her legs. She was only gone for a short time but was deeply embarrassed by what had happened.

'Must have been the heat of the room,' she said to Lorcan. It was stuffy and she admitted she had skipped lunch. He insisted that they went to Cafe Nero for a 'crappyfrappylatte' as he called it and plonked a panini in front of her. 'Eat,' he ordered. 'I'm not going until you've scarfed that.'

Neither of them mentioned the main subject of the meeting, but she did tell him about her visit to Patrick and the nuisance neighbours. Lorcan thanked her for the visit. 'That's above and beyond that is. I'm grateful to ye. Do you know I could almost believe my old Da would be capable of being a vigilante, so I could? He's that angry with people and he is very creative in his mind. Look at that campaign he did in the care home. Jesus, I couldn't believe he'd have done that. If he hadn't been in Seahaven House at the time, I could believe he had capacity, even he's not quite fit enough for the shenanigans on the estate. However, he doesn't know how to use a mobile phone or internet and doesn't have access to the names and addresses of the victims.' He stopped speaking and looked at a spot on the wall with a faraway look in his eyes and a slight frown.

Circe kept quiet and nibbled the panini. It was leathery and greasy. She struggled with the socially embarrassing strands of mozzarella that clung like stalactites to her lips, teeth and tongue. She was relieved that the immediate danger to revealing her identity appeared to be lifted and thought that silence was the best option.

Lorcan looked hard at Circe. 'You don't seem to be eating enough to my way of thinking. Look at that Tosspot shite we had the other day. No disrespect intended, but surely you've passed the danger age for developing eating disorders?'

Swallowing a hard greasy bolus she answered, 'Don't you believe it. I know of one old girl of eighty-five who starves herself so that she can be thin and attractive for her husband. Unfortunately, he's been dead for twenty years, but she hallucinates so well that she can have a full scale row with the air about his philandering. She's in a dementia unit now and is worse than a fifteen year old about her dietary intake. Thanks for your concern, but it's misplaced. I'm fine about eating and just like many women, watch my figure. I've just been a bit busy lately and haven't always remembered to eat properly.'

'Busy with what in particular?' The policeman as well as the man in Lorcan asked the question.

'Mostly Victim Support.'

'Not the kind on the estate then? Not going up there with some dog shite and superglue then?'

Circe gave a hollow laugh. 'Oh, absolutely, and if you ask me they all deserve it.' This was a dangerous comment, but she hoped her humour had saved her and she watched Lorcan grab the remains of the panini.

His mouth was still half full, but his green eyes looked hard into her amber ones. 'That's what you think, is it? That's what you really think? That it's just desserts for the scum of Stoneleigh? That's hardly the way for a magistrate to talk now is it, Ms Byrne? Not when you have access to people's names and addresses too.'

Rising new panic sent Circe into a quick reply. 'Lorcan, for a detective, you do talk crap. We don't have access to their information; the Clerk to the Court holds that. But since you ask I'm not very sorry that they have been targeted, and I'm sure I'm not alone in that regard. But don't start making spurious allegations against me just because Anne Lancaster has put a wasp up all your arses.'

He smiled despite himself at the image and the truth behind it. 'We are trained to expect the unexpected, and anyone who could make an unsuspecting friend and colleague drink wheatgrass is probably capable of anything.'

She got up to go, 'Thanks for the knight in shining armour bit, but I could have done without the massive great panini wallet. I'll go

169

home and get some Rennies down me. Good luck with your investigations, I look forward to hearing your conclusions.'

* * *

When Circe arrived home, it was to a darkening sky that matched her mood. The cats were, as ever, pleased to see her and she crouched down while they butted her hand and whichever part of her body they could nuzzle. It wasn't just cupboard love, they wouldn't eat until she had stroked and loved them. They were purring and winding round her legs as she made her way into the kitchen. The shadows from the tree branches and street light waved through the glass lantern roof. Sometimes it was so well illuminated that she didn't need to turn on the kitchen light unless she was cooking. She had a low level colour changing strip light and tonight stopped the sequence on purple. Rupert, Nigel and Clive were noisily and competitively crunching through their kibbles. Circe could see the phone flashing with messages and knew that there were more on her mobile phone, as well as the insistent emails that her computer would have received. She kicked off her black stilettos and automatically headed for the bottle of Bombay Sapphire which glowed prettily under the light. She'd bought a bunch of mint earlier in the week so she had all the ingredients for a large BSC.

Sitting down in front of the computer and having taken the first large gulp of the drink, she sighed long and hard. On the out breath she was surprised to find her tears flowing. They ran down her face and neck, soaking the neckline of her black top. She completely gave way to sobbing. It was loud and heartfelt. She hadn't cried like that in a long time. The cats came in and stared at her. Rupert even sat on her desk tapping her cheek with his paw. She cried even harder at his feline affection. Who would look after them if she was in prison? What the bloody hell had she been thinking? Risking everything just to get even with those lazy good for nothings. It wasn't worth it, and she stood to lose everything.

All her panic of the afternoon's meeting condensed and crystallised and she felt hollow and desperate. Blowing her nose and taking a big mouthful of the drink she knew that she could so easily have been arrested and not be sitting here this evening. For God's sake what was wrong with her? Was she so desensitised after years of being in court and seeing successive political parties water down sentences and strip police forces of their powers? No doubt that was the basis on which she had started all this. What chance did she have of not being discovered? Virtually none it seemed. All she could do was deny it and get rid of the evidence of her involvement. That was the least that she could do to try and make it harder for them to incriminate her. She lit the fire in the beautifully tiled Victorian grate. The pine cones and kindling soon crackled, and she tossed on a few logs. Circe went upstairs and returned to the fireplace with armfuls of her paraphernalia. She burned all the paperwork and her notes and everything associated with it. On to the fire went the wig and a couple of clothing items. They smelled so bad that it was obvious she couldn't continue as the locals would become suspicious, and the street's Neighbourhood Watch were like the Stasi.

Plan B was to place all the various items into separate plastic bags. The old coat and one 'pay as you go' phone was put in one carrier and the gloves and handbag in another. The old shopping trolley got filled with different plastic bags and she then put on her own coat and set off for a walk just out of her own neighbourhood, disposing carefully of the tied up bags in domestic dustbins under other people's rubbish. She was three miles away from home when she was left with just the shopping trolley. She carefully stood it in the doorway of the Barnardo's charity shop. Making her way quietly back down the street she heard a noise and turned sharply just in time to see an old vagrant wheeling it away. As far as she was concerned it was all over.

When she went back in again through the front door, she made another drink and pressed the messages on the phone. Nigel sat on her lap as she settled down with a pen and paper in case she needed to call back. The first message was another one from her ex-husband. Yet again he said they needed to talk. Circe automatically pressed the delete button. Next the veg box company said they'd had problems this week. 'Don't they always?' Circe told Nigel. The main substance of the message, besides blaming the weather and carrot fly, was to ask if she'd be OK with three swedes and they'd try and ring the changes next week with a few extra parsnips. 'Definitely not,' Circe said crossly to the machine and made a note to cancel her order with them. The only thing that was varied about their veg box were the excuses. The third message was hard to hear. She had to play the first part three times before letting it run. It was a woman crying who then hung up. The call list showed she rang back half an hour later still crying and finally after another hour she left a message in a voice clearly distorted by anguish and grief.

'It's me, Sadie's mum. She's gone and done it! I couldn't stop her and you couldn't either, no one could, she had nothing left. You did your best, but he was too strong for us both. I went in and found her, hanging from the stairs - the neighbours had the kids - just for half an hour she'd said. She'd used his belt, the one he hit her with and the floor was covered with, well it don't matter now. I just wanted to let you know. We both failed, but thanks for trying to help. You can call me when you get this if you like.' She reeled off a phone number as she ended the call.

Circe rang Sadie's mother back on autopilot. It wasn't the first time that she'd comforted a relative of a suicide following domestic violence, but the impact never got easier. She could almost see a vision of herself dressed in her old lady clothes and disguise standing in front of the fire where she had so lately destroyed her alter ego. That was why she'd done what she'd done, to try and stop this by any means at her disposal. But did two wrongs make a right and had she really made any difference? In her heart she knew she had. That was what all the fuss was about. The campaign had made a difference, some victims lives might have changed for the better. Wasn't that worth the risks she'd taken? The alcohol took the edge off the fears that had so paralysed her earlier in the day and she wished she hadn't destroyed her vigilante self. Who was there left to avenge Sadie? Ida Dunmore would have done it. And now she was gone.

Chapter Thirty-Four

ARSON

It was Patrick who'd called the fire brigade. He'd already made himself useful, as Circe and Lorcan thought he might. It was fortunate that despite it being the early hours of the morning, he was up and about in his living room dancing along to his music and movement cassette. He and his late wife had done this for years and after her death he just carried on. There didn't seem to be a reason to stop. She'd always liked doing stretches along with the Green Goddess on television and had got herself a lilac spandex jumpsuit similar to the presenter's, and the unforgiving ones sported by Anneka Rice, so that she would be in the mood to exercise. Patrick and his wife used to look forward to 'Challenge Anneka' when it used to be on Saturday night TV. He particularly enjoyed the part where she barrelled along with her backside level with the camera. For a variety of reasons Patrick never got rid of the garment and when he began to feel more like his old self, he carried on prancing about to the tape and wearing the catsuit. His wife had been very stout and though shorter than him he found it fitted him reasonably well, as it was so stretchy. It was just a little short in the legs and a couple of the seams wanted stitching up, but he liked it a lot and called it his 'happy clobber.' Anyone seeing him in it would blench at his genitals which sagged predictably with age, and consequently some dangled down the left side of the tight legs while the other bits bulged in a changeable sort of way at the front.

He was wearing it when the fire brigade arrived. He'd been halfway through his routine at 3.10am as he couldn't sleep and this, as he told the Watch officer, was how he came to see the flames from the door of the people across the road. He didn't know the residents, but called the emergency services, and now stood with them in the street in his shiny lilac outfit which reflected the flashing lights of the emergency vehicles, so that he resembled a mobile light show. The firefighters ran to the burning house and started shouting to the residents. A police car pulled up since it was a suspicious fire. A woman from the upstairs window was screaming hysterically. After some difficulty she broke the double glazing and was pulled through to safety by the fire crew using ladders and was dispatched to the waiting ambulance. She was screaming drunkenly about her kid.

The officers went about their preparations and the police questioned the gathered assembly of people about the likely occupants of the house. One scruffy man who didn't seem to want to make eye contact with the police spoke gruffly. 'There's these two big dogs; Staffies by all accounts, but don't take my word for it. I just hear 'em bark. And there's a boy of about six.'

Another woman joined in. 'And a right fucking little shit he is. I don't wish him ill, what with him being a kid and all, but I wouldn't rush in there to save him.'

Another added, 'He's a right little scrote is Mickey, but I don't think we want to see him burned to a crisp.'

The firefighters had already noticed the signs of accelerant use and suspected that the fire had been started deliberately from within the premises.

As some of the crew hosed the red-bricked semi-detached house down, others brought out the two dogs one at a time. Both burned and both dead. A gasp went up from the crowd. Dogs had a special place in the heart of Stoneleigh. Patrick stood with the others in his shiny catsuit. He looked odd but not totally out of place as many other people were in nightclothes, or the ubiquitous jogging bottoms and tracksuit tops. Ideal day or night wear, or for the half-life in between. Some of the neighbourhood kids looked excitedly at the scene and one bullet-headed boy said to Patrick, 'What have you got on? You some sort of tranny?'

The old man used the cover of the darkness and the diversion of the flames and smoke to pat him heavily on the number two haircut.

'Ow,' the kid screeched. 'This fucking old bastard hit me.' He raised his voice in appeal to the bystanders who were gathered around the smoking dogs and one of whom laid a blanket over them. A toothless woman of about thirty-five turned and spotted the lad and screeched back at him, 'Oi, what the fuck? That's your fucking house that's burning. Tell them firemen not to bother looking for him

174

in there, when he's fucking out here, the little shit. Did you start this blaze, Mickey? It wouldn't be the first time, would it? You did our shed, but we couldn't prove it, could we? Oi, coppers! Come over here, here's the kid what done it. The little bastard!'

The boy wiped his nose on his sleeve and Patrick could smell the petrol. He'd noticed it often enough back home, there was no mistaking it. Patrick grabbed the kid's arm with an iron grip nearly lifting him off his feet. He was still a strong man, despite the soft image created by the lilac spandex, and dragged him towards a police Sergeant whose head was bent, talking into his Airwave radio.

He raised his voice and his strong accent cut through the noise and the night. 'Here's the fire raiser, the little shite.'

The boy turned and started to run. The officer wasn't quick enough, but Patrick stuck his scrawny leg out with his big trainer which had effect of causing the culprit to fall straight to the pavement. The old man barked at the Sergeant, 'Can't you bloody arrest him now, for Christ's sake, you dozy fecker?'

Obediently the policeman and his colleague took hold of each of the child's arms and went to take him to a waiting police car.

'Do you know how old I am,' Patrick called after them.

'Haven't got time for guessing games, Grandpa, but thanks for your help.' He turned to the crowd. 'Move along now, there's nothing to more to see...'

Patrick snarled, 'Of course there bloody is, there is always something to see.' He went over to the officer who was already struggling with the boy and stuck his face up close. 'It comes to something when a man in his eighties has to apprehend a kid because you're too slow. No need to thank me.'

'We are grateful for the assistance of members of the public and we may well need you as a witness.'

Patrick raised his voice. 'We both know you won't be able to do anything to this little bastard. It was dogs he killed this time but next time it will be worse. He needs stopping.'

Mickey shouted at Patrick, 'What the fuck do you know, you great purple condom? My mum pissed me off and she had it coming to her and I hated those fucking dogs. She loved 'em more than me. You can all piss off.'

175

The police mouthed 'condom' at each other. What didn't this kid know? Except what it was like to be brought up properly.

* * *

The whole story was all over The Argus the next day. There was a large colour front page photograph of the burned out house with big black streaks going up the brickwork and a smaller image of a maroon fleece blanket with two large lumps underneath that the caption cited as being the dead dogs.

As she looked at the newspaper Circe felt sickened and that it just about summarised everything that was wrong with that estate. She put down her cereal spoon and ran her hands through her curls. It was an awful situation. Those poor bloody dogs, not that they had much of a life anyway, but her heart ached for them. Mickey's mother was responsible for what he'd become and Circe didn't have much sympathy for her. Inside the paper there was an interview with Patrick and a photo of him in the lilac outfit. He was quoted as coming out with the kind of invective that was likely to have his own house firebombed, but somehow she felt that anyone looking at him in that catsuit would probably not take him seriously. Well, she hoped they wouldn't. After Sadie's suicide she was confused about things again. Should she have given up her role as an avenging or revenging angel? There clearly was a need. She sent Lorcan a short email.

Seen your Da in the paper. It looks like he saved that mother's life, God love him. What a stroke of fortune that he was there and not rotting in that care home? By the way what's the craic with the jumpsuit? I'm sure it's a good one. If you get the chance give me a ring. I've had a gutful with a client committing suicide and I feel quite helpless. I was supposed to go into court today but don't feel that I can dispense justice without fear or favour, or in fact not bursting into tears. This is very unusual for me and possibly a sign of the times.'

She clicked the 'send' button then wrote to Alice while her cats washed themselves and licked their bottoms on The Argus.

Lorcan was pleased to hear from her but wondered why she chose to share her feelings with him. Surely she must have closer friends and colleagues? Or was it a subtle way of saying that she'd like to change the dynamics of their professional relationship into something more personal? After all they were working closely on a number of issues, although Circe never talked about her private life, nor he his own. But he had asked her for help with old man O'Leary aka the Hero of the Hour. This was help that she had freely given. She had also visited his father herself which was above and beyond. But then she was an intrinsic do-gooder; you didn't get an MBE for nothing, did you?

He replied quickly saying it was doubtful he'd have much time as he had to attend a crisis meeting which had been called relating to the murder of Rita Manser last week.

As she read his reply Circe recalled the case. The sixty-year old had come back from shopping and there was an intruder in the house who systematically sexually assaulted, raped and then murdered her. She squared her shoulders, put on her court clothes and set off.

Chapter Thirty-Five

SANDWICH AT STONELEIGH

Circe had spent the day trying to pull herself together. Did the arson attack on the estate take the pressure off her? What with that and Rita Manser's murder inquiry there might be enough to muddy the waters? She changed out of her 'court clothes' and noticed with irony how much thinner she looked. God, all the effort she'd made with those damn stupid diets and all the time it was the exercise that she got running around the estate and the adrenaline surge that the fear of discovery caused. She checked herself on the scales. Yes, one stone one pound gone. Brilliant! She stared at her naked self, as if at a stranger. Her body wasn't bad for her age, but how annoying it was to see one's pubic hair turn white. Irritably she wondered why she coloured the hair on her head, but no one ever mentions the down belows. Guess that's why it's waxed off. Sighing she bent down and pulled on her pants.

Why am I being so vain when my life could cave in at any moment? And why do I want Lorcan O'Leary around more than anyone else right now? Am I going to confess my misdemeanours to him? Her quick mind ran through the scenario. *No way. Guess I just wanted to talk with someone who wasn't a stranger to tragedy.* She crouched down, noting the noisy explosion of cracking in her knees, and stroked the three cats that butted and writhed affectionately against her. She left the house as ever with drifts of white fur clinging to her clothes. It was ironic that for someone who had recently spent so much time behaving suspiciously and hanging about outside people's accommodation watching their movements, that Circe was so unobservant of her own situation. For as she left the house and got into her Figaro, she was entirely oblivious to the person watching her on the other side of the street.

Force of habit saw her drive up to Stoneleigh, truly revisiting the scenes of her crimes. She parked her car in view of the mini-mart and walked back to Patrick's bungalow. The estate was still the same and the fat girls still smoked with one hand as they pushed buggies with the other. The burned house was cordoned off and the dogs had been removed. The blackened windows stared like reproachful dark eyes. Shivering, Circe knocked at Patrick's door.

'It's yerself,' he said, as he did to most people. Circe wondered if it was to save him having to think of people's names.

'Hallo, Patrick. I see you're headlines in the papers and I must congratulate you for saving the life of the woman across the road. I won't say you saved her son as well, since he appears to have started it.'

Patrick was characteristically modest. He had lived with dramas for too long. As he made her a cup of tea she noticed the lilac catsuit on the arm of his chair. Picking it up, she noticed the holes. 'Hey Patrick, is this yours? You had it on in the picture?'

'That's me movement to music outfit.'

'I see. Would you like me to fix these seams for you? It won't take long and I've got some thread that will match the colour, so you'll never see the repair? I'll give it a wash as there's smuts from that fire on it.'

Patrick's eyes unexpectedly filled with tears. 'I won't let anyone touch it as it was me wife's, but I can see that you'll respect it and only do what you need to do to make it right.'

Circe nodded, 'I'll take special care of it, I promise.' She only stayed twenty minutes then made her excuses to leave and put the catsuit in a plastic carrier bag. 'I'll have it back to you as soon as ever,' she promised and went on her way to the mini-mart.

The owner looked disinterested and could see that she wasn't one of his typical customers. She looked for something to eat and found a cheese and pickle sandwich in a triangular plastic container. The other patrons had fallen silent, turning and staring at her. Weaselly faces and the ubiquitous baseball caps with hoods over them. Perfect for avoiding being identified on camera. Circe paid the assistant in silence wondering if anyone recognised her from court. She didn't think she could go back there. How could she dispense justice on such political lines? It was no justice. Did it make a difference whether she was there, or not? No one would give a flying fuck.

She ripped open the packet of sandwiches and foul air arose as she did. Nevertheless, she bit into one as she walked back to her car.

179

Eating in the street was de-rigeur here. The bread was thick and foetid, like a memory foam mattress and the cheese was grated, cheap and entirely without flavour. Just yellow, plasticky fat. The pickle was the redeeming feature and the sharpness was what she needed to feel in her mouth, but after two small bites she was sated. The bitterness just served to remind her of the situation she was in.

She threw the sandwiches to an ecstatic seagull who was sitting on the grass verge, its legs tired after treadling for worms. As soon as he got his beak around the first one there was a white cloud of his colleagues who swooped and screamed. Fighting and jockeying for the remnants. A parody of the estate.

Chapter Thirty-Six

THE GIN HOUSE

When Circe arrived back home it was late afternoon and getting dark; just before the streetlights came on. She parked the car further up the road than usual, as there seemed to be more vehicles than ever using the street; quite a few had parking tickets on them. It was either expensive 'pay and display', or expensive resident permits - all part of the price paid for living in Brighton and Hove. As she walked back towards her house, she carefully carried the Tesco bag in both arms to protect the contents; cat food, a bag of mixed salad leaves and the turquoise bottle of gin, while a couple of limes and a bunch of mint protruded from the top. The sky was a deepening shade of purply-blue, and Circe looked at the clear definition of the twigs on the elm trees. Her eyes were good for her age and she could see most things clearly, but still she didn't notice someone looking at her and who smiled with pleasure as she went into her house.

Still preoccupied she stroked and fed the cats enjoying the way the shadows from the tree branches danced across their white fur as they noisily crunched through their biscuits. The peripheral under-cupboard lighting was subtle and tasteful. She didn't need to turn on the large statement chandelier hanging over her central kitchen island. Rupert sat on the granite work top and dabbed at the sparkles on its surface. She filled the kettle with filtered water and put her herbal teabag in a mug. She poured half a cup of water on top of it. Leaving the kettle on the Aga she noted that it was still nearly full. It was a waste of money, but she always put enough in as if Alice was still there. She just couldn't break that habit. Circe eyed the bottle of Bombay Sapphire and decided to have a bath before indulging in a proper drink.

Half an hour later as she crossed the upstairs landing in her comfy pink and black checked 'house pyjamas', as she called them, she heard a noise downstairs. Her hair was wet, but before she dried it she thought she had better check out what chaos the cats had wreaked. She was no stranger to unusual bangs and crashes as the cats were frequent perpetrators of all kinds of accidents and incidents. Only two weeks ago Clive had balanced on the paper tray of her printer and had made the whole machine fall to the floor. The carpet still bore the testimony of the ink cartridge stain. More often than not she couldn't identify the culprit. Although the damage was apparent, usually things like a smashed plant pot, lampshades askew, cushions scattered, the offending feline would be long gone and innocently asleep elsewhere in the house.

Cocking her head, Circe listened. Very often whichever cat was responsible would cleverly run in the opposite direction to the carnage making a connection to the scene of the crime difficult, but now she didn't hear any furry footsteps. She heard the noise again. What was it? A sort of scraping and banging sound. They'd had a fox get in when Alice was little and it sounded just like that, as the poor creature crashed around trying to escape. Freeing it had been the easy part, it was the odour that took a long time to eliminate. However, she loved foxes and it didn't change her mind about them.

Her concern grew as she realised that two of the cats were with her and it wasn't like Nigel to make that much noise. Circe grew afraid but also angry. No one had any right to be in her house. God it wasn't even six o'clock in the evening; a bloody strange time for burglars. She grabbed her hairdryer and started slowly down the stairs. Every one of them creaked. Blasted Victorian houses. As she reached the bottom step she heard what sounded like one of her kitchen utensils falling to the ground. Sighing with relief she called Nigel's name. Unfortunately, she didn't look behind her or she would have seen his brothers arched and stiff with fear and would have realised that it wasn't a playful accident. She heard a loud wail from the kitchen and knew at once that it wasn't the normal Siamese meowing cry, but a dreadful heart stopping scream born of some kind of terror. Her blood ran cold and she was now very frightened. What could it be? She ran across the hall and the Persian carpet deadened the sound of her footsteps. But now Circe's progress as she heard a man's voice. An artificially jolly voice.

'Hallo, love. Who's this Nigel then? Man of the house is he?'

Chapter Thirty-Seven

SEEING THE LIGHT

Circe took a step backwards feeling a sharp pain in the ball of her left foot where it landed on a lone cat biscuit. A small, but astonishingly painful weapon against the bare foot. The shock and discomfort pushed her adrenaline one step higher.

'What the fuck are you doing in my fucking house?' she screamed.

A man of about twenty or so years lounged in the doorway. 'Nice jammies, lady. You look even better close up. Not young, but not too old. Just how I like them.'

Jesus he wasn't a burglar, he was a rapist! In a split second she realised that her mobile phone was in her bag upstairs and she wouldn't be able to reach the landline, as he was between it and her. She was alone. He started towards her slowly. She could see his greasy brown hair and that he was older than she had thought, not that it mattered. He was nearer to thirty than twenty-five, and his unshaven face was the colour of putty. How had he got in? Had he broken a window? If so, someone might hear and they might come and help her. Could she stall him? Was it best to pretend to humour him and feign niceness and cooperation? Try to keep him talking?

He grinned confidently displaying a missing front tooth while the others sat randomly alongside like off balance gravestones, badly discoloured and resting loosely on inflamed gums. *Drugs*, she thought. *There'll definitely be no reasoning with him.* She could see everything from his dirty fingernails, as they extended towards her to the oily sweat on his ugly dissipated face. One of the cats growled behind her. She'd never heard them make that noise before. Siamese had a wide range of calls but not that weird growl. It was answered with a muted howl of anguish from the kitchen, but its owner didn't appear. Something must have happened to Nigel. Her stomach lurched more for the cat than for her own immediate danger.

In the next instant Circe felt herself quite disconnected. For some time the guy ropes that held her anchored to so-called normal life had slackened and then snapped. She floated free uncaring about the consequences. What did it matter? What did any of it matter? He took another step forward. His dirty trainers on her stripped and beautifully polished wooden floor. Despite everything she didn't want to be raped and murdered. She owed it to Alice to do her best and she wouldn't give in without a fight. The red mist rose and swirled upwards within her. The fear receded, and anger took its place. How dare this filthy bastard come into her house? How fucking dare he?

Circe and Alice had been to a series of women's self-defence classes a few years ago. It had been Circe's idea as she had wanted some peace of mind that her daughter would be able to protect herself when she went to Cambodia. Alice had only gone to keep Circe happy. Surprisingly, it had been quite good fun despite the seriousness of the subject. They had learned blocking, throws and how to use their voices so as to give the appearance of being more confident than they were. They learned that the victim's fear is like a drug to the attacker. It gets them high and they may take even more courage from the perceived weakness and shock of the quarry.

Circe roared. A volcanic bellow with the white hot molten embers of her anger coming up in waves and springing into new life. A solar flare of heat whipped through her and shimmered out towards the intruder.

Lee Phipps had trodden on the cat as he jumped down from the worktops of her kitchen, having made his entrance by breaking the sash window. He was no great expert at gaining entry and had left his DNA at properties many times. However, the overcrowding in prisons, on the few occasions he found himself there, usually meant an early release and he was free to reoffend. He'd kicked the broken cat to one side, but it was his foot shoving its food bowl in the dark that spoiled his surprise for Circe. He didn't like the way she shouted at him. He was high and horny and low on smack.

Her voice was shrill, 'What are you doing here? Get the hell out of my house.' She hurled the hairdryer she was still holding at him. It hit his chest without injury and dropped to the ground breaking in two.

He laughed. 'Come here love, I won't hurt ya. You're just my type. I'll bet you'll be glad of the attention. You be a good girl now.'

The confident and excited smirk allowed a pause for just a fraction of a second. Circe was ready when he lunged and quickly grabbed his arm, putting it in a lock. He was bigger and stronger though and tried to put his grubby hand over her mouth to silence her banshee screams. She bit it. He stank of tobacco and reeked of oniony sweat. Trying to move away he slipped on the rug lying on her well-polished floor. Recovering his balance he pulled a hank of her long copper hair which tore at root level from her scalp. She fought and screamed, pulling his hand down on her head, as she'd been taught, and writhed his fingers loose. Hair would re-grow, and right now she was choosing life.

Breaking free he stood facing her with his arms out to block her way. She pulled the cord on his hoodie which whipped into a makeshift garrotte. While he squirmed away he pulled at her pyjama top and she heard the button ping off and land somewhere on the wooden floor. Her knee found itself automatically going for his groin and he instinctively moved into a protective crouch, just loosening his grip a little, which was long enough for her to sidestep him and she ran towards the kitchen. It housed plenty of weapons. There might be a saucepan she could grab, or even the gin bottle, or perhaps she might make it out of the back door.

Nigel lay snapped in two by the fridge. It was obvious that his spine was broken. She could hear Lee's curses and panting as he ran after her going round the central island to grab her from behind as she gasped in horror at her beloved cat. His back was L-shaped and his legs were the wrong way up behind him. Nigel's head raised slightly to look at her and his eyes were filmy with both terror and tears.

Circe's assailant grabbed her again and she struggled to free herself as they wrestled. They were both mortally tired. The sweat was hotter and more foetid now. His blackheads stood out and a herpes blister cracked and bled. Spittle flew from his mouth as he laughed while wrenching at her clothing. He enjoyed the pain her injured cat caused her and he stretched out his leg and stamped on its body. 'I fucking hate cats and their owners' he gasped. Whipping round Circe grabbed one of the Sabatier knives from the wooden

185

block on the side. He promptly wrestled it from her. His hands were cut as he pulled the knife towards him twisting it away from her. With one big surge of energy Circe kicked his legs sideways from under him and he fell backwards onto the black and white tiles. 'You fucking bitch,' he screamed.

Snatching the knife back from him, and cutting her own hand in the process, she moved away as Lee swung back his leg to get to his feet. Circe had a moment to make that decision. One moment that was going to change her life. She was no longer in fear and was now in control. She looked at him and then her mind was made up. Like lightening Circe thrust the knife *'through from the left side of his body,'* as the coroner later said, *'to the right groin with the single knife wound continuing through his genitalia and piercing the femoral artery causing a fatal loss of blood.'* She didn't have to, but something in her made her want to do this more than anything else. He'd given up his rights to life the moment he broke in to her house and bugger what the law said.

Lee Phipps was trying to pull the knife out and was moving his legs up and down sliding on the blood and was now making whimpering, groaning noises. She took a wooden Lakeland chopping board and hit it against the end of the knife's hilt and felt it sink in another two inches.

Her bare feet struggled to keep her upright. She slid in the sticky warmth of his blood.

'Help me. I'll go to prison, just don't let me die.' He beseeched her.

'How many women have you raped, you bastard? she shouted. She wanted to be not just the executioner, but the confessor too. That Catholic training ran through her like letters through seaside rock.

His eyes were on the pumping blood, 'Dunno - a few. I can't help it. I didn't mean to kill that woman - it just happened and I wouldn't have killed you unless you'd fought me. I've gotta have the control. Help me love.' He whispered now, all control lost.

Panting from her exertions Circe barked, 'What good would that do? Have you released early only for you to reoffend again, having convinced the dozy parole board that you've changed.' Circe knew he'd have to bleed out soon. Even if she called an ambulance it would be too late. 'Just tell me - why old ladies?'

His voice was fainter still, 'They're so bloody sure of themselves, old bitches, living their smug bloody lives.' He couldn't help the ghost of a smile at the memory despite his circumstances.

'You're not sorry are you?' Circe felt safe enough to lean forward noticing that the blood smelled of iron and his breath of the devil. 'You'd just keep on going. What mercy did you show even my cat?'

'Pussy sacrificed to get more pussy.' He drawled now. The room was getting dark and Clive jumped onto the worktop his bloodstained paws sliding on the surface. The cat's body knocked sideways into the recently boiled kettle on the Aga as he veered away from its heat. Circe could have steadied it and her hand shot out automatically as she rose from her crouching position, but she didn't. Her shaking fingers stayed still as the lid burst open with the weight and force of the contents and the man looked up for one last time as the steaming water hit his eyes. They turned opaque, like fish eyes as they boiled in his skull. He was now out of pain and began his onward journey, just as Circe was starting hers with his blood not just on her hands, but on most of the other parts of her kitchen.

She thought quickly and started by placing one of the biggest knives in Lee's hands, having torn a decisive rip in her pyjamas. She threw a couple more around in the water and blood-soaked debris. Got to look like self-defence. Was he left of right handed? Yellow nicotine stains on the right. She put some of her loose hairs in his fingers and threw some plant pots around, while the earth cascaded over surfaces and the floor mixing with the broken glass. She further ripped the front of her pyjama top knowing it was tearing and reddening the skin of her neck and then ran bloodstained into the street and grabbed a shocked young woman who was walking home from work. 'Call the police,' she screamed, as she fell over a tree root on the pavement. 'My cat's been murdered.'

Chapter Thirty-Eight

BRIGHTON DETECTIVES

The police arrived in nine minutes and the ambulance in twelve. The two response officers entered the house and stood in the kitchen doorway. The smashed window and havoc gave them a fairly swift idea of what had happened, but the bloodied figure on the floor was the surprise. The male officer knelt in the blood and water and searched for a pulse and after a time shook his head at his colleague.

They looked at the slight red-haired woman crying hysterically and the female officer led Circe into the living room and sat her down. Her partner got on his Airwave police radio and called for assistance regarding a death in unusual circumstances. He secured the scene and went to his car for the roll of incident tape. There was already a group of neighbours and passers-by asking him who'd died. A young man was photographing the house. The press would be onto this directly. He was pleased to hear sirens coming as he needed help. It was his first body too.

The ambulance crew pronounced life extinct. The two officers in the second car were CID and one of whom was DC Steve Tibbs on late shift. The second was DS Martin Potter. They both exchanged glances as they stared down at Lee Phipps.

'Well, well, look who it isn't,' Tibbs said quietly, with barely suppressed glee.

'Fucking result,' Martin Potter replied in a hushed whisper. They struggled to wipe the smiles off their faces. Closing the kitchen door they high-fived. The feline wailings brought them to their senses.

Steve Tibbs loved cats and was shocked at what he saw. 'The cat needs putting to sleep even I can see that there's nothing that can be done. Let's speak to the victim.' They both walked round the dead man and into the living room. Circe was arguing with the female officer that her cat needed treatment. He was surprised to see it was her at the centre of this incident.

'Ma'am,' Tibbs began softly. 'Please let me help that lovely cat of yours. Am I right to take it that the cat is yours?'

'Of course he's fucking mine. He needs help.'

'I love cats too and every second is causing that creature more pain. I know someone in the emergency vets who will give him peace. Let's take him there right now. Let's get that sorted first, as that's a priority. He read the cat lady part of her very well.

Crying uncontrollably Circe allowed herself to be led into the hall where the young response officer had a blanket with the bloodstained cat already wrapped in it. Nigel looked at his mistress for the last time as she kissed his warm head that would shortly be rendered cold by the efficiency of the vet's euthanasia. She whispered in his ear.

'Best if I take him now,' the officer responded to a head jerk from Tibbs. Cradling the blanket bundle he took Nigel from his home for the last time. The broken cat looked back at Circe and she collapsed screaming. They called a doctor who prescribed Valium to sedate Circe and Zopiclone for night sedation, should she need it, over the next few days.

The female officer, Jan, asked her if there was someone who could come and be with her. Maybe a friend or relative?

'No, there's no one.' Circe answered then paused. The Chair of the Bench would need to know all about this. 'Call Joyce Bagshawe. Her number's on my phone.' She handed the handset to the officer who came back shortly.

'Joyce sounds very capable and is on her way over. You need someone you know to be with you.'

Photos were being taken of the crime scene and the CID officers first thoughts were that it looked like an aggravated burglary with a view to committing rape, sexual assault or GBH. In the light of the situation involving a known rapist and magistrate, there was going to be massive national media interest. The local press were already outside. Inspector John Crook, who was the CID supervisor and duty officer was called.

His instructions to DS Potter were clear, 'The case needs very careful handling. Everything has to be done right and we mustn't assume anything. It's a death in unusual circumstances and we need to investigate everything thoroughly. No need for the Major Crime Team to investigate, but out of courtesy I'll update the duty Senior

Investigating Officer and our Divisional Commanders. I want you to be the officer in this case and keep Steve Tibbs on the team. Both of you report directly to me. In the light of the attempted sexual assault use the Victim Suite and call out Dr Hathaway and see if she can deal with this personally.

'There is likely to be quite a lot of public interest in what has happened, and I want to make sure we have a comprehensive package for the Coroner. Arrange a Home Office post mortem for as soon as we can, and make sure the forensics are all in good order. I'll brief Chief Officers and handle the press. I'll also speak to Ms Byrne tomorrow. That's all for now, but just to say, well done and good work.'

Circe was taken to the Victim Suite and seen by the female doctor, Dr Hathaway. Despite assurances that she was fine and nothing had happened, the officers had put her in a car with the Bench Chair, who had just arrived. She was a redoubtable matron of the old school. Calm and practical and just what was needed in a crisis.

This left the officers clear to do their tasks and preserve everything for the coroner's court. Evidence needed to be secured, keeping in mind that they didn't yet know what had happened. Tibbs was phoning the coroner's office when Lorcan let himself in under the fluttering tape.

He looked quite distraught and not his usual jaded self.

Steve Tibbs ended the call and said, 'We've got a good one here. How come you've arrived on the scene? You're off duty?'

'Jan phoned me as she saw my number on Circe's phone and probably thought a friendly face would be needed as looking at you great old bruisers would make her feel worse.'

'Circe has gone to the Victim Suite.'

He paled visibly. 'No... surely–'

Tibbs cut in. 'It's a precaution. We don't think she was sexually assaulted, but as it was an attempted rape, we need to check everything.'

'How badly is she hurt?' Lorcan almost barked the question.

'Hard to assess her physical injuries and defence wounds, as she's been so upset about her cat.'

He told the story and Lorcan's face contorted with undisguised anger. 'Where is the bastard?'

Tibbs thumbed the kitchen.

Lorcan never thought he would get to see the inside of Circe's house particularly under these circumstances. He'd hardly dared to hope they had any chance of, well, anything. But he did hope, despite himself. She probably would have been horrified if she'd suspected. He caught sight of two more cringing cats and bent down. Their blue eyes shone red in the lighting that was set up for the photo shoot.

'Jaysus. These need caring for out of here.' He saw a cat box in the corner of her study and gently picked the two terrified cats up and put them in on the blanket. It was a tight squeeze, but he couldn't find a second box. He took a litter tray and food bowls, sadly noting the one he was leaving behind and set off back to his home which was secure and peaceful.

He gave them some cold chicken from his fridge and turned the TV on for them. Bending down he stroked and petted them. 'Ah it'll be alright lads, so it will. Ye'll see yer Mam soon.'

He went back to the crime scene and it was being dealt with very professionally. Bidding his colleagues good night and taking a last look at Lee, as he was conveyed to the pathologist's office, Lorcan looked round. He stared at the house and took in the plush carpet and the tasteful fixtures and fittings. He also noticed Alice's coat hung on the inside of the front door.

'Shit,' he said to himself, and walked down the path.

Chapter Thirty-Nine

THE VICTIM SUITE

Lorcan arrived at the sexual offences suite. It was an old police house converted for the purpose, and he was admitted at once. He waited in reception and recognised Bench Chair, Joyce Bagshawe. She was on her phone and waved his greeting away as if he were an annoying gnat.

He placed himself in front of her. 'How's Circe? What's the story? What happened?'

'And you are?' She peered over her reading glasses at him. He'd never felt so politely disrespected before. He'd had all other types of abuse but this was a class above.

'DS Lorcan O'Leary. I work with Ms Byrne on the Police Authority.'

She grunted assent and he sat down next to her. 'How is she?'

'How do you think, officer? A rapist attacked her.'

The door opened at the end of the corridor and Dr Hathaway came out. She knew Lorcan well and he raised a hand. The doctor came towards them. He explained his reason for being there and she checked with Circe and then beckoned him into her room. 'She would like to see you.'

'Well really!' Mrs Bagshawe began.

Circe was wearing a hospital gown but appeared to be making to get dressed.

'Thanks for coming,' she said, turning her reddened eyes on him. He thought she seemed very calm.

'I'm so sorry,' he said lamely. 'So sorry.'

'Did you see what happened to my cat?'

He was surprised at this question and though he hadn't really, he nodded. He'd got the idea, and to be honest the cat's demise was the least of it, or so he thought. There was a man dead for God's sake and Circe nearly raped.

Circe ran her hands through her hair dragging some out with the wrenching motion. 'He killed him. He deliberately bloody killed him. And kicked his broken body. How could he do that?'

The tears began cascading down her white face. Lorcan's hand reached out into the air close to her then used it instead to illustrate his reply. His fist clenched as he said, 'Your assailant, your man there, was a fecking bastard. We knew him well and what he did to your cat was just an example of what his character was like, right enough. I could lose my job for saying what a great fecking job you did on that piece of shite tonight. It couldn't have happened to a more deserving fuckwit. You did the world a favour, but I'm of course sorry your wee cat didn't make it. Its whisker was worth more than the whole of that whole sack of...'

He broke off as her tears began cascading down her blanched cheeks growing in volume and intensity and he could see the power of that emotion rising. He didn't know quite how to behave. He didn't have that script. If truth be told, he didn't have many scripts.

He held both arms open. 'May I give you a hug? You're the bravest person I know, but I don't know what to say to yous?'

She accepted the embrace in the non-threatening way it was offered. He kept his body at an angle so they weren't facing each other directly. It wasn't male and female. It was just two colleagues united in a desire for justice. His battered heart bled for her and his slight touch opened her chasm of grief wider.

'Why didn't I die, Lorcan? Why did I have to bloody live? Why me?'

He knew what this was about. Everyone knew, but no one dared say anything. Circe wouldn't have any mention of it. It must never be discussed. But he was in the white water rapids now that was for sure, and no raft in sight. What did he have to lose?

'How about you tell me? How about you just let it out? You're a brave woman, so you are.' You've just taken out a scumbag and saved society so much pain. You can do anything Circe. You're strong.'

She wailed, 'I'm not. He was nothing, I don't know why I fought to live. I've nothing to live for...not since...'

'Yes?' Lorcan encouraged, they were near to it now. They were so close and there may never be another opportunity.

Circe's tears and snot ran down her face, mouth and chin. He pulled out a bunch of medical wipes from the side and said, 'Tell me.'

Circe kept asking questions almost to herself. 'Why couldn't Alice have survived? Why did she have to die when those fucking locals jumped her? Why me and not her? We both did that self-defence course? She had her life ahead of her and I have nothing...'

She was screaming and crying now, knocking over instruments. Dr Hathaway ran back into the room.

'It's OK,' Lorcan said, 'I've got it...' She raised an eyebrow and Lorcan gave her a thumbs up above Circe's tousled head. 'Just give us a wee bit of space. She'll call if she needs you.'

He said to Circe, 'Just tell me. I've heard the story from others but want to hear it from you.'

Circe fell to the floor hitting it with her fists. 'They killed Alice. Killed my daughter. She was just helping the victims of the Khmer Rouge and two fucking drunken youths ran her over one night and raped and killed her.'

Lorcan pulled her up and back into a chair and just held her.

Sobbing she half whispered, 'What do you think that flight was like going to identify her body? What do you think? Crying for fucking hours. Being stared at. People looking at me as they were going on holiday, or maybe on business, choosing their fucking meals and drinks. I had stress diarrhoea and was hyper ventilating and weeping, knowing what every inch of that planes journey was taking me to. Changing planes at Singapore, I didn't want to get back on it. I didn't want to get to Cambodia. I didn't want to see the truth. I didn't want the plane to land so I wouldn't have to identify my ravaged, damaged daughter who was so perfect in every way. And then to have to come back with her ashes in my suitcase. A souvenir of South East Asia. And no, they never found the bastards who murdered her. That's fair, isn't it? They could even have been among the gawpers with their impassive faces when I identified Alice.' Circe gasped for breath. 'And so that's how it was, Lorcan. It's so terrible. I don't want it to have happened, and so that's why I drop the odd email to Alice's address. I imagine her writing back. She was always so positive and said things would always be alright. But they weren't, and she was wrong and I'm so unhappy to be proved right.'

Circe's tears ran harder. 'And another thing! Would you believe that in her little room they found a half-starved cat that she'd been caring for until she died. It was black, and she called it Midnight. It only had one eye and was in such a bad way when she took over its care. I had to find someone I could pay to keep looking after him. I hope that woman keeps her word. No one had fed him until I got there. Can you imagine?'

There were a lot of things that Lorcan could imagine, but Circe's cat obsession now made perfect sense. Children. They were just like children, large eyed and affectionate. She needed them and if that was the vehicle to access her emotions, then whatever bloody worked was just fine.

He couldn't say things would be OK; they never would be. A man had died following a break-in at her home. It was also a wicked turn of fate that her daughter should die at the hands of rapists, but Circe deserved to live, not just survive, like a lot of other people in similar circumstances.

Circe finally stopped crying. Lorcan took her by the shoulders and looked into her bloodshot eyes.

He whispered, 'You don't need to answer this, but I'd just like to know if there was a choice tonight...if you had a choice. When he...'

Her eyes met his. Her eyelashes were clumped together with tears. In their depths, though, there was a glint. She didn't speak.

'Right enough. That's me answered. I'll make sure we get this wrapped up as soon as possible.'

'Lorcan shouldn't I...?'

'Not on my watch.'

He got up. 'I'll get that old Mrs Bagshawe in for yous. Stay with her tonight. I've got your two cats and they'll be getting some of my takeaway. I'm guessing they like kebabs?'

Circe started arguing and Mrs Bagshawe was ushered in.

Chapter Forty

QUESTIONS ASKED

The investigation into the death of Lee Phipps went smoothly. The CID team and forensics prepared the case and the coroner set a date.

A more concerning problem for the police was the press interest. The Argus was the most cooperative. The paper had a good relationship with the Force and the storyline was supportive: *Convicted Criminal Dies in Attack on Local Magistrate.* All the rest of the media ran with the story and it was featured on national radio with the strapline *JP nearly raped by offender that the criminal justice system failed to stop.*

Ann Lancaster sat with her fingers steepled. John Crook eased his way into her room wearing his oiliest smile. Steve Tibbs walked in confidently, with Lorcan hanging back looking for the lucky bit of carpet. He superstitiously believed that he wouldn't be berated if he could find the join in it that was about three metres from her desk. It was also out of the firing line.

'Gentlemen, please take a seat.' She waved to the chairs which put them well below her body height.

There was a knock at the door and an immaculately attired Adrian Hoy, known as 'Ahoy' to the team, peered round the door.

The senior scenes of crime officer was bending so low as he stuck his head round, that he was level with the door handle. 'Ma'am your staff officer said it was OK to come in, and so here I am! All ready to be debriefed!' He smiled engagingly at the ACC's stony face.

Impeccably dressed Adrian made his entrance with his arms outstretched. One of which held his file. 'Lots of goodies in here,' he announced, still smiling with perfect teeth glowing against his fake tan.

Lorcan looked at the file held in the clear nail varnished fingernails. '*Feck me*' he muttered to himself. He didn't know what the results were and could only hold his breath till he involuntarily coughed.

Adrian looked at him distastefully and whispered to him. 'If you don't mind me saying, you look a bit naff, old chap. All that white hair over your clothes. No wonder you're coughing. You want a Sticky Buddy you do. It's brilliant! It's a sort of clothes roller that you run up and down yourself and the hairs just...'

'Thank you, Adrian.' The ACC cut in. She missed very little.

'Oh, excuse me.' He put on a hurt look.

'Speak to me.' She turned to John Crook. He outlined the case and progress to date. Her steely blue eyes alighted on him and he falteringly came to a stop. 'Ma'am?' he whispered.

Her voice was firm and unwavering. 'What I'm thinking is, and I know this may sound strange as none of you have mentioned it, but isn't it an unfortunate coincidence that one of our Police Authority members and a senior Magistrate with a somewhat formidable reputation for tough sentencing should be attacked in her own home? And him with such a long list of convictions and yet free to re-offend?'

John Crook cleared his throat. 'His previous is indeed extensive. However, we don't have him for rape and assault as yet.'

'Did you even have him in your sights? I asked you why he went for Circe Byrne. How did he know where she lived? What was the intelligence? What do you think it looks like when a pillar of the community is attacked in her own home? She's a champion of victims for goodness sake. And now she's one herself!'

Lorcan sneezed, 'Sorry Ma'am.'

'And I had a journalist, from the radio, asking for an interview on keeping law enforcers safe. For Gods' sake, just what am I supposed to say? Why her, gentlemen? Why Circe? Someone just speak.'

Lorcan sneezed again. With a flourish Adrian handed him a perfectly folded handkerchief. 'Keep it officer, you sound like you've got something coming on.'

Lorcan dabbed his red eyes. 'No, you're alright.'

Adrian was firm. 'Be my guest.'

Not to have accepted it would have been to untick a diversity box. Best not to do that, and especially in front of the ACC.

'Thanks, Adrian.' Lorcan stuffed it into his pocket.

Steve Tibbs answered for the group with uncharacteristic boldness. 'Ma'am. I was there, and from what I could see of the

197

scene it just seemed just like a random attack. There was no evidence of any planning. He just got into the house, probably to burgle...'

'Has Circe said if he spoke or gave any indication of motive? '

John Crook said that Circe's statement indicated he admitted murdering the elderly victim in Worthing.

Adrian said, 'Can I pipe up now?'

Ann Lancaster nodded. Adrian brandished the file with a theatrical flourish. 'Well now! It's all here! Lee Phipps has his DNA on so many incident scenes. It was in the body of Rita Manser, who was raped, and he is also implicated in several other cases. He seemed to have slipped through the net, and we didn't have the time or resources to join everything up. But the good news we have now!' He beamed at his stony faced colleagues.

Chapter Forty-One

CONFESSIONS

Lee Phipps's confession and disclosures were a massive relief to the Force, and Lorcan in particular. It made things tidier.

The press was sated with the satisfaction of a crime solved and one prevented. Though no one said it, everyone including the Stoneleigh community, thought he deserved it. 'He had it coming,' they said emphatically in The Dog. 'That's taking it too far. Magistrates are bastards, but that's too much.'

The mood on the streets in Stoneleigh was one of unease. Some new drug dealers and traffickers had moved in on what seemed to be a vacancy in the supply chain, since the locals were windy and uncertain. Business was not brisk and there was a feeling of tension in the air.

Lorcan called his father and asked him over to his flat. Patrick was understandably shocked and suspicious. 'What are you up to lad? You never ask me round to yours.'

'I need your help, so I do. Just pack an overnight bag and I'll pick ye up.'

He collected the old man and explained that he had cats that needed feeding and company. 'I've never heard screeching like those two. They miss their mistress. I'm allergic to them too. I'm on bloody antihistamines, so I am.'

Patrick scowled, 'I couldn't believe it when I heard about the attack on the news. She's a nice wee lass. She's mending my exercise outfit.'

Lorcan's eyes rolled. 'Don't hold your breath on that one. She's in a bad way.'

As he settled the old man in and showed him the food in the fridge, his father rubbed his son's hair. Lorcan sat down and the tears sprang to his eyes. 'Now don't you start being nice. I can take anything but that, you old fecker.'

He left his father with a doorstep sandwich, a bottle of Guinness and a feeling of worry that circled his bowels like a writhing serpent.

At work every minute was an hour. The celebratory mood failed to lift his spirits. Steve Tibbs was jubilant. 'Got the bastard, Lorcan. No complicated trial and prison sentence. Result!' He punched the air with a hand that was holding a custard tart, and it broke under the force of his paean of triumph. Lorcan took a direct hit and the yellowy slime slid down his white shirt.

'Thanks, mate,' he said, smearing it as he tried to wipe it with the kitchen towelling, extending the mark. *Brilliant* he said to himself. *Bloody brilliant.*

* * *

Circe said she would see Lorcan at 1.00pm and was expecting the cats to be delivered back. However, he wanted her full attention; those two wouldn't let him have a word in edgeways, and Circe would be diverted with her happiness to see them. He'd drop them back after. If, of course, he was allowed back there. It was the time for secrets to be shared. But if they weren't, wouldn't that be better?

He looked in the mirror in the gents. His green eyes stared back. He still looked OK for his forty-nine years, but he was moving into that crumpled face and body that heralded middle-age. His mid brown hair had a few grey ones. Tibbs called him a silver fox, but he only said it to wind him up.

When he arrived at her house, Circe opened the door and he saw her look past him for her cats, just as he looked past her down the hall, so recently the scene of her fight.

'I'll be getting those lads for you shortly. I just wanted a wee word with yous first. That alright?'

'Sure. As long as they're OK and you're not breaking bad news that they've escaped from your house or something?'

'They're grand and looking forward to seeing their Mam.'

The house was immaculate but with an unmistakeable chemical smell that heralded a crime scene clean up. The police had great respect for the specialist companies that sanitised crime scenes after the event. They worked in appalling conditions and situations. There was no glamour in clearing up, especially in extreme cases, such as when a body was found in summer after it had lain there for three weeks on the kitchen floor. There was one company the Force nicknamed 'Kill and Clean' which provided some specialist grisly clean-up operations.

Circe had a tastefully expensive, three wick Jo Malone candle burning. Instinctively, Lorcan knew this was for the dead cat rather than to cover the odour. Sure enough Nigel's photo was placed next to the candle.

'You OK?' he asked, rhetorically. He felt helpless, not knowing what else to say. His famous blarney seemed to have deserted him entirely.

'Getting there. Still can't believe most of it. Is it too early for a drink?'

'Not in the circumstances.'

'Like to try my favourite gin drink?'

'I'd love to.' He didn't like gin but wanted to be close to everything that she liked.

When they were settled and he was drinking the BSC with loads of mint, he couldn't help but say, 'You really like your greenery don't you? If it hadn't been in Tosser's salads it's now ruined what would otherwise be a perfectly decent drink!'

Circe smiled. 'Sorry, I should have offered you something more ordinary. I can see that.'

'It's not a problem. I need me palate broadening, so I do. How are you really doing? I hope you didn't mind me talking about Alice?' His eyes flew to the small colour photo of her on the mantelpiece. No drama there, just a picture of a young woman.

Her eyes filled with tears and she sighed deeply. 'I needed to face it, Lorcan. I wouldn't let anyone help me. No one understood how I felt. The injustice of it all.'

He let her talk till she had no more to say and the room had grown dark and the streetlight made the tree's branches cast shadows on the wall. He slid his arm along the back of the velvet settee and rested it on her shoulders.

'Not being unprofessional, am I?'

'Don't think I'm the one to talk about that do you? After what I did?

'Want to let me know what really happened? If you don't want to that's OK too....'

'Yeah, might as well.' She got fresh drinks. 'I don't know how many other people I can tell except a judge.'

'No, Circe. You're a hero. No trial, no judge. You're just telling me so you don't have to keep it all in. And then if you like I'll share me own demons and you won't feel so bad when you hear my story. On the same terms, of course. It goes no further. I also need to tell someone. My old Da knows but has probably forgotten along with many other things.'

'I don't think he forgets like you think he does.'

Circe told him the full unexpurgated story of Lee's entrance and departure. She left nothing out. Even the Lakeland chopping board got a mention.

He stifled a smile at that, but winced at the boiling water. Men were often squeamish when it came to eyes.

'You did well. He properly deserved it. One for the old lady in Worthing.' He raised his glass.

'And for Nigel.'

'And Nigel.'

'I should confess it and take my punishment, shouldn't I?'

'Do you think anything would be served by that?'

'Justice.'

'Was Alice's death just?'

Circe sighed. 'I don't think there is justice anymore.'

'There is, but it is very watered down and not liberally dispensed. We do work hard in the police, as you yourself know, but the politicians have hobbled us, cut money and reduced sentences for convicted criminals, so we are where we are. Talking of which I would really, truly like to kiss you.'

If she hadn't already drained her glass Circe would have spilled the drink.

'Would I be the first murderer that you've kissed?'

'Probably. At least the first that I know for sure.'

'It's bad isn't it?'

'Not in the great scheme of things.' And he kissed her without regard for her previous crime, her status, her loss or her sadness. He kissed her hoping he could somehow console and comfort her.

Afterwards, in her high thread count bed that felt like silk, they were both quiet. He cleared his throat. 'So now you need to know something about me.'

'You're in the Force so I'd assume your character and references were pretty good? I kind of took that for granted.' Circe felt vulnerable now.

Lorcan responded. 'Well now, I could say the same for you, being a Magistrate, MBE, Police Authority member and so on and so on.'

'Fair play. Things change and things happen.'

'Right enough they do, and that's what my story is. I'm not such a young man anymore and I want you to be in what's left of my life. To share it and to love me as I already love you.'

She blushed and pushed her mass of auburn curls back. 'Let's take it slowly and see how we go after you've told me your own secret. Can't be worse than mine.'

He shrugged heavily. 'I've lost a child too. My son was killed.'

Circe clapped her hands to her mouth. 'I had no idea! I'm so sorry.' She knew enough of Victim Support to let him talk.

'No one over here knows this. Only Patrick. Back in the day Northern Ireland was another place. I dated a girl. She was sweet and kind and wouldn't hurt a soul.'

Circe's battered heart stabbed at hearing this. God she was jealous. This man was already under her skin!

'Long story short. She was Protestant and pregnant. Both her Da and brother were pretty involved in the Troubles. They didn't have any time for Catholics, even lapsed ones. I was on duty when the serial came in that she was found naked, tarred and feathered, and the five month foetus beaten out of her. I had to keep my grief to myself and within a couple of days there had been a Protestant 'investigation,' if you take my meaning. The sectarian groups there set about hurting enough people to yield the name of the culprits. I knew that the man who killed Victoria was likely to be executed that night. I had intelligence to that fact. I had the name. I could have tried to prevent the death. I could have got him to safety. Maybe arrested him – done it the right way? But no, I did nothing. I let him have what was coming to him. He was a mate of her brother who would rather see her dead than with me. I won't go into detail, but that lad met the kind of bad end that only those troubled times could summon up.'

Lorcan paused and wiped both is eyes. 'I applied for a transfer. My life wasn't safe. Proper coward, aren't I? But my family had seen enough. My Mam had broken her hip avoiding an angry crowd, and she stumbled and fell. They spat on her. She got a thrombosis two weeks later in hospital and we lost her. Me old Da was never the same and the sisters left the area. We were all broken. My guvnor was happy to see me transferred. He said he never trusted anyone who wasn't ballsy enough to stay Feinian. Truth was, I'd lost my faith in everything. Religion means nothing to me. Fecking nothing.' The tears ran down his face.

Circe pulled a robe on. 'Somehow I don't quite believe that. But that's certainly a terrible, terrible thing to have gone through and I for one, don't judge you.'

* * *

When he got home Lorcan found a scene of complete chaos at his flat.

Patrick was on the landing roaring at him. 'Don't ye ever look at your blasted phone, boy?'

Social Services had been granted entry following a report, allegedly to rescue the crying babies that were being told to *fecking shut up'* by Patrick, so Lorcan's neighbour confirmed.

Going back to Circe's house, Lorcan thrust the cat box with the two yowling creatures at her. 'Jaysus, just take them, I've me Da in the car and he needs to be back on the estate. It's all kicking off.'

Chapter Forty-Two

A CHILD GOES MISSING

Lorcan dropped Patrick a couple of roads away from his house so he wouldn't be seen with the old man as he ambled along picking up estate gossip. Patrick had been told as much as Lorcan knew. A young girl had gone missing and he was to keep his eyes and ears open.

Twelve year old Kaycee Slater hadn't come home the day before. It seemed she'd gone to the mini-mart for some sweets and hadn't been seen since. Her family were well known to Social Services and her biological father was in prison. Her mother Emma now lived with 'Uncle Bob' who was itinerant and violent. Within a short time the local women mobilised search parties and set up a headquarters in the community centre.

They weren't really cooperating with the police, who were coordinating the official operation. Lorcan was run off his feet and the press and media were in a frenzy. There was the feeling that this kind of situation was well rehearsed. Yet again, the mother and stepfather appealed for Kaycee's safe return. There was something so familiar about the mother brushing away tears and holding her daughter's favourite toy. 'She might be twelve but she still sleeps with her toy elephant every night.' Watching the recording, Lorcan grimaced. If the kid was found there would be a load of bullying after that revelation!

If there was one thing the estate did well it was drama, and it swiftly galvanised itself and searched through garages, communal bins, waste ground and the scrubby woodland near the recreation park.

That night there were two clear moods in the community. Anger and sorrow. A significant group organised an ostentatious candlelit vigil, where a shrine of cheap stuffed toys were placed in front of the mini-mart. Mr Ahmad was less than pleased with the unwanted publicity, but business was brisk, so he smiled and welcomed them all in. Police checked his CCTV footage and although it was grainy and indistinct there was no sign of Kaycee on it. It seemed she never got as far as the shop.

In no time T-shirts were being dispensed with a photo of Kaycee on it. It was one where she'd gone to a friend's party and was wearing makeup. Not the usual school photo, but one which made her look older than her years. Despite all police advice to the contrary, her mother insisted on it being used. Kaycee was not a regular school attendee so there wasn't a recent image of her in uniform anyway.

The flyers blew round the estate as the dogs and police searched. News items had the ravaged faces of the family pleading for Kaycee's safe return, while forensic psychologists were profiling the performances.

The duty inspector followed standard search procedures and examined everything in the home and the family. They checked her friends, information from Social Services and the school and education service. Lorcan was asked to look at all the intelligence and coordinate the searches. As was the usual official custom and practice with a child possibly being abducted by a stranger, there was a Detective Superintendent overseeing the operation and there was considerable national press interest.

Watching yet another appeal Lorcan stared intently at the step-dad's face. 'Are those real tears? What do you think?'

Tibbs said, 'You know he's a real scumbag, but somehow I don't think he's involved. Drinks on me if I'm wrong.'

'I don't like to say this, but I agree with you.' Lorcan bit his pen. The habit was acquired mainly to deter colleagues from stealing it. Police were not always to be trusted around stationery.

After a further two days there was no progress in the investigation. The community was weary and despairing. Everyone knew the rule. Every hour after the first twenty-four made it less likely that the child would be found alive. The damp toys at the shrine stared sightlessly at the growing pile of cigarette butts in front of it.

Lorcan's phone rang and he answered irritably. 'Not now, Da, I'm up to my bloody neck, so I am.'

Patrick snapped back, 'Yes boy, and that's why I'm calling. I've heard some gossip about that wee girl that's gone missing.'

'What? Tell me.'

'It's just craic at this stage from an old lady. I know you're busy so I wanted a chat with Circe. I'm calling to ask you for her number. I'm sure she won't mind you giving it to me. Or can you ask her to ring me? You carry on with what you're up to and I'll speak to her. If there's anything in it, we'll tell you. There's a lot of rumour round here and it's hard to tell fact from fiction. That's it, get her to phone me and I'd prefer it if you didn't say anything to your police mates just yet. It's not that simple. It might need careful handling if there is anything and we don't even know if there is yet. A woman's touch is what's needed.'

If he hadn't been so swamped with other cases alongside this emergency and top priority investigation then Lorcan might have pressed Patrick further. But it sounded like one of his father's usual off the wall hints, rumours and conspiracy theories and he just didn't have time for that. So it was the human part of him that was happy for any contact with Patrick to be diverted to Circe, and especially now. He called her at once.

'It may be nothing but me old Da wants to speak to you about women's things and Kaycee's disappearance. Can you drop everything and give him a ring? Off the record? I don't think it may be much, but just in case, let's humour him. It goes without saying that if there's anything relevant, however insignificant it may seem, then it's a police matter and I would appreciate you letting us know at once.'

'Of course.' Circe headed off to Stoneleigh, and Patrick showed her into his shabby, but clean property. He was obviously managing to care for himself.

'It's a bad business Circe. Four days now is it that the wee girl's been missing?' But what he had to say then surprised and gave hope in equal measure.

'Now you see there's an old girl I've been talking to at the bus stop. A bit of an outsider with a recluse of a husband. Calls herself Elsie Standish. Got a bungalow not far from here. It's near where some lad got knifed.'

'Yes, I know it.' Circe was waiting for Patrick to get to the point. Maybe he wasn't doing as well on his own as she thought.

He grabbed her arm and lowered his voice even though there were just the two of them there. 'What the old girl, this Elsie, said was that she thinks the girl is in one of the flats across the way.'

Circe spoke loudly. 'For goodness sake you should have told this to Lorcan. It's for the police to deal with.'

'Slow down girl, it's not as easy as that. There's complications.'

'And they are? Come on Patrick tell me what you've heard. I'll give you my opinion then.'

'OK. So what Elsie said is in confidence. She's very nervous like and doesn't have many friends in Stoneleigh. So she curtain twitches a lot of the time, reckons it's better than the telly and you learn a lot. She sees comings and goings and all sorts really.'

Circe could hear Patrick's breath getting faster.

'Just what has she seen, Patrick? Has she seen Kaycee?'

'Yes, me darling. That's what I'm trying to tell yous. But first you must promise you'll not tell the police.' Patrick sniffed and looked towards Circe. 'Elsie doesn't want to be implicated in any way. If people find out they'll destroy her, and she can't start again with a new identity. She's too old she says. It's got to be under the radar like.'

Circe felt Ida Dunmore emerging in her mind. What would she do? She shut her mind off and said to Patrick, 'I understand the seriousness of the situation, but you have to trust me. I'll be the judge of whether the police need to be called despite the risk to Elsie. You have to remember there's a missing child here. That has to be our priority. Now what's is the intelligence you've been told then?'

So finally the old man told her that the young girl was with what Elsie believed was a boyfriend. For the last few months Elsie had seen them meet up by the stabbing shrine outside her bungalow and go over to the young man's flat. It was always during school hours and the girl looked very tarty. Hardly wore any clothes, no matter what the weather. Painted face. The boy looked much older, in a hard living sort of way. She could see Kaycee in his flat closing the blinds when they got there. She'd always come back past Elsie's bungalow by herself at night.

'What's his name?'

Apparently, he's called Jamie. A common enough name with no clue as to his last one.'

'Can we have a chat with Elsie herself?' Patrick phoned the old lady and she came round within ten minutes. Her apron was still on underneath her coat.

'Thanks for coming,' Circe said to Elsie.

'You're not the police, are you?' she whispered.

'No, I'm Circe and I'm here to help.'

Elsie swallowed. 'Promise you won't say anything to anyone? I'm so scared, but I want to save that girl. He's a bad man. Jamie, she calls him. It started about a year ago before he was seeing her. He always seemed to be hanging about when I came out to get my pension money. First time he pushed me into a bush in someone's garden and the thorns cut my legs. I got cellulitis. That took a long time to clear up and next time he just held his hand out and said, 'Money, old woman. Give me your money.' He raised a fist and I was so scared I gave him my purse. It had my bus pass and everything in it. I tried to avoid him, but he always seemed to be waiting for me and watching from his flat window. He bullies and terrorises me. We go hungry as he takes my money. I can't tell anyone. But in the last few days it's been so peaceful. I think they're both in the flat. I've seen it all on TV and in the papers, but he'd know it was me who told the police, so I just wanted this nice man,' she indicated Patrick, 'to go and get young Kaycee out.'

Circe stepped in. 'It may not be that easy, and we would want to protect you, as you ask. There are procedures for doing this and the police are the right people to take care of it. However, I think we can assume that although this is a case of sexual abuse of a minor, her life isn't in any immediate danger?'

'She was kissing him this morning.'

'Well, aside of the fact that's all illegal, it seems that we have a little time to bring this to a conclusion that will protect you Elsie, as well as get the girl the help she needs. Not to mention bringing old Jamie to justice.'

While Patrick put the kettle on, Circe asked Elsie for a few more details. By the time the builder's tea was poured, she had decided that Ida Dunmore would make one last appearance. She told Patrick she'd be back in a couple of hours, just before nightfall. Circe had little time and made her arrangements, flying around town buying what she needed. In and out of charity shops again, but on this occasion there was no time to wash Ida's clothing and she paid more for a grey curly wig than she'd have liked. All sorted.

And so it was that with a capacious shopper she knocked on Jamie's flat door. After a long time the door opened. She had a bottle of vodka in her hand and slurred, 'Is William here? He wanted this. He'll be angry if he doesn't get it.'

Jamie reached out and grabbed the bottle. 'Yeah, I'll give it him, don't you worry, love.' Circe suddenly pitched forward. 'I'm a bit dizzy. Let me sit down for a while. Get me breath back.'

Her purse had fallen into the hall and Jamie kicked it further backwards out of her reach.

'OK, just for a minute. Wait here.' Circe sat on the floor of the cramped and dirty hall while Jamie opened the sitting room door a crack and said something to the occupant. It all went quiet and the music was turned off. Circe pretended to faint and lay unmoving on the floor. He picked up the bottle of vodka and swigged and swigged. He hit the floor himself not long afterwards and Circe got up and opened the living room door. There was Kaycee in a fluffy robe. She didn't look scared to see a nice little old lady, smiling at her. 'Get dressed sweetie, your boyfriend is flat out drunk and I need you to see me home as I'm feeling a bit woozy and I've got a cat that needs feeding. He's a nice cat. You'll like him. Blue eyes and he doesn't half talk.' Kaycee disappeared to get dressed and the two of them stepped over the comatose Jamie and went to Patrick's house.

Clive, who she had dropped off earlier as bait, obligingly meowed and chatted with Kaycee while Circe phoned Lorcan to update him. Before he arrived Circe slipped back out and returned to Jamie's flat. He was deeply unconscious. The GHB had done its work. Thank goodness for the gay sex shops in Kemptown. She'd not been sure of the dose for a whole bottle of vodka so went in heavy to be sure. She unbuttoned his flies and he didn't move at all. She pulled out a permanent marker from her bag and wrote *Rapist* on the skin of his groin. Pausing as it dried, she stretched the skin on his penis and with a small, sharp paring knife from Lakeland she carefully cross hatched the shaft. That wound would open every time he had a dirty thought, masturbated, or attempted sex. Shuddering at the unpleasantness of his member, she then rummaged around in her bag for the home tattoo kit with which to make her writing more permanent. She just had time to do a practice buzz into the ink when the door crashed open. It was Lorcan who pulled her off him.

'Are you fucking mad, woman? That's too far.'

'It's never too far, it's just deserts and a warning to other women. Whatever their age.'

'Stop now, I'm telling ye! Clear up this stuff. Kaycee's with Social Services, and the police will be here any minute.' Instantly Circe was up and out. As she went down the narrow pathway her disguise was so good that Steve Tibbs politely stood to one side to let her pass. Walking slowly back to her car, which as ever, was a distance from her target, she went home and changed. She then went back to Patrick's to collect the cat.

'How did you do it?' He smiled.

Circe tapped her nose. 'Can't say.'

Chapter Forty-Three

THE BURNING TIMES

The bonfires raged over the estate again that night as child pornography was destroyed. In some places it looked like Guy Fawkes night. Police noted the fires and called on the men who lit them soon after. It seemed that Jamie was twenty-nine years old and in with a set of paedophiles from the estate. It wasn't discovered who had drugged and assaulted him, but many of the estate men claimed the attack as their own handiwork. Because despite their best efforts, the police were unable to say for sure who had inflicted the wound on his penis that was ulcerated and septic for a long time. Jamie could remember nothing. Kaycee was taken into care and opted for a termination.

It was considered by the local community that the police had done a good job in finding Kaycee and arresting the perpetrator. The mysterious little old lady who had helped was never identified. Each description of her varied, but it was agreed that no one on the estate could say they knew her. She didn't go to bingo and hadn't been seen in The Black Dog, although there was a drink behind the bar for her if she ever did turn up, so the landlord told The Argus.

As John Crook said to his team. 'We got the right result, but the means have yet to be understood.' The Detective Superintendent took the plaudits, but with a cautious smile. Within two days there was a massive drugs deal on the estate that took everyone's mind off it. Two people died of extra strength heroin. Business as usual in Stoneleigh.

* * *

Circe took Patrick's lilac catsuit round to him. She'd cleaned and repaired it as best she could.

'Thanks! That looks great. I can get back to me dancing now. And Elsie is happy that Jamie has been caught. She's free to get her pension and says she has a new life now.'

Circe smiled. There were dark rings under her eyes. 'How's Lorcan?'

'Looking shite, like you do. What's wrong? You two had a row? He's not a bad lad. His heart's in the right place.'

'So is mine, as a matter of fact.'

* * *

Ann Lancaster went into the CID section at Brighton police station unannounced. The officers were predictably surprised and worried to see her in equal measure. Dirty cups overflowed on untidy desks and the remains of a two day old pizza lent its foetid odour to the stuffy and airless room. It had very sick building syndrome and this area was on life support.

She stood with her back to the window declining a stained seat. She engineered her face so it was in shadow.

'Good morning. I wonder if any of you detectives can guess the reason for this visit?'

There was a collective shaking of heads and a barely suppressed burp from someone who had just wolfed a McDonald's breakfast at his desk.

John Crook swiftly tried to take control. 'A pleasure to see you Ma'am, maybe you've looked in after seeing the District Commander?'

'With that level of astuteness, I can really see why you've reached the rank of Detective Inspector, John. You are of course correct. But I also wanted to come and thank you personally as a team for all your recent good work on a couple of difficult cases. I'm aware of the extra hours and effort you all put in and just to say you got good results. Well done.'

The hard-bitten officers were shocked and an intake of breath and smiles went round the room. The ACC opened a window behind her and a blast of cold air rushed in. 'That's better,' she said as a few papers blew on to the grubby carpet. 'And another reason for being here is to give you the heads up that there will be some organisational changes coming. Some efficiency savings need to be made that'll be affecting this department. Can't say what they will be yet, as nothing is finalised, but you'll be informed as soon as we've made a decision. So watch this space.'

She swept out and a fulsome breaking of wind followed her departure. Tibbs pulled the window shut.

'Feck me. What's going on then?' Lorcan asked. 'She actually praised us and then dropped the bombshell leaving us to search for where the hole is going to be. Start worrying guys, details to follow.'

John Crook leant on the glass door of his partition. 'It doesn't look good, so we just wait for the rumour mill to kick into action. But we did get praise, so let's be grateful for the crumbs too.'

Steve Tibbs looked at Lorcan. 'Pub tonight?'

He inexplicably looked at his watch. 'Let me come back to you on that.' He had a Community Engagement Steering Group meeting that afternoon and Circe was supposed to be there.

* * *

Neither Circe or Lorcan looked at each other during the meeting. She felt her phone vibrate towards the end. Unobtrusively checking the message she could see it was from Lorcan.

Any chance of a drink with you tonight? Nothing that needs a kettle boiled, I'm thinking. And probably not vodka either. Or wheatgrass. Perhaps just a pint of Murphys for myself and maybe a shot of vitriol for the lady?

Circe laughed out loud attracting bemused glances from her colleagues. It was all very unprofessional.

Four hours later Circe heard the news from the Chief Constable who called her even before Lorcan had a chance to update her. It seemed that a police car had been following a stolen car which had been driven dangerously. It had eventually struck the metal safety rails on a pedestrian crossing. The occupant were pronounced dead at the scene and was named as Darren Sutton. Police had followed all the correct procedures, but it was still an official requirement that the case be referred to the Independent Police Complaints Commission for investigation. So Darren Sutton was dead! Was this his karma?

Drinking her gin as a pre-load before going out, she reflected that he deserved everything that happened to him. She couldn't find it in her heart to feel anything but relief for his passing. Women would be safer now and the Court list a lot shorter. She toasted the mirror, hope hell is waiting for him, she thought.

Lorcan drove her up to The Devil's Dyke pub high on the Sussex Downs. The ice age glacial gouges in the landscape were in shadow and they could see the glittering lights of the city and estates below. He cleared his throat. 'I've a proposal to make since I don't seem to be able to get you out of my head. I may be making some assumptions, but feel we are both kindred spirits, though one of us has a very devious streak.'

Circe looked up at him crossly.

Lorcan ploughed on. 'However, I think that it may be a good career move for us to start again in another part of the country. There are going to be some changes in Sussex Police that don't look very good. So maybe it's time for a transfer to another Force and a new challenge would be good for me.'

Circe's heart rose in her chest. 'Strange you should say that. My house is already on the market. I couldn't go on living in it now I've come to terms with Alice's death, and also after the break in.'

'You're a very fast worker.'

'Speak for yourself.'

'You could also transfer magistrate benches, if you wanted, and I imagine you'd be bringing Ida Dunmore with you? We could maybe find a new city that needed sorting out?'

'Or a village maybe. There's a lot that goes on in the country. And there are two conditions.'

'Only two?'

'That we have an annexe for Patrick.'

'OK, but he'll drive me mad. What's the second?'

'That you have hypnotherapy for your so-called dislike of the cats. It's all in your head, all that sniffing and sneezing.'

Lorcan raised his eyes and his beer glass.

'To justice.'

Circe raised her gin in a return toast. 'To justice!'

Lorcan held her gaze. 'And just for the record *my* condition is that I never want to see you with another man's cock in your hand.'

'Fair enough. I'm sticking with veganism now anyway.'

'Brilliant' said Lorcan draining his glass.

THE END

ACKNOWLEDGEMENTS

In writing this book I drew upon my knowledge of the Magistrates Court system having served as a JP for many years, but all characters and situations are totally fictional. I do however believe people benefit from visiting the public gallery of their, now sadly not so local, courthouse. On offer is a free seat in the 'Theatre of Crime' to witness how justice is dispensed. No booking required!

I need to insert a disclaimer. I was not paid, or sponsored, by Lakeland. It's just that their catalogue has products which are versatile, and therefore perfect for my vigilante character to use in her campaign! Lakeland does not in any way support their merchandise being used for nefarious purposes! I was also not sponsored by any gin company!

I would especially like to thank Sussex Police's former Chief Superintendent Peter Coll who reviewed the book professionally. He was Superintendent Crime and Operations in Brighton and Hove from 2000-2003. He provided valuable advice with his martial arts experience, and extensive knowledge of policing and anecdotes. Remaining errors are entirely my responsibility!

My thanks go to my daughter for her meticulous help on an early draft and to 'Nurse Ratched' for her unwavering support and medical input. I am especially grateful to my husband for uncomplainingly checking each edit and making divine Earl Grey tea. It isn't easy living with someone who writes on the dark side.

The police, and Sussex police in particular, will always have my continuing admiration. I have watched with sadness over the years how the police 'force' has become a dreadfully underfunded and maligned police 'service.' The men and women who work for them are amazing. It is the persistent failure of successive governments to place the victim at the heart of the criminal justice system that means we are beset by pitifully low prosecution rates, weak sentencing and inadequate punishment.

And so this book is dedicated to the victims of crime who have so little voice now. It shouldn't take a vigilante to wreak revenge, but perhaps Circe's campaign is understandable in the circumstances. Maybe she's moving to a place near you soon?

Thanks to Peter Clinton peterclinton@gmail.com for the cover design.

I'm always very happy to hear from my readers, so do please get in touch at www.lucyrutherford.co.uk

Thank you for reading my book, I hope you enjoyed it as much as I enjoyed writing it. Won't you please consider leaving a review? Even just a few words would help others decide if the book is right for them.

Many thanks in advance!
Lucy Rutherford

Lightning Source UK Ltd.
Milton Keynes UK
UKHW020620030519

342063UK00011B/986/P